THE WAY WE BARED OUR SOULS

A NOVEL

WILLA STRAYHORN

razOr
bill

A division of Penguin Young Readers Group

Published by the Penguin Group
Penguin Group (USA) LLC
345 Hudson Street
New York, New York 10014

USA / Canada / UK / Ireland / Australia / New Zealand / India /
South Africa / China
Penguin.com
A Penguin Random House Company

ISBN: 978-1-59514-735-6

Printed in the United States of America

1 3 5 7 9 10 8 6 4 2

For Latham, Zoe, and Harper

IT FELT AS IF WE'D just been here, on this same dirt floor, within these same adobe walls, in this same spectral formation.

But it had been a full week since the subterranean ritual, and everything had changed since then. For the most glaring example, I needed only to look around the ceremonial kiva at the stricken faces before me. Only four of us remained in the ghostly underworld of our initiation. Where Kaya, our fifth, had sat beside me on a blanket last Saturday night, there was now just a depression in the dirt. Kaya, the girl who felt no pain.

Now she would feel nothing, ever again.

What would Jay say? He had warned me of the consequences, but I hadn't listened. He had entrusted me with his magic, and I had let him down. Could he have been completely wrong about me? He'd told me that I had a powerful soul, but now I just felt muted and buried, crushed by the earth above me. Maybe I'd never been equipped to lead my friends to better lives. I'd wanted so badly to be healed that I'd let myself get carried away—and had doggedly carried others with me. And we definitely weren't noble Indians of the Southwest communing with the benevolent spirits of our ancestors. We were just four kids from Santa Fe High crowded around a fading fire in the New Mexico desert that served as our city's suburb. And now we'd lost one of our own. I'd lost her. Me. My fault. Not Jay. Not his mystical coyote. Me.

I was Kaya's murderer.

Across from me and through the thickening smoke, Ellen looked berserk—more jittery and unmoored from reality than she'd ever been in her burnout days—and this despite the fact that most of the drugs had been flushed from her system. Except for the ones she took for her incurable disease. Or rather, for *my* incurable disease. If it was still my disease. Confusing, I know, but bear with me. A lot of crazy things happened that week.

Ellen's bleached blond hair was tangled with sage and juniper from scrambling down the mountain the night before. The mud on her face had hardened, like the aging adobe slathered on every building in our city. I wrapped my Navajo blanket around her shoulders. She accepted the offering numbly, lost in her own anxious world. I almost wished she would lash out at me, as she used to when she was under the influence. Now, her distance felt unnatural.

Not that any of this was natural. Death seemed the most unnatural thing of all.

When Ellen adjusted her arms I saw the turquoise horse figurine she clung to. I looked down at the object I gripped in my own hand. It should have been a deer totem, but instead it was a shard of bone. Which, I didn't realize until now, was drawing blood from my palm. And I was the one expected to save us?

"Lo," Thomas said, his voice muffled by his zipped-up hoodie, "you're bleeding again." Was it my imagination, or had some of the solicitude left his voice? As a child Thomas had been through a war, practically a genocide, and yet even he was shell-shocked by recent events. You can only see someone bleed so many times in a week without getting caregiver fatigue.

"Here," he said, offering me a fresh white towel from his backpack. I shook my head and tucked the sharp object back into my pocket. I didn't want to soil something so pure.

"Serves Lo right," Kit said, prodding the fire with a stick. He had revived his old resentment. The joyful, manic energy he'd been cultivating for the past week seemed to have taken a sinister turn. He ran his fingers through his stubby Mohawk, which barely moved under the gesture. He also hadn't seen a shower for a couple of days. We'd all been too busy trying to survive. Trying, and failing, to keep each other whole.

"Leave her alone," Thomas told Kit. But judging from his weak, exhausted voice, I could tell his heart wasn't even in that small defense. Kit could probably shove me violently against the kiva's sacred wall right now, and Thomas would scarcely budge. I deserved all that and more. Thomas knew me better than anyone else in the world at this point, well enough to know that he would be wise to be done with me.

He'd been a foot soldier for a psychotic warlord, and I'd still never be good enough for him. We were both killers, but at least he could cite force and coercion as an excuse for his fatal mistakes.

Judging by the buttery light filtering through the hole above our heads, the desert sun was finally rising. Kaya should have been waking up right now to the dissonant hum of her alarm clock. Her mom should have been in her bedroom to take her temperature and check for any cuts and bruises that might have accrued in the night. But now Kaya was beyond injury.

My eyes climbed the ladder rungs that we'd descended to get into the ceremonial chamber the night before. We were buried together in this dark interior, but I could still see the peekaboo brilliance overhead. Another blue-sky day in New Mexico, big surprise. It was the Land of Enchantment, after all. I guess I couldn't expect this climate to reflect the tragedies I created. Santa Fe boasted three hundred days of sunshine every year. I boasted one stupid decision to haunt me for the rest of my life. However long that might be. My days were numbered differently every day.

"Please just bring her back," I murmured, but to whom, I wasn't sure.

Then the opening darkened, and a pair of legs appeared on the ladder. For one ecstatic moment I thought they belonged to Kaya, but then I recognized the weathered hiking boots, the worn Levi's.

Jay.

The ring of desert sunshine formed a halo around his head as he seemed to drop effortlessly from the sky. When Jay touched down I immediately felt more grounded. Maybe he could miraculously undo the damage I'd inflicted.

Jay quietly assessed the kiva's inhabitants. "Where is your fifth?" he said. Ellen began to cry.

"We were hoping you could tell us," I said. I closed my eyes and tried to see Kaya's face, but it was pushed aside by images of deranged coyotes and angry bulls, machine guns and burning men. . . .

I felt a hand on my shoulder. Jay studied me softly. He seemed to understand my guilt, my fear. Our overwhelming loss.

"You already know," I said. He nodded.

"It's over, Consuelo," Jay said. "It's time to reverse the ritual." I crumpled to the ground. My selfish experiment had reached its ugly, bitter end. Jay reached out to touch my quaking back. I raised my head. "It's not just Kaya who departed our circle last night," he continued. "You have all let your centers weaken. It's time for you to reclaim your souls. Only then can you see your friend again."

See her again. Maybe we could resurrect her after all.

Jay's coyote trotted up from some dark recess of the kiva and licked my bandaged forearm, around the puncture wounds that she'd made the night before. I petted her absentmindedly on the scruff of her neck. I knew she wouldn't try to hurt me.

Thomas, Ellen, and Kit regarded me through the smoke, hungry for whatever wisdom I could deliver. It seemed they still saw me as the natural leader of our spiritual outfit, even though I'd failed them miserably. We were all suffering beneath our burdens, but right now the heavy, subterranean silence weighed on us the most. I had never felt more lost, more disconnected from people, from my own strength, from daylight itself. I took a deep breath and prepared to speak.

"I got you into this," I said, pulling a precious object from my pocket and extending my wounded, lifeless hand toward the flames. "And now I'm going to get you out."

2

"HOW LONG HAVE YOU BEEN experiencing symptoms, Consuelo?"

When Dr. Osborn finally removed his flashlight from my retinas, the exam room filled with white dots. I squirmed on the paper sheet that lay between my undergarments and the exam table, really wishing that I hadn't chosen to wear my fluorescent orange underwear under my jeans to the hospital that morning. But I hadn't expected this neurology exam to be so comprehensive. So full-body. After all, I wasn't really sick. I just had weird headaches now and then. And shaky hands. And blurred vision. And sometimes shooting pain down my right arm that was so violent I had to stop whatever I was doing and envision rainbows and puppies to keep from throwing up. Okay, so maybe that did sound sort of bad.

"I'm not sure," I said. "Maybe a couple of months now?"

The doctor grunted. This wasn't Dr. Sue, my usual pediatrician who still insisted on sneaking me a lollipop after appointments and who spent most of our time together pumping me for gossip from Santa Fe High School. This was a specialist—one totally lacking in bedside manner—and you had to take numerous turns and elevators through a labyrinthine hospital in order to reach his exalted offices. And somehow I didn't think he'd care about my negligible love life.

"Do you remember the first time you felt something might be wrong?" said Dr. Osborn. He was now (sadistically?) banging his rubber mallet against my bare knee. I resisted the urge to kick him lightly on the shin and blame my reflexes.

The first time. . . . Jeez, that was hard to answer. I supposed it was over summer break. I was trying to swim laps when my legs started trembling in the pool. Or when my favorite trick hula-hoop suddenly began skittering to the floor because my hips couldn't keep up with its rotations. Or when I stopped dancing solo around my bedroom altogether because my body no longer felt like my own.

The backs of my thighs began to sweat onto the filmy white paper. Why did the doctor sound so foreboding? So concerned? I thought this appointment was just a precaution before I got too busy with junior year. I'd be taking the SATs this fall and needed to be at the top of my game so I could get good grades, get a good boyfriend, get into a good college, get a good job, have a good life, et cetera, et cetera. I didn't have time for serious illness. I didn't even have time for a head cold.

"Lo?" Mom said. For a second I'd forgotten that my parents were there with me in the exam room. I wrapped my cheap, hospital-issue gown further around my back to ensure that my obscene underwear stayed hidden from all three adults. Mom sat in the armchair in the corner, twisting her hands together and looking at me expectantly. I'd spaced out for . . . some length of time—not an uncommon occurrence those days.

"Sorry," I said, glancing at her and then at my dad, who stood frozen next to her chair. He tends to turn to marble whenever he's worried about something or is overthinking his fatherly thoughts. "I was just . . . trying to remember."

Mom settled back in her seat but continued to fidget. Like mother, like daughter. I tucked my gown further beneath me and sat on my restless hands.

"I guess when I first felt different . . . ," I mumbled at Dr. Osborn, getting distracted by seeing my own reflection in his giant silver belt buckle. Only in New Mexico would your neurologist be styled like a cowboy. "Well, it actually wasn't long after . . . Aunt Karine died." I looked at Mom; as I expected, hearing her sister's name had made her wince. It was our unspoken rule that we never mentioned Aunt Karine within our triangular family unit. But Mom quickly collected herself and waved at me with subtle encouragement. She looked so young, so pretty, so capable in the pink scrubs from her overnight nursing shift. I know it pained her that she couldn't heal me.

As I spoke, Dr. Osborn seemed to be preparing to listen to my heartbeat, but the cord of his stethoscope got tangled in his bolo tie.

I forged ahead while he fumbled.

"So maybe around the Fourth of July or so? I was making coffee in the kitchen and felt a sort of . . . spasm in my arm that made me drop my mug. And I'm not clumsy at all usually." Dad raised an eyebrow. At least he still had his sense of humor. "Despite what *some* people think." He winked at me.

Then I didn't like the pensive way the doctor was looking in my direction, so I started to babble. "The mug pretty much shattered on the floor. Even now, like three months later, I'm still stepping on shards of porcelain every once in a while, in my bare feet. Did you know that, Mom? I've tried and tried to clean it up. I think the Dustbuster must be defective. Guys, can we get a new Dustbuster?" I clasped my hands in front of my heart as if I were asking for a pony for my birthday. "Pretty please?"

Mom nodded absentmindedly. The mug that I'd broken had been one of her favorites. I'd had it printed with a photo of the three of us and given it to her for Christmas one year. Dad had called it the Holy Caffeine Grail.

Dr. Osborn seemed to have given up on my heartbeat. His bolo tie had cast too stubborn a web.

"It's not unusual," he said, "for this disease to manifest first in loss of coordination."

This disease. He said it like it was an established fact. I knew it ran in families, but. . . . He must have noted the sudden look of horror on my face because he quickly backtracked.

"I'm going to schedule you for a series of more-conclusive tests a week from Monday." He made a note on my chart. I imagined it was a brainstorm about a new line of clinical wear that combined medical functionality with Southwestern fashion sensibilities. Lab jackets printed with Aztec designs. Fringed cowhide face masks. Hygienic paper shoes that could fit over cowboy boots and spurs.

Okay, then. Monday after next. A Monday would decide my fate. Couldn't it at least be a Friday, so I wouldn't have to go to school the next day? Or even a Sunday, so I could go to church beforehand and pray to the Virgin Mary like Mom was always doing? I'd never prayed before, but surely it wasn't too late. God, if you're out there, please grant me a Dustbuster and perfect health.

"Meanwhile, Consuelo—" the doctor said.

"It's just Lo," I interrupted, surprised by how irritated I sounded.

I should say something about my name: Consuelo McDonough. We're Anglo, not Hispanic, but when my parents came to Santa Fe years ago on their low-budget honeymoon, my mother embraced Southwestern culture to an extreme. She's sort of obsessed with the Spanish missionary history of the city and never strays far from the kneelers of our local Catholic churches that the conquistadors founded. When we moved here from California when I was in kindergarten, I found that my name helped me fit in immediately. Santa Fe is about 50 percent Hispanic, after all.

"Of course," the doctor said, finally returning his rubber mallet and flashlight to his lab coat pockets as if he were a Wild West outlaw holstering his pistols. "Just Lo, then. I'll make a note. Just Lo, until your next appointment, I need you to keep up with the vitamin and dietary regimen that I recommended, and don't hesitate to be liberal with the pills I prescribed if you're in pain. The steroids especially. Later we can talk rehab, support groups—"

Dad cleared his throat loudly. Bless him. He's a fire ranger, and he was missing work to be with me. I used to think his job was romantic. Then I got older and realized that it's not exactly a privilege to be sent into raging infernos by the Forest Service. It actually sounds pretty hellish. Dad is part of an elite crew of "hotshots" who hike toward the flames and then dig a line to break the progress of the fire. I sometimes wish he had an office job. Pencils rarely burst into flames.

"Right," Dr. Osborn said. "There is plenty of time to discuss those matters. And of course it's all contingent on next week's paraclinical tests. Meanwhile, do you have any questions for me, Consuelo?" I didn't correct him this time. I shook my head. I just wanted to get out of there.

"Then you're free to get dressed. Mr. and Mrs. McDonough, may I speak to you in the hallway for a moment?"

My parents left with the doctor. In a daze, I began to reassemble my outfit. Faded black jeans. A vintage rock T-shirt that was always slipping off my shoulder. It wasn't until my boots were laced up that I realized I'd forgotten to put on my socks.

Focus, Lo. I tried to imagine a drug I could take to feel at home in my body again, to feel less scatterbrained and off-kilter. It'd be called TranquiLo™. Side effects included drowsiness, loss of appetite. . . .

I ran into my parents in the hallway, and as soon as I saw their bleak faces, I knew I didn't want to engage with them. I told them I was in a rush to make it to the end of fourth period, and then fled the hospital into the vivid New Mexico sunshine before anybody—or anything—could slow me down. I wouldn't make history class, but I'd get to lunch before the bell, and I desperately wanted to see my friends, eat some potato chips in the courtyard, laugh about stupid teenage stuff, and forget the morning ever happened.

———

I made it to lunch period just in time to get faux-stern reprimands from my best friends, Alex and Juanita, who were sitting on the courtyard concrete in the midst of an epic hair-styling session. Alex had her legs wrapped around Juanita's hips for better leverage and was putting the finishing touches on a long, silky braid.

"Lo! You're, like, four hours late," Alex said as she looped the finished braid around the back of Juanita's head. "Pretty tardy, young lady, even for you. What gives?"

Alex and I had bonded freshman year over a fetal pig dissection in the world's grossest biology lab, and my social life hadn't been the same since. Alex is pretty and blond, and she brought me into her exclusive circle of rich Anglo kids and hot athletes who make up the picnic society around our school's circular courtyard fountain, which we'd redundantly nicknamed "Agua de Water." At lunch we also threw coins in the water, wishing for things like calorie-free guacamole and our favorite movie stars to fall in love with us via our Twitter accounts.

"Yeah, chica," Juanita said, jumping up and swinging her arms around me after making sure her hair was in place. "Where've you been? Alex won't stop going on about kissing Brett last night, and I need a buffer from her blah blah blahs." Her hand made a motormouthed puppet. "Oops, sorry," she said to Alex. "I guess mind-numbing boredom is the price to pay for your beautician services."

Alex laughed and threatened to muss Juanita's hair. "Damn right. Anyway, you're just jealous that you missed the show last night because you had to help Ellen barf out her guts in the bathroom."

"Oh no," I said, snapping to attention. "Again?"

"Yup," Juanita said. "This is *after* she decided to make a fool of herself with Jason's karaoke machine. But we'll talk about that later. It merits serious discussion. Meanwhile, Lo, for real, where've you been all morning? Chemistry felt ten hours long without you."

"I didn't tell you guys I had a doctor's appointment?"

The truth was, my parents were the only ones who knew about my Mysterious Symptoms. I didn't want anyone to think I was a weirdo. Or overreact and get worried when I might not even have anything wrong with me at all. I just wanted to be normal until I couldn't be normal anymore. I wanted to be normal until my normalcy dried up like the river that ran through the center of town. And besides, I was probably fine. I was going to ask my parents if we could get a second opinion from a doctor whose belt buckle didn't weigh as much as a car engine. Better yet, I'd get better before my next appointment. I was probably just eating too much sugar, or there was toxic mold in my bedroom, or my hormones were out of whack. . . .

TranquiLo. You're at school now, in public. I dug around in my backpack for my lunch, only to realize I'd forgotten to pack one.

"Oh my god," Alex said, her blue eyes fixed on me in shock. I stopped in my tracks. For a second I thought she knew my secret, like she had gotten hold of my medical chart. Then she lowered her voice to a whisper. "Lo, did you go to the gyno this morning? Did your mom take you to get a prescription for birth control?"

I laughed, relieved. Alex knew perfectly well that birth control was the furthest thing from my mind, especially since I was a virgin and didn't have a boyfriend, despite what my DayGlo underwear might suggest.

"Yeah, right. Just a routine checkup," I said, feeling a little guilty about lying but deciding that the alternative— making my friends worry—was worse. "So tell me about Brett," I said, changing the subject. "Dish, Alex. I hate that I missed Weekends on Wednesdays last night." I might have changed the subject a bit too effectively, because for the next four minutes, Alex didn't stop talking about the star soccer player's "pillowy" lips and "rock-hard abs." I took this to indicate that she'd been reading too many of her mother's romance novels. (By which I mean the novels that her mom *writes*, not ones she keeps on the shelf. Slightly overweight and incredibly awkward, Mrs. Karen Reynolds is known everywhere besides her church and the dentist's office as Cate Mayweather, best-selling romance author.)

Before I could interrupt Alex's monologue, Ellen Davis arrived on the Agua scene like a bucking bronco.

"Who's seen my backpack?" she practically shrieked, stopping short our conversation, such as it was. I looked around for the bag in question, but someone was sitting on or near every backpack in the vicinity in a proprietary way.

I hadn't hung out much with Ellen recently. We didn't have any classes together that semester, and I'd been distracted by my symptoms since the start of school. Ellen used to be attached at the hip to me, Juanita, and Alex, but she'd started going off the deep end last spring. Though we hadn't said it to her explicitly, we were all really worried about her. Her pill problem was the worst-kept secret in our crowd. So far her mom, a wealthy state delegate, and the nosy guidance counselors at school didn't appear to have gotten wind of her addiction, but Ellen routinely came to class either high on something or in a stupor that no amount of caffeine from the cafeteria vending machines could shake.

And last spring Ellen had discovered heavy-duty painkillers. Serious stuff, like Oxy and Percocet. So I was definitely worried about the road Ellen was on. But—and I hated to say it, because lord knows I'd had my own mood swings lately—she'd also been acting like a real bitch. After she wrecked her brand-new car last April driving to school on a handful of Xanax washed down with lite beer, we all rallied around her. Even though Mrs. Davis told us it was "only a fender bender" (false) and that they "had enough flowers already, mostly from the capitol building" (brag), we visited Ellen in the hospital anyway. But she was a nightmare patient, cursing us out right and left. She wouldn't even accept Juanita's get-well flower bouquet, saying that the smell of roses "made her want to vom." It got so bad one day that we decided we wouldn't come back to visit; we clearly weren't helping her and were maybe only making things worse. Ellen had been drifting further and further from us ever since.

Now she seemed to be on something far worse than pills. She'd lost a bunch of weight, for one. Her jeans sagged off her hips, and she'd already been pretty thin to begin with (her mom basically stocked the fridge only with flavored seltzers and imitation eggs). For two, her skin, which had always been clear and sun-kissed, was now ghost-white and splotchy. Her bleached blond hair was all over the place, and she had a wild look in her eyes that scared me. She seemed to be staring right through us.

"No one has your backpack, crazy," Alex said.

Ellen whirled around to face Alex. Her forehead had broken out in a sweat, and various stains showed on her baby blue tank top.

"Then where. The eff. *Is* it?" Ellen said.

"Probably where you saw it last, chica," said Juanita's sometimes boyfriend Luis LeBlanc, who was approaching from a nearby picnic table. Ellen responded by grabbing Luis's baseball cap and tossing it into the fountain like a Frisbee.

"Damn, girl," he said. "Chill." For a second it looked as if Ellen was going to retrieve the hat, but then I realized she was just leaning over the Agua wall to scoop up the coins at the bottom of the fountain. When she was satisfied with her handful of nickels and pennies, she held them aloft.

"Hey," I said automatically, "those are someone's wishes."

"Yeah?" Ellen said. "Well, I wish you'd all just disappear." She hurled a couple of pennies across the courtyard, pocketed the rest of the coins, and stormed back into the school. I was stunned. Luis muttered some profanity and made his way back to his table, shaking the water from his cap.

"What the hell was that?" I said.

"Meth," whispered Alex.

At first I thought she was joking. Then I saw her exchange a grave look with Juanita that indicated she wasn't.

"You're serious?" I said. Sharp-as-a-tack Ellen, who starred in the fifth grade play, won the middle school science fair three years in a row, and had scored practically all the goals on our childhood soccer team, was on *meth*? What was a sixteen-year-old girl, by all accounts clever and accomplished, doing on such a savage drug?

"Unfortunately," said Juanita. "I got it on good authority. Granted, my brother can be kind of a dick, but he's not a liar, and he knows a lot of people. Last night he told me that his friend Angelina accidentally walked in on her using in the bathroom of Stoops. Caught her in the act."

"She's sure?" I said.

Juanita nodded soberly. "No wiggle room."

"I only just heard about it this morning," said Alex. "But it seems so obvious now. You should have seen her last night at the party, Lo. She was totally tweaking."

I could barely process this. "I know that she hasn't been handling her alcohol lately—"

"No shit," said Alex. "She can't go out without getting totally obliterated."

"And she's been downing all those pills. But . . . Jesus. Meth? Really?"

"Really," said Juanita. "Apparently that complete ass she's been hooking up with—Mike what's-his-face—gave her her first hit." Boyfriends were supposed to introduce you to cool new bands and video games and car mechanics and stuff. Not meth.

"I feel like we need to do something," said Alex.

Of *course* we needed to do something. But clearly we were out of our league. Sure, we weren't innocent to the fact that kids our age dabbled in drugs. But that mostly stopped at smoking pot and snorting Adderall occasionally. Crystal meth was way out of the range of substances that could optimistically be called "recreational." People didn't do meth in moderation. They did it until it destroyed them.

Just then, a shot of pain bullied its way through my head, making me feel like my skull was clenching up and trying to squeeze my brain out of my eye sockets. I reeled backward into the fountain wall and put my head between my knees.

"Lo?" Alex said, as if through water. Electrified water. "Are you okay?"

"I'm fine," I said. "It's just. . . ." Tears came into my eyes, summoned both by pain and by my frustration that I was alone with this secret. "Period cramps," I said. "They're really bad this month."

"Awww," Juanita said, putting her arm around me.

"Um, I know I just got to school," I said, "but do you guys mind covering for me? I think I have to ditch."

"No problem," Alex said.

"Then I guess this is where we part," said Juanita, making a teardrop with her manicured fingernail. "Until later, *señorita, mi corazon.*" Heart, *corazon.* Brain, *cerebro.* I knew a woefully small number of words in Spanish, but I liked to use them in conversation because they always struck me as jauntier than English. I made a mental note to memorize all my body parts in Spanish. Then maybe I'd look upon them more cheerfully if they began to fail, one by one.

Shut up, Lo. Quit with the self-pity. *Bienvenido. Buenas tardes. Mucho gusto encantada.*

"Feel better, babe," said Alex. "A heating pad and some ibuprofen always help me."

"Thanks, guys," I said, making my way toward the courtyard exit. "You're the best."

"I know!" said Alex. "Finally somebody gets it!"

"Don't forget chocolate and mafia movies!" shouted Juanita at my back. "I swear on my heart that *The Godfather* trilogy healed my eczema!"

I smiled back at her through the pain.

From school I drove straight to the pharmacy. Fernando's Pharmacy, in the boonies of Santa Fe, where I could be anonymous. I didn't risk running into anyone from Santa Fe High there, and the pharmacist never batted an eye when I picked up my arsenal of drugs from behind as well as over the counter. While Alex and Juanita shelled out for new clothes and pedicures every week, I bought ibuprofen, fish oil, super B-complex vitamins, and protein bars with my parents' credit card—all staples of my morose survival diet.

As I barreled down the freeway past outlier shopping malls, used-car lots, and Mexican buffets, I tried to get out of my own head. I thought about Ellen. I was furious at myself for being oblivious to her downward spiral. The meth explained so much about her recent behavior. But I couldn't get over how . . . *serious* it was. And way too much for me to handle, especially when I wasn't doing so well myself. But Ellen was tough and distinct and endearingly obscene. She was my friend. I couldn't allow her to fall apart.

3

ARMED WITH OTC PAINKILLERS AND a red basket's worth of obscure supplements big enough for a horse to choke on, I started out for home.

The route back from the pharmacy ran along the perimeter of a semi-wooded park that Dad called the "Tinderbox." For years he'd been trying to get the Forest Service to do a controlled burn of the sage and thick underbrush, to no avail. Now we were in the midst of one of the worst droughts our region had ever experienced, and it was way too late and too dangerous to think of burning anything on purpose. The last monsoon sea=son hadn't provided us with a thorough soak, and Dad worried that the arid aspens in the Sangre de Cristo Mountains would go up in flames. I envisioned a single match obliterating every tree from here to the Pacific Ocean.

But I didn't see any fires that day as I drove and washed down my brain-boosting vitamins with a sports drink. Nor did I see smoke when I scanned the scraggly, desiccated treetops.

I did, however, see a large mammal dash in front of my car, leaving me only milliseconds to avoid hitting it by swerving into the opposite lane.

Orange pills flew all over the passenger-side floor, where they were swallowed by coffee cups and candy wrappers. "Cheese and toast," I blurted, then almost laughed when I realized that I'd instinctively used my mother's version of "profanity."

TranquiLo. Focus. Collect yourself and your medicine.

I pulled over and looked in the rearview mirror. Standing just where my car had passed, so close that it could probably sniff my wall of bumper stickers (**one nuclear bomb can ruin your whole day. IF YOU CAN READ THIS, I'VE LOST MY TRAILER.** horn broken, watch for finger.), was a coyote.

I'm not scared of coyotes. Unless you're an escaped housecat or an infant abandoned on a picnic blanket, you have no cause to fear them. Coyotes are everywhere in New Mexico, including downtown Santa Fe, where they frequently wander past tourists in the midst of dream-catcher-buying frenzies. Still, it's not like I would ever try to hand-feed Milk-Bones to one. Being prolific doesn't exactly make them docile. You just have to be sensible enough to stay out of their way.

Or not.

I stepped out of my car. The coyote didn't flee, nor did it freeze with fear. It just gazed at me steadily, reflectively, somehow demanding my full attention in return. Its eyes seemed to issue a gentle challenge: *Come here,* they said. *Let me see who you are and what you're about.*

Let's get in each other's faces and make sure we're both fully alive.

Was I losing my mind? Hallucinating? My nerves were already frazzled by . . . the obvious. And the not so obvious. You start the morning with a visit to the neurologist and you never know what's going to happen. I felt raw, unmoored, as if I could burst into tears at any moment. And I had never been a crier.

I inched around the car, my legs shaky from the near-accident and not, I told myself, from the Maybe Sclerosis. I crept toward the coyote and was about to say something pretty nutty considering the context, something along the lines of "Here, pup. Do you need a friend?" when another un-expected body appeared through the trees, this one human. I felt an electric shock plunge down my right leg like a live wire and exit via my boot. I hated it when that happened.

The man jogged casually toward me, indicating with a wave that everything was okay—stellar even. Though I'm understandably wary whenever strange men appear out of nowhere and make a beeline for me, his smile immediately put me at ease—as much as I ever felt at ease in my own skin those days. The expression on his face was . . . transcendent.

His silky dark hair hinted at Native American blood, but I couldn't determine his ancestry for sure. He wore his hair almost to his shoulders, with one funky ponytail on top of his head that resembled the crested plumage of a bird. He looked like a refugee from a local college—the kind of school that taught classes like "Personal Communication in a Machine Age" or "Feminist Puppetry in Elementary

Education." Whether he'd be an older student or a young professor, I couldn't be sure exactly.

"I see you found Dakota," he said in a throaty, harmonious voice that either indicated depth of life experience or decades of smoking. I suspected it was the former. "Or she found you."

"This coyote belongs to you?" I said, feeling shy all of a sudden.

"Well, not exactly. This coyote belongs to me as much as she belongs to you, and as much as you belong to that thirsty tree over there. Today Dakota just happens to be walking in my world. Better than me walking in her world, I suppose. Otherwise I'd be biting the heads off chickens." He chuckled.

Biting the heads off chickens? Who was this guy, a voodoo priest? After a long pause, he must have registered the confusion in my face. "She likes to join me on my . . . outings," he went on. "We enjoy each other's company, is all. We're connected."

I'd never been allowed to have a *real* pet because Mom was allergic to dander. But I sort of knew what this guy was getting at—every morning I brightened when I saw the lizard I called Seymour strut across my bedroom window screen in search of flies. And then there was our backyard population of chickens, a bonanza of feathery heads I was in charge of naming and feeding. Few sunrise pleasures could compete with letting Pollo Hermano eat grain from my hand.

I couldn't put my finger on why, but I felt calm around this guy. I used to think I could read energy fields, the colors and auras that surrounded people. It was probably something that my old friend Kaya had suggested once, or maybe it was something I read about in a book a long time ago, but every now and then I still thought I saw lights around certain people. Or, if the person was really special, I heard music. And this man radiated a sort of soundtrack. Like, a violin concerto wrapped in a sixties rock show.

"I'm Jay," he said, pausing the music but not the spell he'd cast on me.

"I'm Consuelo," I said, suddenly dizzy. "Lo." I stepped back and braced myself against the hood of my station wagon so I wouldn't faint. Jay looked concerned but didn't move.

"I don't know if you saw," I said, "but I almost hit . . . Dakota on the road just now. It was a really close call, actually. Kind of rattled me." I felt like I was snitching on his animal buddy, but I needed Jay to know how close Dakota had come to dying. So he could maybe protect her in the future.

"Sorry about that," Jay said, throwing me another charismatic smile. "Dakota isn't great at formal introductions. She must have been pretty desperate to meet you."

I liked the notion of a creature being so eager to make my acquaintance that she would hurl herself in front of my car. As long as there were no casualties, of course.

Dakota trotted up to us and presented her head to my hand. I hesitated. Dad always taught me that if a wild animal acts too friendly or fearless toward humans, it might have rabies.

"She seems to like you," Jay said. "She wants to smell you and size you up."

"As long as she doesn't want to know what I taste like," I said. I imagined that, right now, licking me would be like licking a tablet of Advil.

I felt the hot breath exhaling from the coyote's nostrils, giving the tips of my fingers individual steam baths. Jay smiled down at her as a new mother might smile down at her newborn. I lightly ruffled the bristly hair between Dakota's black-striped ears. I relaxed again.

"Why did the coyote cross the road?" Jay said, chuckling to himself as if he were about to unleash the king of corny dad jokes.

"I don't know," I said. "To get flattened by a used station wagon with a million ironic bumper stickers?"

Jay smiled. "To make a new friend. You should feel special. I had to woo old Dakota for weeks before she'd approach me, and she was just living in the cave next door."

"You live in a cave?" I said.

"Doesn't everybody?"

"Not the last time I checked. Wait, are you Batman?" I was joking, but Jay would actually make a pretty good super-hero. He seemed intensely moral, and he had an awesome sidekick. Why not?

"Not that I'm aware of," Jay said, "but I *have* been inhaling a lot of bat guano lately. Of course, if that's how super-heroes got made, comic books would be a lot less popular."

"Yeah," I said. "Like Superman stepped in a radioactive cow pie and that's how he got his X-ray vision. I think most teenage boys would pass."

"How about you?" Jay said.

"Me?"

"What's your superpower, Consuelo?"

Well, let's see. I could dance alone in my room "Maniac"-style to the same song a hundred times in a row. Or at least I could last spring. I wondered if that still counted.

Suddenly, Dakota gave a sustained cry, shrill as chalkboard fingernails. I jerked my hand away. She barked gruffly and backed away from me.

"What happened?" I said, trembling with self-doubt. I thought Dakota liked me. "Did I do something wrong?"

Dakota growled and lowered herself into a menacing crouch. Was she getting ready to attack? Jay shook his head casually, as if to indicate, *What can you do? Coyotes will be coyotes.* Then he looked down at me, and his face went grim.

"What happened to your blood, dear?" he said.

"What . . . what do you mean?" I said. Could he actually see that I was suffering?

"You're unwell," he said. "You're . . . afflicted. Is it your blood, sweetheart?"

"My blood? Of course not," I said. But for some reason I felt Jay wasn't going to let me beat around the bush. The morning's doctor appointment came flooding back to me. For the first time, to the first person outside my family, I needed to confess what was going on with me. I felt that perhaps the secret of my Might-be-Sickness would be safe with him.

"It's my brain," I said.

It was actually a relief to unload.

"Yes," Jay said, considering me, all of me, every neuron. "I see that now. I can see how your energy is tainted." Dakota whimpered and looked inquisitively at Jay, as if she thought I was contagious and meant to suggest that they should both remove themselves from my presence, on the double. Then Jay laid his hand on my shoulder. I didn't shy away as I usually did when strangers touched me. "You're in pain," he said.

I nodded. My pain had never felt so immeasurable.

"Pain is a funny thing," Jay said. "It can control your entire environment. It can turn the sun to the moon. It can make the blue sky black."

"I know what you mean," I said. Even though it sounded melodramatic, lately it was like my entire world was filtered through pain goggles. The world just looked different to me now. Somehow . . . faded. Like all the colors had been put through the wash too many times.

A bolt of nerve lightning shot down my leg, and I grimaced.

"I'm sorry that you're suffering," Jay said with deep compassion.

I felt validated that Jay had grasped what I was going through in a heartbeat, there with the hot canine breath on my hand. He saw my pain, but he didn't try to identify it to show me how smart he was or to make me feel uncomfortable. He simply acknowledged it while reserving all judgment. I somehow felt secure there in the little triangle we made of strange Tinderbox hippie and moody coyote. I felt that I could stand there forever and be healed.

"You know, dear," Jay said, "your essential well-being is much deeper than the burden your body carries. You do not have to be tyrannized by your disease."

I smiled. That sounded reassuring. But I wasn't sure it was true.

"Do you believe in souls?" he said.

I looked intently into his eyes and saw something radiant there. Something almost . . . nuclear. Which wouldn't exactly be surprising considering the proximity of Los Alamos. Who knows what's in our water supply? "Unknown environmental insults" are another possible cause of MS.

"Of course," I said. I'd always assumed that souls were the deepest, most profound part of us, the core part that couldn't be undone or dissolved. My soul was what fueled my need to hula-hoop for hours or to hug my parents or to leave a nice note in someone's locker. A soul wasn't necessarily divine, though at times I'd felt it stir when Mom dragged me to St. Francis for Sunday Mass. It responded to the candles and the stained glass and the low hum of love that filled the cathedral. But that all sounded too cheesy to discuss with my friends.

"Good," Jay said. "Then you'll believe me when I tell you that yours is in jeopardy."

"What?" That was a bold statement. "How do you figure?"

Jay smiled in his saintly way.

"Something is ailing you," he said. "Something is targeting your body, and you're letting it penetrate your soul, little by little. You need to stop it in its destructive path before it's too late. Build a line of defense around your soul so it will stay intact, no matter what threatens it."

But I might be diagnosed with a disease that was attacking my body on multiple fronts. How could I be expected not to think about that, worry about that, obsess about that?

How could I prevent it from getting to me? But, in a way, what he said felt... true.

"It's changing me," I said, on the verge of breaking down and burying my face in the coyote's fur. "I feel it. I experience things... differently now. There's, like, a dark shine on everything. And I don't know what to do. I don't know how to stop it. I don't know how to get better."

"Your soul knows how to get better, if you would only listen to it."

I wondered what that involved. Tarot card readings and séances, like Kaya and I used to do during our "mystical" phase? Bible study? Stream-of-consciousness journaling? I was at a total loss. And then the pain picked that exact moment to return with a vengeance. I cradled my arm in front of my chest as if it were a baby. A baby that was being poked with a thousand sharp needles.

"I... don't know how," I said, and began crying, stupidly. Maybe that could be my superpower: filling up infinite empty bottles with tears. This was all too much. The pain, the coyote, this mysterious man, the way the near-accident had made me put the brakes not just on my car but on my whole life.

"You know more than you think," Jay said. "I can tell. Dakota and I have mingled with a lot of souls over the years. Yours is powerful. And highly reactive."

I wanted to tell Jay to repeat that to my muscles and my neurons on the off chance they'd listen.

"But," he continued, "it is also entirely exposed right now. It's vulnerable. And you're in danger of compromising it."

I nodded, overwhelmed.

TranquiLo. Take two dozen and call me in the morning.

"I have something for you," Jay said.

He drew a small object from his pocket and held it out to me. It was a horse figurine carved from crystal the color of turquoise, and it was beautiful.

"For me?" I said.

"Yes, dear. A symbol of your journey."

"Why?" I said, ignoring the "symbol" aspect. "A present? You don't even know me."

"It's not forever," he said, tenderly placing the horse in my hand. "You'll give it back when you're done with it. After your energy is healed."

"How do you know I'm going to be healed?" I said. Maybe he knew of magical herbs and potions that could mend my body and allow me to start over fresh. What was this unfamiliar feeling? Hope? Why did it have its locus in a total stranger? But the man no longer seemed like a stranger. He seemed like a friend. Like an uncle, perhaps.

Jay merely smiled. "We can all be healed," he said. "At any moment. You just have to change your perspective. You'll learn. You'll see." He placed his hand on the coyote's head. Dakota seemed much calmer now. "Your pain. My pain," Jay said. Dakota whimpered again. "Her pain. The mountain's pain when it's burning. The caterpillar's pain when it's transforming. It's all connected. It's all one. And transparent. You just have to see it clearly."

I didn't know what to say. *See* pain clearly? Wasn't feeling it clearly bad enough? Plus, if I did have MS, one of the first things to go would be twenty/twenty vision.

"I was meant to meet you today," Jay said, once again disarming me with his beatific smile. He was like the pope of the desert. "You need my help. You need to feel the universe's larger plan for you."

"A plan? For me?" Lately it felt as if the universe only cared about me as far as it could throw me. Suddenly I was afraid that Jay was going to recruit me for Teen Bible Study.

"I may not look the part," he said, flicking his ponytail, "but I know some things that might be useful to you if you're willing to open your soul to them. I perform rituals. Ancient, time-honored rituals, born in these deserts by their native inhabitants. And one of these rituals can release you from your burden."

My eyes must have widened a bit too much because Jay immediately altered his tone.

"But be warned. I'm offering you powerful medicine, and power can easily swing between positive and negative. If you give it a chance, however—if you embrace it with a full heart—the ritual can eliminate your pain and disease and teach you to accept everything fate throws your way. With joy."

Okay, so maybe he was talking about something more like a hippie support group. I could get on board with that. In New Mexico everyone is familiar with the mumbo-jumbo vocabulary of spirituality, but that's different from actually believing in sacred healing and medicine men and stuff. Still, I couldn't help picturing Jay waving a turkey feather over my head and pronouncing me cured. I imagined him banging on a painted drum until the evil spirits were expunged. Clearly I didn't know anything, really, about shamans or rituals.

"But is that . . . allowed?" I said soberly, to be respectful. Jay looked at me curiously. "For me to be included? Even though I'm not . . . ? I just thought those rituals were sort of trademarked by the Native Americans."

Jay smiled indulgently. "The spirit world is for everyone, Consuelo. We're all related. Our underlying energies are one. Remember? Speaking of which, when I perform the ceremony, you must have four friends with you, four friends who are similarly suffering and who also aim to safeguard their souls."

I slipped the turquoise horse into the pocket of my hoodie.

Four? Four friends who'd be willing to do an ancient Indian ritual with me? When one of our favorite pastimes was belting out rap songs from the back of a pickup truck while we drove from pool to pool? I knew Jay's cure seemed too good to be true.

"I can see you're wary," he said. "But it would benefit you to trust me. I may not be Batman, but I know how to channel the superpowers. Think it over. If you decide to participate, meet me at Pecos Park on Camino de las Madres on Saturday evening. Sunset. I'll lead you to the pueblo ruins where we will make our magic. Remember, there must be five of you. A full star. That's essential. You have nothing to lose but your burdens."

He gave a little whistle, and Dakota stood at attention, then the two of them turned to walk back into the Tinderbox.

Back in my car, I lost track of how long I sat in thought. What kind of madness was I entertaining here? No matter how kind and trustworthy Jay's eyes were, it didn't change the fact that he was a New Agey witch doctor who'd come out of the woods with a freaking pet coyote, and now he was headed back there as if he were on some kind of twenty-first-century, dope-driven vision quest. There was still a chance that modern medicine would save me. Or that I didn't have MS after all. It was only Minor Silliness. Mañana Sadness.

And there was another major hindrance to following his instructions. I didn't have four friends with problems.

4

IN THE FRONT OF THE classroom, Indians were being massacred. A movie screen had dropped from the blackboard to show an all-too-realistic reenactment of the 1864 "Battle" of Sand Creek, the ruthless murder of more than a hundred Cheyenne and Arapaho people—mostly women and children—by American soldiers at a peaceful encampment in Colorado. The film was part of our section on the history of Native Americans in the West. Gun and cannon fire lit up the screen, terrified women shrieked words I didn't understand, teepees burned to the ground, wounded old men were mutilated as they begged for mercy, and then someone dimmed the lights. I saw the flashing explosions. . . .

And then I saw nothing. The room went completely dark. I lifted my hand to my face. Nothing. I was blind.

Though I'd already been frightened by the scene in front of me, somehow not being able to see it was a thousand times worse. The military gunfire continued to blast into unarmed Indians. The detonations and the screaming were all amplified now that I couldn't temper the horrible sounds with images. For a second it felt as if the mayhem was actually *in* my body. But no, it was just a movie. I couldn't lose my mind along with my sight. Not now. My eyes were intact—just completely blinded.

Again.

This had happened once before. The last time I went dark was right after someone switched on a strobe light during a Justin Timberlake song at a Weekends on Wednesdays party. But then, my vision had come back in seconds.

This time was different.

This time, it wasn't going away. And the longer I waited, the worse the feeling got. I sat very still in my seat and listened to the kaleidoscopic sounds of gunfire and screaming. I knew I had friends on either side of me, but that almost made things worse—to be surrounded by people I cared about but couldn't see. I felt like I had disappeared. Like I was a black hole. Soulless.

The bell rang, and the movie cut out. What would I do now? The room filled with the sounds of shuffled papers and hitched-up backpacks as everyone prepared to file out to their next class.

"Aren't you coming, Lo?"

"No," I said, looking in the direction of Alex's voice and her violet-scented body spray. I knew that the room would be empty next period. "Not right now, anyway. I feel pretty nauseated—same thing as yesterday, you know? I'm just going to chill here for a few minutes."

"Do you want me to stay with you? Or take you to the nurse's office?"

I could hear her voice, but did she even exist? Did I?

TranquiLo. Take with water. Do not operate heavy machinery. Limit exposure to sun.

"No thanks," I said. "I just want to be alone, I think, until it passes." I didn't ask if Mrs. Laramie was still in the room because I didn't want to betray my blind condition, but judging by the quiet, Alex and I were the only two people still there.

"Okay," Alex said with concern in her voice. "Feel better, doll. I'll let Mr. Rodriguez know that you're running a few minutes behind for English."

"Thanks, Alex," I said, closing my eyes to another blanket of darkness and resting my cheek on the cold desk. "For everything. I mean it." Alex rubbed my back, then departed, taking her floral-smelling skin with her, leaving me in a state of nothingness.

———

About an hour (I think—I couldn't consult a clock) after the final bell rang, my sight came back. First the enameled wood of the desk shuddered into view, and then I slowly raised my head to the window and saw the sun penetrate the venetian blinds. The sun. I would never complain about it again.

Before I could start contemplating a life of solar worship, I was assailed by a rush of horrific thoughts. What if I'd been walking down the hallway when the blindness struck? What if I'd been driving? I would've plowed into a roadside saguaro stand or something. I could have *killed* someone. What if my parents found out things were this bad? Or Dr. Osborn? No, my current condition was totally unsustainable. I wouldn't be able to hide these symptoms for much longer. Everything was going to change. Life as I knew it was going to be totally upended. I'd never felt so scared, so disoriented. I gathered my things and rushed down the empty hallway and out into the parking lot. I had to do something, and I had to do it immediately.

The way I saw it (now that I could actually see), I had one option, as crazy as it sounded. Well, maybe not so crazy for Santa Fe.

Jay's ritual.

But to do that, I'd need four friends.

I couldn't imagine taking Juanita to meet Jay. I loved her, but for one, she'd never take something like this seriously, and for two, what was her burden? That she'd recently gotten stuck behind a minivan full of kids in the drive-thru of Taco Sandy's? That Luis persisted in buying her regular instead of diet at lunchtime? That her boobs were so big they caused her mild back pain? And Alex had nothing wrong with her except for what she termed her "spaghetti legs." Everybody loved her. She was . . . happy. Like a character at the end of one of her mother's romance novels. My friends weren't shallow; they just weren't searching for answers right now. They didn't even have the questions.

No. If I was going to find real suffering, something more akin to mine, I would have to get creative. I would have to find the outsiders, those who didn't drink from the agua of our lunchtime clique.

Like Jay said, I had to save my soul.

And to save my soul I needed to take a big risk. I needed to convince others to save theirs.

And suddenly I knew just the person who could help me do it.

—

I drove past my own house and parked three doors down, in Kit Calhoun's driveway. Kit and I had grown up together and were in the same year in school, but he and I hadn't talked much since our ill-fated "romance" three summers before. Today, however, he was my gateway to Thomas Kamara.

I was perhaps a little *too* well aware of the fact that Thomas had been hanging out in my neighborhood recently, always glued to a skateboard. Kit appeared to be teaching the Liberian orphan how to emulate Tony Hawk. Thomas was a fast learner. He also happened to look amazing with his shirt off. I'd seen them in the middle of my road, doing ollies and kickflips and skating in the empty pool in Kit's backyard, which had been converted into a half-pipe. A lot of kids used to congregate there for long skating sessions, but Kit was more of a loner these days. Thomas, another notorious loner, seemed to be the only one allowed in.

How can I describe Thomas? In brief, he was a really hot student from Africa who looked half the time as if he wanted you dead and the other half as if he was about to hand you a bouquet of flowers and sweep you off your feet. There was just something so intense about him. Vibrant. Even when he seemed clouded or out of it at school, Thomas still had this piercing quality to him. And then there was the matter of that poem he wrote, the words he'd never meant for me to see. Right now it was those words more than anything that steered me toward him. But more on that later.

I let myself in through the Calhouns' side gate, my childhood route, and walked around the house to the backyard. There was Kit, not skateboarding, exactly, but straddling the rusty diving board with his wooden deck on his lap, staring into the empty deep end of the pool. He was either lost in thought or ignoring me on purpose.

I suspected that Kit harbored some malice toward me. Which was understandable for two reasons: One, I might have been responsible for both his initiation into romance and his first broken heart. The summer between eighth grade and high school—the summer that decided many social fates—Kit and I hung out almost every day. In the not-too-distant past, Kit's swimming pool had been filled with water and was a huge draw for me and the other kids in the neighborhood. Kit, on the other hand, had less appreciation for it. "I wish I could drain it and turn it into a skatepark," he'd always say. Eventually, he got his wish.

But back during those lazy summer pool sessions, Kit and I got to know each other, floating head to head on inflated rafts in the blazing desert sunshine, drifting with the music that was always playing from his stereo. We talked about our parents, what we thought high school would be like, where we saw ourselves five years after graduation. We'd seen all the same high school comedies and romances and had read a lot of the same books. We felt qualified to declare to each other what mistakes we wouldn't repeat.

"You're going to get popular and forget about me," Kit had teased. "You're going to be one of *those* girls. I've got a bad feeling, Lo. You'll start dating a generic senior quarter-back on the first day of school. His name will be Rocco, and he'll think Pink Floyd is a flavor of ice cream."

I laughed and dismissed that prediction, throwing a beach ball at him. "Well, *my* crystal ball tells me you're dead wrong," I said. But secretly I thought that all sounded pretty great. Not the forgetting-about-Kit part, obviously, but . . . just . . . meeting new people, trying different things. And it turned out that Kit wasn't too far off in his prediction. Except it was a junior lacrosse player named Simon, and it was the second week of school.

I'd never revealed this to Alex and Juanita, but Kit and I had kissed a little bit before that summer was over. I'd never kissed anyone before and . . . maybe I needed some-one to practice on so I wouldn't embarrass myself at the high school parties in my fantasy future. I admit that sounds awful, really mean-girl of me. But it's the bitter truth. One day I just grabbed Kit in the pool and got to know his lips. They were soft, eager, and tasted a little like sunblock and chlorine. It was nice, but I didn't feel that spark I'd read about in so many nineteenth-century novels, and I didn't want to go into high school already attached to someone. Still, I thought we'd stay friends after I told him that even though I really cared about him, I wasn't ready to be his girlfriend, that I wanted to start the new year with a clean slate.

But he wanted nothing to do with me afterward.

And though I made small efforts here and there, I all but avoided him because I felt so guilty for hurting his feelings.

And then there was the second reason Kit was cagey and despondent, around not just me but everyone. He was in mourning. The previous year he'd fallen completely Mohawk over Vans for Lucita, a beautiful Zuni girl and a recent transplant to our school from the Four Corners area. She had eyes that everybody wanted to wallow in, eyes like the deep end of an inground swimming pool.

But Lucita died.

She was driving home to the rez from Kit's house one night and she ran off the road. She overcorrected and flipped her car. She wasn't wearing a seat belt. I don't think she was texting at the time or anything. It was just one of those stupid errors that inexperienced drivers make, like not yielding to school buses or taking twenty minutes to parallel park. Except this time the mistake was fatal. On a weeknight after school when everyone else her age was joyriding, eating junk food, drinking, evading homework, figuring out what to do next to prolong the bliss of not doing anything much, Lucita bled out on the shoulder of an empty road.

Gone.

Ever since Lucita's death, Kit had mostly isolated himself. I never heard music from his backyard anymore. He barely said a word at school, unless he was in American history class, during which he seemed universally outraged, especially about our government's treatment of the Indian tribes.

So I wasn't all that surprised when Kit started hanging out with Thomas last spring. But it wasn't as if they were having long, intimate discussions over milk shakes. Actually, I'd never even heard them talk about personal things. They just seemed to be trying to leave all their feelings on the pavement. They were both so distant. I guess I was starting to relate to them.

I wondered how much Thomas knew about my history with Kit, or if Kit had ever said any resentful things about me. If Thomas thought I was a bad person who broke people's hearts for no good reason. Well, I truly hoped not.

I was going to need his help.

"Kit?" I said now, unsure of my right to be in his backyard. He finally looked up, but he did it with such sluggishness he seemed barely alive.

"Lo? What are you doing here?"

"I'm actually looking for Thomas," I said, "but I take it he's not here."

"Kamara? You guys know each other?"

"No . . . not exactly," I said, remembering lines from Thomas's poem: *He thinks you must be deaf / Not to hear the shots, / See the blood.* For a second I thought Kit was going to give me the third degree, but then he visibly lost the required energy.

"Nope. I'm alone." He sighed. "But have a seat. Stay a while."

Okay, so maybe he didn't hate me.

I sat down on the edge beside the diving board. To populate the silence, I started tossing twigs into the pool, and from there I kind of understood why Kit was wearing that look of fierce concentration when I arrived. That gaping void of a view was rather entrancing. Such a deep, seductive sanctum. All sun-bleached concrete cut through with black tire marks. A person could easily disappear in it.

"I still don't know how you convinced your mom to drain the pool," I said, making conversation. "We used to have so much fun swimming."

"Yeah, well, she was sort of desperate to do something to make me feel better since. . . ."

I nodded. So we were going to go there.

"I understand. And I'm so sorry, Kit. How long has it been now?"

"Eight months, three days, and two hours since the car accident. Eight months, three days, and forty-five minutes since she died."

I looked up at him. I was crushed about my aunt Karine's death too, but I wasn't keeping such a morbid and precise timeline.

"I see," I said. Lucita had been really special—like movie-star special—and Kit had adored her. I hadn't known any other high school couples who seemed so in love. Seeing them hold hands down the hallway, or make themselves a table for two at lunch, or dart around Kit's front yard playing with squirt guns, it had almost made me feel . . . well, not exactly jealous. But as if I had missed out on something wonderful. And then all that happiness was obliterated in a random instant by the side of the road. I tried to visit Kit after it happened, but he refused to leave his room. In many ways, he still hadn't emerged.

"I was going to teach her how to skate," Kit said softly now from his diving board perch. "I'd finally convinced her to try it. The week she died."

"Kit, I'd . . . I'm so sorry. I want to talk more about her, and I want you to know that I'm here for you always. I feel like a colossal jerk, but the thing is, I'm in a bit of a rush, in a deadline situation, you know? I need to find Thomas as soon as possible. Do you know where he is?"

"Oh yeah. Your mysterious quest for the mysterious Thomas. Well, um, it's Friday so he's probably helping with the sunset tour at the balloon field."

Oh, right. Thomas's adoptive parents ran a Christian-themed hot-air balloon business just south of downtown. It sounds crazy, but this isn't so remarkable in Santa Fe. Everyone's parents seem to have some wacky job or another. Luis LeBlanc's mom sells meteorites in the plaza. Mrs. Laramie's husband paints old RVs and fills them with scrap metal as installation art pieces. Then there are the bodice-rippers by Alex's mom, which you can buy in airports all over the country. By comparison my parents' careers are snore-inducingly normal, even though they flirt with death and fire every day.

"Okay, thanks," I said. "I'll try there." I got up to leave. Kit just nodded and resumed staring, idly spinning the wheels on his skateboard. I felt bad leaving him like that, but I also knew that sometimes, when you were really missing someone, you just wanted to be alone with her absence.

"Listen, Kit," I said, "if you ever want to talk. . . ."

"Talking doesn't really help," he said. For a split second I heard Jay's voice in my head. *Four friends who are similarly suffering.* Maybe now wasn't the time, maybe it would never be a good time, but I wondered about taking Kit to see Jay with me.

"Well, you know where I live," I said. Kit showed a hint of a smile. He didn't just know where I lived; he knew which first-floor bedroom I slept in. He used to wake me up some mornings before middle school by tapping on the window.

But now that seemed like an eternity ago. Now we were separated by much more than panes of glass.

5

AT PSALMS OVER SANTA FE, the Dent family does a booming business at sunrise and sunset, when the local scenery is at its most picturesque. I was used to seeing the giant canvas balloons overhead when I fed the chickens in the morning or came home in the early evening from lady dates with Alex and Juanita. The structures made me think of massive sea creatures floating through the brine, like whales or giant squids. Oddly enough, I'd never actually seen the balloons land, only rise and sink.

I parked at the far end of the vast Psalms lot and sat in my car for a few minutes, trying to build up some nerve. *TranquiLo. Remember: no risk without reward.* No, that didn't sound right. The opposite of that. *Lo contrario.*

Finally, I got out of my station wagon, bypassed the main office, and went straight for the balloon launch site. You didn't have to worry about airfield security at Psalms, though it would be sort of funny to have to remove your shoes and go through a checkpoint before boarding the balloon basket. And then be asked to turn off all electronics upon takeoff and landing.

Settle down, space cadet. Sketch comedy is not your forte.

Thomas was at the periphery of the bald, bone-dry airfield, hunched over some kind of metal burner. In the center of the field Mr. Dent helped a group of middle-aged passengers weighed down with cameras board the basket of a half-inflated balloon designed to look like an ice cream cone dipped in rainbow sprinkles.

I have to admit, I was kind of jealous of these tourists. Even though I don't lust for the Southwestern landscape, as so many flocks of visitors seem to, early September is by all accounts an ideal time to have a bird's-eye view of the region. Monsoon season had just ended, and though we were still suffering from an unusually arid climate, the colors were beginning to change in the foothills of the Sangre de Cristo Mountains.

I looked away from the Baskin-Robbins balloon to find that Thomas had stopped what he was doing and now had his gaze set squarely on me. He wore his customary uniform of Converse high-tops, a white V-neck T-shirt, and cutoff jean shorts. And of course the usual dark hoodie that hid his face at school.

When you say the war is over,
He wants to argue the point. . . .

I knew Thomas's story partly from my mom, who went to the same church as his parents. The Dents used to travel worldwide as missionaries, but their hands were currently pretty full with one biological son and six other young children they'd adopted or were fostering. Not to mention the responsibilities of running the airborne ops at Psalms Over Santa Fe.

But Thomas seemed to be the exception to their happy family. He was the newest, and chronologically the oldest, addition to the Dent melting pot on de Gama Street, and as far as I could tell he hadn't yet assimilated into the Smiling Grateful Children Club. Just two summers ago he'd been re-located to whitewashed Santa Fe from Liberia, where rumor was he'd been a child soldier in the Second Liberian Civil War. At school, people said that he'd killed people. Lots of people, maybe even his own parents.

I'd never heard Thomas talk about growing up in Africa. Actually, I thought, as I prepared to ask him the biggest favor of my life, I'd never even had a proper conversation with him. I only knew of his experience secondhand, through the rumor mill and my mother's friends at St. Francis. At school Thomas kept quiet, aloof. He was jumpy in class, easily rat-tled by loud noises, as if his finger were still on the trigger. His body still seemed poised to dodge bullets or dive into ditches. Everyone (except maybe Kit Calhoun) was too ter-rified to ask him questions or even to stand too close to him in the cafeteria lunch line. Because he kept so silent, I guess everyone assumed the worst. That Thomas could snap at any moment, as if he had some machete muscle memory and might stab them with a cafeteria fork.

But what I first noticed about Thomas was how good-looking he was, especially on the one or two occasions I'd seen him smile. Like the first time I met him, sort of, when

I found him standing alone by Agua de Water at the end of lunch period.

"Why do people throw away their money in the fountain?" he'd said as I walked by him *very* slowly.

"I guess because the hope of having their wishes fulfilled is worth more than their money," I'd said. Then I'd pulled some change from my pocket and handed him the sole quarter in a constellation of pennies. "You try."

That was the first time I saw his dimples, and the golden undertones that lit up his skin when he was thoughtful.

But none of my friends had ever mentioned Thomas's beauty; their fear of his war-torn past pushed him right into the category of weird and undateable.

Which I guess is why I'd hesitated to tell my friends that I thought Thomas was hot. Like, smoldering hot. I worried that they might judge me strangely for it. That was my weakness. And I hadn't told them about his poem that I'd found, about how much it had affected me. Ever since I read the poem, whenever Thomas walked into a room, I felt his energy more than ever. Like an electric charge. His eyes were usually downcast, and his body language made him all but unapproachable, but it seemed as if he hid universes beneath his skin. Galaxies. He didn't radiate blandness like my ex-boyfriend, Jason Sibley, or Juanita's boyfriend, Luis, or the other varsity guys at school. Thomas was different.

But I won't lie. He scared me a little bit. But not for the reasons he scared everyone else. I was scared because his presence made me seek the same vital qualities I saw in him—even the painful ones—in myself. And perhaps I wasn't ready to face them.

Or, now that I was on the verge of diagnosis, to lose them.

Over the last year, Thomas had started to make casual friends, and once in a while our social circles overlapped. He'd been to a couple of Weekends on Wednesdays, though he didn't really chat with anyone and he usually left early, long before I'd get up the courage to talk to him. So why did I think I could summon the guts to speak to him one-on-one now? *Mano a mano*. *Tête-à-tête*. No, French didn't put nearly the same positive spin on things as Spanish.

But it was way too late to backtrack now. Before I had a chance to bail, I was standing close enough to kiss him, staring at the cloud of dust my feet had thrown up.

"Hi, Thomas," I said. He squinted, as though willing me to shrink into a bug or turn around and walk away, a thousand miles away. As he crouched over the burner with a faint shimmer of sweat on his forehead, I thought he'd never looked more handsome, or been more disconcerting.

"I, um, thought I'd find you here," I said.

"Oh?" Thomas said, revealing no emotion, good or bad. He waited, still affectless, for me to continue. I shielded my eyes from the glare of the sun that seemed to penetrate my neurons themselves, causing a migraine. My vision blurred slightly, and my knees weakened like a wave had hit them. But there was no place to go but forward.

"Which of course begs the question," I said, trying to fill the embarrassing silence, "of, um, why have I been looking for you?"

"You tell me," Thomas said, keeping his eyes steady on me. "You never have before."

He had me there. But in all fairness, Thomas didn't exactly make himself easy to befriend. He always seemed light-years away. Which is precisely why I knew we could help each other.

"Well, did you ever think that maybe you're sort of hard to talk to?" I said, smiling. "Like maybe you're willfully intimidating?" Was I bordering on flirtation?

"Am I?" Thomas said, lighting the burner with such vigor that I could feel the heat on my bare legs.

"You're just . . . you know. . . ." Suddenly this was coming out all wrong. I didn't know how to finish. I didn't have the words. How pathetic I must appear to him right now. I might as well be blind again, considering how much I was stumbling.

My eyes wandered to the people climbing into the generous scoop of balloon. For a second I wanted to trade places with any one of them, even if it meant changing schools, changing faces, changing histories. I just wanted to feel strong again, like I would remain whole until graduation.

"I see," he said, solemnly fiddling with the balloon apparatus. Though his English was impeccable, his accent was slightly foreign—possibly French—and it made me melt a little.

Focus, Lo. You can do this.

"Listen, Thomas," I said, regrouping. "The truth is . . . I have a proposal for you. And, well, I don't know what you're going to say. It's kind of heavy."

"Let me be the judge of that."

"Well, it's about this condition I have."

"Condition?"

"Yeah." I wanted to stall for time, but Thomas's eyes were expectant, burning into me. There'd be no equivocating. "I just found out that I might be . . . sick. Like incurably, neurologically sick." There. I'd said it. MS. My Strain. My Substance. *Mucho* Sorry.

For a millisecond Thomas seemed like he might be genuinely troubled. But then he knelt back down to the ground and began puttering with the burner once again. Moving on to the next task. This hurt my feelings.

"Hello?" I said. "Sick girl here." Wait, I hadn't meant to sound angry.

Thomas's eyes had gone cold again. "What do you want me to do about it?"

"It was stupid of me to come," I said, whirling around. So much for risks reaping rewards. I felt exhausted, hopeless. What had I been thinking? This wasn't gorgeous, untouchable Thomas's problem. This was mine alone. I couldn't expect him, of all people, to care. The migraine began spreading down my spine, if that were even possible.

"I'm sorry," Thomas said, making me slow down and stop. His voice was loud, clear, almost yearning. I turned around to face him again. He was still squatting in the dirt, not making eye contact, but he'd put down his tools.

Not me, of course.
I am not at war
Anymore. . . .

"About what, exactly?" I said.

"That I was callous. . . . That you're sick. It's just that . . . I've . . . seen too many people die. I can't . . . get close. My instinct is to turn away when someone I like. . . ."

He trailed off, and I got confused. Someone he . . . *likes*? Was he referring to me? He didn't even know me. How could he like me? We'd barely had a conversation. His life experience was so vastly different from mine. He was an ex–child soldier from Africa. I was an economically comfortable white chick with parents who still made me a basket full of jelly beans every Easter. I owned four Joni Mitchell records, for god's sake. I could keep eight hula-hoops going at once. Thomas and I were the dictionary definition of "worlds apart."

"I have a favor to ask you," I said, gaining nerve and brushing aside Thomas's confusing comment for now, though I feared I was still blushing from it. "But I don't have much time to spare, so please be honest with me. And promise that you won't do anything that you're not one hundred percent comfortable with."

Now it was Thomas's turn to be confused. "I promise," he said.

I took a deep breath. "I know you've been through a lot. The war, coming to the States, the adoption."

Was I saying too much? Thomas's face became forbidding, maybe even angry. It wasn't really fair to know all these personal details about him secondhand. But I'd already warmed to my speech, so I kept going.

"You've got some things that probably weigh on you," I continued. "Heavy things. And so do I, though probably . . . to a much lesser degree. So I'm just going to say it. Tomorrow there's a ceremony in the desert that could maybe take . . . that weight . . . away. I'd be healed of my disease. Potentially. And you'd be, you know. . . ."

Truth was, I didn't really know what Thomas would be released from after the ritual, because I didn't know what exactly he was afflicted with now. I was confronting him out of the blue about his sorrows before he'd even shared them with me. Maybe now he never would. I lowered my head.

"Come here," Thomas said. "I have something to show you." He grabbed my hand and practically yanked me across the airfield toward an isolated red balloon. I looked around for Mr. Dent, but he was already high above our heads with the tourists. I'd been so absorbed in our conversation—in Thomas—that I hadn't even noticed their ascent. Now Thomas and I were alone together in the field with this menacing red contraption.

"Get in," he said.

Though earlier I'd been longing to go up in the air, these weren't exactly ideal circumstances. I'd made Thomas angry, had triggered something in him. I didn't truly know him, not beyond my own haphazard guesswork, and I couldn't predict what he would do.

I sleep in a bed.
My new mom makes me a sandwich.
There are no machine guns at my disposal.
But that is me. Not him. . . .

"No thanks," I said. "Maybe we could get coffee or something instead? Frozen yogurt?"

"Get in," Thomas repeated, and this time the command had an almost military ring to it. I obeyed, climbing into the basket. He followed me inside, latching the short wicker door behind us. Then he lowered his black hood and turned on the burner. A long, jagged scar I'd never noticed before stood out prominently on the back of his neck.

"Thomas, what are you doing?" I was really starting to feel anxious now. It seemed as if my enigmatic classmate intended to launch us into the heavens. Thomas untied various ropes around the basket. When he got stuck on a particularly stubborn knot, he pulled a large hunting knife from his belt and sliced the rope clean through. Then he cranked the burner under the balloon, and I felt my body begin to lift off the ground. My stomach leapt the way it did in fast elevators. I wanted to grab for the ropes that Thomas was dropping one by one to the earth, but my hands had gone numb. I leaned into the corner of the basket to try to secure myself by my elbows in the shaky vessel as we jerked skyward.

"Consuelo Katherine McDonough," Thomas said, "you don't know what you're asking me. You're out of your depth here. You have no clue."

I looked over the basket edge and saw the ground floating away. I closed my eyes. Could Mr. Dent see us? Would he and his passengers descend to save us?

Wait, Thomas knew my full name?

"You're right," I said through gritted teeth. "This was a mistake. Please put me down." What if the breeze blew us into an electrical line or something, caught us on fire, caught everything on fire?

"What do you know about my life?" Thomas said. "That I came from a war zone, that I'm an orphan, that I should be ever so grateful to be safe in the US of A? To be taken care of by Big Daddy America?"

I nodded my head, barely listening, still unable to open my eyes or hold on.

"Can I tell you what you *don't* know?" Thomas said. "When I was a boy, rebel soldiers killed my parents in front of me. They shot them and then burned them in our house outside Monrovia while they were still alive, screaming. My little brother, Henri, and I escaped through the jungle, but we heard their agonizing cries as we ran. And then they stopped."

In one of my nightmares, my father burned alive in the forest, unable to halt the flames of wildfire. Here in the real world of Thomas and the sunset and a rising balloon, I opened my eyes. Thomas gripped the cord that fed gas into the burner. The flatness in his gaze was gone, replaced by something feverish and urgent.

"After weeks alone, starving, Henri and I were picked up by an opposing army. They said we could avenge our parents' murders. That the men who had killed them were less than dogs and we needed to get retribution before they slaughtered more members of our families. The army soldiers marched us into a military camp and gave us guns. I'd never seen a gun up close. It was heavy. Savage. A few days later my best friend from school arrived at the camp. When I saw him I embraced him. I thought he'd died in the fire that had consumed our village. My commander saw our embrace. He didn't like that we were still . . . human. He handed me a machine gun and told me that if I didn't shoot my friend on the spot, he would kill me. . . . Shall I continue?"

I nodded. The earth was farther away every second.

> *I am a broken T.V.*
> *Not like the nice ones in America.*
> *Like the ones I watched in Monrovia.*
> *My static is loud, violent.*
> *Black and white.*
> *Good and evil.*

"Henri was standing right there. I knew that he needed me." Thomas's eyes were lit up as if he were reliving the scene in real time. "I was his big brother, his only family left. And so I shot my friend. I shot him in the leg, and he fell to the ground, screaming in pain. My commander cracked my head open with the butt of his machine gun. 'In the heart,' he said, pointing at my friend's chest. I told him that I couldn't do it. My friend was writhing on the ground, begging me to spare him. Blood was shooting from his leg. I must have hit the femoral artery by mistake. I didn't know anything about the body's most vulnerable points . . . at the time. The commander grabbed my hair and jerked me to the ground, began kicking me in the ribs again and again. My little brother cried for him to stop. The commander shook the gun in my hands. 'Kill your friend,' he said. 'Or I'll kill your brother.' I aimed the gun and shot my friend through the chest."

I trembled in the corner of the basket, wanting Mom and Dad, wanting to be grounded again, feeling my body convulsing beneath me like a storm cloud.

"That was the first person I killed," he said.

"Why are you telling me all this?" I whispered. I was one hundred feet above the ground, a killer's captive.

"Because you don't know what you're messing with. You're in over your head. When I fall asleep at night, I see my finger pulling a trigger again and again. I see the blood of my friends pouring from their bodies like sap from trees. I see myself grinding an old man's face into the ground until he chokes on mud. And sometimes I think I'm capable of doing it all again. For no reason whatsoever. Just because."

He still gripped the knife that he'd used to cut one of the tethers. He stepped closer to me.

"My new siblings are afraid of me," he whispered. "They hear my screams at night. In those seconds before I wake up, I'm fighting for my life. Every time. If they got near me in those seconds, when I'm still un-conscious, operating on instinct, I fear I might break their necks."

His eyes welled up with tears.

"You say you might be dying," he said. "But I'm already dead. I have nothing to lose."

Just then I felt a violent jerk on the basket. I stumbled headlong into Thomas's chest, my stomach barely missing his knife. We had stopped ascending. One rope held us tentatively to the ground.

"If I'm going to do this ritual with you," he said, "and try to lift the . . . weight, as you call it, then I need to know that you're not afraid of me."

"I'm not afraid of you," I said. And I wasn't. I could feel the chill of the knife through my T-shirt, but his chest was warm, inviting, safe.

"I'm a monster," Thomas said.

"It's okay," I said. "Maybe I'm a monster too." We slowly began sinking.

6

WHEN I CAME HOME FROM the airfield with an assurance from Thomas that he would join me in the morning, and would approach Kit about coming too, I found Mom sitting at the kitchen table in her church clothes, an empty bag of barbecue potato chips in front of her. She looked up as if she'd been waiting idly for hours for me to walk in the door.

"If this is an intervention," I said, kissing the top of her head and wiping the crumbs from her cheek, "you are way off the mark. I'm not pregnant, nor am I an alcoholic. But give me a few more months. Isn't patience one of the cardinal Catholic virtues?"

Mom smiled. "Very funny, sweetheart. It's not an intervention. But, believe it or not, Miss Independent, your dad and I are worried about you."

"Isn't that how every intervention begins?" I said. "In fact, I think there's a show on MTV about this. Where is Dad anyway?" I began filling a glass from the faucet.

"He's on the mountain with his crew."

I bristled, and the water overflowed my glass. "On the mountain? Why?"

"There's a small fire up there today. They're just rerouting and containing it. But he'll be fine, dear. You know how cautious your dad is. Safety first."

This was true. One Christmas he'd given me and Mom life jackets, and we'd never even been on a boat before. He made sure the trunk of my car was stocked with bright orange safety vests at all times, in case I got a flat tire or something and needed to await help on the side of the road. The giant signal flares he'd given me for my fifteenth birthday were supplements to this little kit. He probably would've been quite disturbed if he'd known that I'd just been up in the air with a teenage balloon pilot. But right now the memory was too charged and too confounding to share with anyone.

"Consuelo, your dad and I know that you don't want to talk to us about your symptoms. But we think it's important for you to talk to *someone*. A friend or. . . ." She let the sentence fade into the kitchen linoleum. I had a feeling she was about to say "relative," but we both knew that Aunt Karine was the only family member I had a history of opening up to. And we both knew she was dead.

"I'm trying to respect your wishes," Mom continued, "but I don't think it's healthy to keep this possible threat to your health a secret. You go back to the hospital for testing in just over a week. I think you should be prepared for the eventuality that your life is going to change. Maybe radically. And if that happens, you're going to need support. Why not ask for it?"

Little did she know, support was what I was trying to get, except I was going through coyote rather than human channels.

"When . . . your aunt was dying," Mom said, still unable to say her sister's name, "she surrounded herself with friends. You know how much people liked her. She was just a . . . a warm soul." Mom paused for a moment, digging around in the potato chip bag before remembering that it was empty. "And I know that having a support system comforted her. As she made her . . . transition."

"'Transition'? Mom, that's an extremely poor euphemism if I've ever heard one." She was a nurse who dealt with life and death every day, but she still couldn't accept her sister's mortality. Could I?

Aunt Karine had been independent, feisty, had lived all over—even on a houseboat in a Mexican lake. All my life she'd sent me letters and postcards chronicling her extensive travels. She'd been an adventurer and an iconoclast and even knew how to hula-hoop with fire.

Then she'd died in hospice care in the spare bedroom across from mine.

My aunt was only thirty-three when she succumbed to multiple sclerosis. And we never had time to get used to the idea of her dying. She was Mom's kid sister and had been in exemplary health her entire life. She'd been living in an apartment in San Francisco, thriving at her job as a community organizer and moonlighting as a street performer, visiting us at least twice a year in a whirlwind of pure energy and eccentric gifts like sock puppets and glow-in-the-dark models of the Golden Gate Bridge.

Then, last spring, her vision started to blur. Her legs got shaky. Maybe because she was this fetching, vibrant, positive person, the doctors were reluctant to run the serious tests. They didn't see the red flags. Instead, when she mentioned spinal pain and lumbar soreness, they thought she might have slipped a disk. But they wised up eventually.

It's not that an earlier diagnosis would necessarily have prolonged Karine's life. MS is incurable, and my aunt had an extremely acute, accelerated form. She was wheelchair bound within a month. Wheelchair bound, the woman who seemed to live half her waking hours dancing on air. The woman who could compel a crowd of total strangers to attend to her movements on the sidewalk. The woman who had first taught me how to hear music with my whole body. The woman who sounded to me like a symphony.

Not long after the diagnosis, it became clear that Aunt Karine couldn't care for herself or remain in her San Francisco apartment, so my parents flew her to Santa Fe and moved her in with us. Karine tried to insist that we turn her over to a nursing facility, but my mother wasn't entertaining that idea for a second. She seemed to think that only under her own personal supervision would her little sister get better. Mom is a nurse, after all. She had faith in her medicine, and she had faith in the healing powers of Santa Fe.

Karine had lots of friends in the area, as she seemed to have in every area—a gaggle of cowgirls and artists and dancers and buskers and Indians from four surrounding states. They would stream in and out of our house to say hello. Then, when Karine's medical situation became more dire, people began streaming in to say goodbye.

Which was more than I could do.

Mom grew quiet at the kitchen table, and I immediately felt bad for reprimanding her. She took a sip from her can of ginger ale, then cleared her throat and brushed the oily crumbs from the front of her dress.

"My point is, I know it helped Karine to keep her lines of communication open, to talk to her friends."

"Maybe," I said. But I'd now told two people besides my parents and the doctor about my symptoms—Jay and Thomas—and I didn't feel much better, physically anyway. My head still throbbed. I still felt pins and needles on my arms at random moments. Like this one, for instance.

"Do you ever talk to Kaya Johnson anymore?" Mom said. "Maybe she would have some insight into what you're going through since she also has a . . . condition."

Kaya! Of course! The most obvious person ever. Due to her rare form of congenital analgesia—an inability to experience pain—Kaya literally could not feel a knife cut into her skin. She would be perfect for Jay's ritual. Her condition informed her entire existence, and not in a good way. I knew in my heart—and from long association—that she would give anything to feel something. In addition to that, she was Pueblo on her mom's side and Navajo on her dad's (who lived with his second family on the rez). I couldn't help thinking that her Native American heritage might make her more receptive to my proposal.

"You're absolutely right, Mom," I said. "You're a wise woman. Maybe even a saint. Kaya is exactly the person I need right now."

Maybe I was overdoing the gratitude a little, because

Mom seemed astonished that I'd taken her advice. "Oh," she said, seeming self-conscious. "Okay. Well, please give her my love. I haven't seen her in so long. She's such an exceptional person." She balled up the potato chip bag in one hand and clasped my hand with the other. I gave her a kiss and dashed out the door.

———

I drove to Kaya's house, which was on the outskirts of town—not far from Fernando's Pharmacy, in fact. Even though it was a warm Friday evening, I knew that Kaya would be home. With the exception of school hours and doctors' appointments, she could pretty much always be found at 57 Crockett Way. Mrs. Johnson had outlawed any hobbies or after-school activities, deeming them too risky for her daughter's fragile state. After all, a stray projectile at a football game had the potential to give Kaya lasting organ damage. And Mrs. Johnson didn't trust other people to monitor Kaya. Which wasn't so paranoid of her, really, considering kids used to stick paper clips and sharpened pencils through Kaya's skin in the back of the elementary school classroom to see if they could get her to cry. (They never could.)

I should explain something about Kaya's condition. When she was three, her mother, oblivious, sent her to pre-school with a broken arm. After a few days, a classroom aide thought the arm looked a little wonky and took Kaya to the school nurse, who immediately sent her to the hospital for

X-rays. For a full week, little Kaya had been playing, sleeping, and eating breakfast cereal with a compound radial fracture. The pain would have leveled any other kid, but Kaya hadn't complained once, so her mother had no idea the arm was broken. A few weeks later Kaya almost bit her tongue clean off, never feeling a thing. You could still see the stripe of scar tissue whenever she licked an ice cream cone.

By the time her rare condition was identified and precautions were put in place, Kaya had experienced the full range of covert injuries. She'd stepped on rusty nails, dipped her hands in boiling water, scratched her soft spots during nightmares until she stained her sheets with blood, and had at least one emergency eye surgery for an infection caused by a foreign ocular object she couldn't feel.

I never saw Kaya cry. Not at sleepovers when other girls began teasing her about the gloves she had to sleep in so she wouldn't scratch herself raw. Not on the playground when she fell over—and once knocked out a tooth after jumping off the swing set into a concrete barrier. Blood poured out of her mouth, and she just kept playing as if nothing was wrong. At the time I was more upset than she was—I started weeping and then got a sympathy toothache that lasted days.

When Kaya was five or six, Mrs. Johnson became hypervigilant. For instance, she was the first one to rush to Kaya on the playground that day and scrabble around the sand pit looking for the lost tooth. I still remember the way the silver rings on her fingers flashed in the sun as she dug frantically through the sand.

But her overprotective single mom couldn't shield Kaya from getting a reputation as a Grade A weirdo. Kaya was the white buffalo of our town. To most people, she was sort of creepy, but also sort of sacred. Locals were proud to claim her, in a queer way—she'd even been featured in a *People* magazine story about teenagers who can't feel pain—but they kept their distance because she was taboo. No one wanted to be the white buffalo. Or even party with the white buffalo. Better to corral her off, keep her as offbeat eye candy.

Mrs. Johnson was portrayed in the *People* article as a sort of beleaguered, woe-is-me single mother who was both gifted and cursed with this special-needs daughter. She struck me as the type who was always aiming for the sympathy vote. I didn't entirely trust her, and I didn't think Kaya did either. Unfortunately, when I rang the doorbell, it was Mrs. Johnson who answered.

"Hi!" I said, trying not to betray the unkind nature of my thoughts.

"Consuelo McDonough. It's been a long time." Kaya's mom paused, maybe waiting for me to give an explanation, but I said nothing. "What brings you here?"

Over the past few weeks, I'd realized that certain people made my symptoms flare up. Mrs. Johnson, for instance, made my middle finger twitch ever so slightly on my right hand. But she was Kaya's maternal security detail, and I had to be civil.

"Oh, I'm just here to see Kaya," I said politely. "We're . . . working on a school project together. Is she home?"

Mrs. Johnson eyed my backpack, as if to check it for sharp objects. Like I was going to smuggle in a chainsaw to hack her daughter to pieces. "Kaya," she yelled up the stairs. "Your old"—emphasis on the "old"—"friend Consuelo is here." The trepidation in her tone made me wonder if she secretly wished to keep Kaya in one of those giant sterile bubbles.

"Thanks," I said, still trying my utmost to contain my frustration at having a bodyguard between me and my oldest friend in Santa Fe. "Okay if I just go up?" Before Mrs. Johnson could answer I was rocking the stairs two at a time, like I used to.

"Be my guest," Mrs. Johnson murmured as she retreated toward the kitchen. "But bedtime is promptly at ten. And I don't want her leaving the house."

I pushed Kaya's bedroom door open after a cautious knock, and she started. Apparently she hadn't heard her mother announce me, due to the headphones in her ears.

"Lo?" she said timidly. "What are you doing here?"

I plopped down on Kaya's purple beanbag—no hard edges in her bedroom, obviously.

"I need to talk to you," I said.

We probably hadn't spoken more than twenty words to each other in a year and a half, and now I was in her bedroom, where we used to play with plastic show horses and magic kits for hours on end. Then, when we were a little older, where we tried to summon the spirits of the dead with a Ouija board and predict our futures with tarot cards. I'd still never met anyone else with a similar lust for paranormal experiences. But it had been years since I'd even read my horoscope in the newspaper.

"Whoa," she said. "Is there a blue moon this month that commanded you to come here or something? Is everything all right?"

I'd forgotten how pretty Kaya was. I used to tell her that all the time—how I wished I had her high cheekbones, fawn-colored skin, and intense cat eyes. Though I felt pretty good about my physical appearance, sometimes I still coveted her looks. My strawberry blond hair and green eyes often drove me nuts—I was a freak Irish girl in the midst of the Southwest. But the same shy body language that Kaya enlisted to protect her fragile person—head lowered, arms crossed over chest, shoulders hunched, et cetera—also served to camouflage her finer features. Now, swiveling around in her desk chair, she brushed her black bangs from her face as if she wanted me to notice those cat eyes once more, as if she wanted to show me that she was still the same pretty person I used to compliment. Then her hand shot nervously back into her lap.

"Listen, Kaya," I said. "I'm sorry to barge in here like this. I know that we've . . . drifted apart. But there are only a few people I can trust at this point, and you're one of them."

Kaya had never been judgmental. I used to open up to her about every crazy thought and feeling that passed through my brain, and she'd just roll with all of it even when she couldn't relate. I tried to do the same for her. I missed that about us. But standing here in front of her now, I suddenly felt as if my success with Thomas had been pure luck.

I was supposed to pitch Kaya some story about a magical coyote and a mesmerizing forest gypsy and a five-person sacred ritual, and she was supposed to jump on board without asking too many questions. None of which I could answer, of course. I was about to call to order a wing-and-a-prayer sort of meeting, and I didn't have any words. Where to begin exactly? *So this coyote . . . ?* I decided to skip the preliminaries.

"I've got a major problem."

Kaya looked at me skeptically. I didn't blame her. How could she know anything was wrong behind the shiny veneer of Agua wishing-well happiness I usually exuded at school?

"That makes two of us," Kaya said. *Touché.* And it was true. Kaya had problems that even her mother didn't know about. I knew from personal experience that she could be . . . reckless with her anesthetized body. Years ago, right around the time Kaya and I stopped hanging out every day, she told me that sometimes she cut herself at night, hoping that she'd find out what pain was. I all but freaked out when she showed me the fresh lacerations, all jagged from the serrated steak knife she'd used.

I shuddered involuntarily at the memory. I couldn't handle any more knife imagery that evening. I squeezed my eyes shut for a moment and breathed deeply. *TranquiLo.* For an extended second the perfume of Kaya's bedroom brought back memories of sleepovers, late-night psychic readings, intimate secrets, and laughter that erupted volcanically whenever we were together.

"It sucks that we're not friends anymore," I said suddenly.

"We're not friends anymore?" said Kaya innocently. "Then what am I supposed to do with all the bracelets I made you at summer camp?"

We both smiled. We had always shared a borderline cheesy sense of humor.

"I'm serious," I said.

Kaya shrugged. "My current lifestyle doesn't exactly support a wide social circle. By the way, did my mom happen to frisk you when you came in?"

"Nah," I said. "She only asked to neutralize the three grenades I was packing."

At that moment Kaya's mom knocked on the door, and we both started giggling. Mrs. Johnson had obviously been creeping because we hadn't heard her approach across the aged floorboards.

"Kaya?" she said. "Are you all right?"

"I'm fine, Mom," Kaya said. Then, quietly to me, "Ugh." We heard footsteps retreat reluctantly down the hall.

"Man," I said. "You'd think one of us would've sensed her presence. Aren't we supposed to have psychic powers?"

Kaya and I used to visit a psychic once a week. Santa Fe was full of people eager to read our palms, predict our rosy futures, and above all take our allowance money. Kaya liked all that pseudo-mystical stuff. And for my part, I just found what psychics had to say more interesting than what Mom's favorite Catholic priest intoned on Sunday mornings. (Forgive the sacrilege.)

"What?" said Kaya. "You didn't know she was out there? I did."

"I was too busy, um, reading your next-door neighbor's mind. Chester isn't sure how to tell his wife that he's leaving her for his llama trainer."

"Makes sense," said Kaya. Her tone was flat, and I got the feeling she was done joking around.

"So you've got a problem, huh?" she said. Maybe I was psychic after all. "Not that you don't deserve every happiness," she continued, "but most girls, as you must know, would kill for your problems. Which span the spectrum of midfielder to point guard to quarterback." I wasn't sure if I deserved all that, but Kaya was allowed to be hurt that I hadn't been around. I hadn't tried hard enough to hold on to my friend.

"I wish," I said, ruing the lack of boyfriends I'd actually had, despite appearances. Boys and I always seemed to break off at the friend mark. Or at least at first base. "I don't think my life was ever *that* idyllic. In any event, it's kind of a shitshow now."

"Yeah, well, like I said before, I can relate," Kaya said. She shuffled some oversized tarot cards on her desk, and I decided to change the subject.

"So I take it your mom is as . . . involved as ever," I said.

"Actually, she's been trying to give me a looser rein. I talked to her about it. She's even letting me have a birthday party next Friday night, out at Shell Rock? You know, the picnic area out there? A band is going to play and everything. I'm really excited." I must have looked hurt, because then Kaya backtracked. "I hadn't invited you because. . . . Well, you're invited now. If you want to come."

"Sure," I said. Kaya smiled. She hadn't had a birthday party in years. I guess you could only be so festive when you were essentially isolated from anyone with nails and teeth. "I'd love to come," I said. "You should be celebrated, Kaya."

She shrugged her shoulders again and nervously began tapping the tarot cards on her desk.

"Let's read each other's fortunes," I said. "Like old times."

Kaya smiled. "Okay," she said, nostalgia overcoming us both.

"You first." I took the tarot deck from her and began shuffling the cards.

"Don't cut them like you used to," Kaya said. "I mean, I'm older now. I don't need you to baby me."

"You knew about that?" I said. In junior high I used to hand-pick the cards so Kaya always got feel-good images like the Magician and the High Priestess. Then I'd interpret them as positively as possible. I shouldn't have cheated, but she was already feeling gloomy about her life and her future, and I'd wanted to give her something to look forward to.

People should always play tarot with friends. You get better fortunes that way.

"Ask your question," I said. "But don't tell me what it is." Kaya closed her eyes, trying to commune spiritually with the cards as I spread them on the desk. This time I didn't cheat, and I drew Death first.

"See?" I said, troubled but trying to hide it. "This is precisely why I'm bad at this game."

"Don't worry about it," Kaya said. "Sometimes the Death card can mean something positive. You know, like transformation, regeneration, et cetera. Or, I'll get run over by a steamroller tomorrow. Hard to say."

"Let's stick with transformation," I said. "Next." I drew another card. The Hanged Man in reverse. "Okay, granted I'm a little rusty, but I think this means you're about to let go of something you've been clinging to, like maybe a feeling or a relationship. Orrr . . . ," I said, "in the spiritual realm, I think it means something like beliefs from your childhood are going to come back to . . . sort of . . . haunt you. Also, you should eat more vegetables."

"What an excellent reading, Lo," Kaya said. "I wonder how the cards knew about the cupcake diet I've been on lately."

"Magic," I said.

"Amazing," Kaya said. "Uncanny. Your turn."

She expertly shuffled the cards and then closed her eyes before she chose one.

"Okay," she said, "is your question about love, money, health, spirituality, or what?" I thought for a second. Somehow I felt that my current crisis transcended my physical health. That it affected my soul, like Jay had told me.

"All of the above."

Kaya laid the card face up on her desk. "The Ace of Swords," she said. "Interesting. That means you need to be brave." She drew another card. "I see you riding a horse," she said. "Like a warrior." I fingered the turquoise horse in my pocket. I'd automatically grabbed it off my dresser that morning—for some reason, it felt good to have it with me. Kaya placed a Devil card on the desk. "This card means— let's see—that you're going to find freedom. From what, I don't know. But it's going to come at great expense. . . ."

"Where do you see that?" I said, suddenly feeling panicky. "How great?"

"That's what the Devil card means, Lo," Kaya said with composure. "It also implies some form of self-bondage. Like, to an idea, maybe. A belief that is preventing you from growing." Kaya had always known more about the tarot than I did. Now it seemed she was an expert.

"Freedom," I said. "Go back to that. Do you really see freedom in my future?" I wondered if that meant freedom from suffering. I wondered if that meant death. I began to tear up.

"Lo, what on earth is going on?" Kaya said, interrupting her reading. "Why are you here, really? I know it's not to get your fortune read."

"I . . . I'm sorry, Kaya. I came here because, well, to be honest, I think I might have multiple sclerosis. And I wanted to talk to you about it since . . . it's a neurological disease. Sort of like yours."

"Oh my god," Kaya said. "Are you serious?"

She listened attentively as I told her about my symptoms and my appointment with Dr. Osborn. The more I talked, the more I calmed down. Kaya had always been a great listener.

"It's really not so bad," I said. "Some aches and pains in the morning. Nothing a few ibuprofen can't fix." Kaya had never even had to take an aspirin. "But I'm especially worried because it runs in families, and my aunt died of it. . . ."

"Karine died?" said Kaya. "Oh my god, Lo. No one told me. When?"

"Late July."

"I'm so sorry. I didn't even know she was sick ..."

"I ... thought you knew," I said.

"No! I would have....."

"Please don't worry about it," I said with finality. I couldn't think about Karine on top of everything else. Kaya shrunk back into her cushy desk chair with its rounded arms.

"It's weird," she said thoughtfully, "because I made you a painting not long ago. Before I knew. It must have been right around the time that she died." She rummaged in a plastic container under her round desk and pulled out a scroll of paper. "You can look at it later," she said with embarrassment as I began to unroll it. I pouted but didn't open it any further. "So what are you going to do?"

I took a deep breath and told her about Jay's ritual.

"That's the story," I said. "Thomas Kamara and I are meeting Jay tomorrow at sunset. What do you think?"

Kaya looked at me, seemingly enraptured with the idea of experiencing something new and quite possibly dangerous. "I'll do it," she said.

"Kaya, thank you. You have no idea what this means to me," I said. "Let me throw your cards again. I think I did it wrong last time."

As I shuffled, I noticed for the first time that on many of Kaya's cards, blood stained the white space around the images. I looked more closely at her hands. Her cuticles were torn to pieces, as if she'd stuck her fingertips in a blender. I remembered something else Kaya had said in *People*: "Sometimes I don't really consider my condition the absence of pain. I consider it the presence of something else. Something magic."

7

ON SATURDAY MORNING I AWOKE at dawn more nervous than I'd ever been in my life. It wasn't just the prospect of investing my future in Jay's ritual, and it wasn't just my physical condition that made my nerves feel tattered. It was that I was about to see Thomas again. I kept remembering how good it had felt to lean against him in the hot-air balloon, hunting knife and all.

But I had to stay focused. Knock on wood, I was going to be responsible for a group of four (if the wild-card candidate I'd decided to approach that morning agreed) burdened kids who didn't really know each other. With the exception of Thomas and Kit, I was the only tie that bound us. And I wasn't even sure I could get them all to show up. But the day was bright and beautiful, and I felt hopeful despite my poor odds of success.

My wild card? Ellen Davis. Though frankly I was pissed that she of all people was making decisions that even a lobotomized goldfish wouldn't consider, I also genuinely hurt for her. I had to think that she could come back into the drug-free fold and be her sweet, cheeky self again.

And okay, maybe I wasn't just pissed at Ellen. Maybe I was furious. But I also knew that I needed to try to understand where she was coming from or I'd get nowhere.

I knew where she would be that morning. Lately she'd been forsaking our Agua group's weekend routine of making up silly biographies about Plaza tourists and trying to sneak into rock shows in favor of hanging with her boyfriend, Meth-Head Mike, and his dropout friends in a fractured parking lot behind the abandoned chili canning factory on St. Bonaventura Drive. Gross.

During my drive to St. Bonaventura I thought about what to say. It would be easier if Ellen hadn't been so volatile lately; I had no idea how she would react to my proposal. Or what state she'd be in when I proposed it.

Where the road and the railroad tracks intersected, a weather-worn billboard advertised a holistic medical retreat in nearby Abiquiú. New Mexico was supposedly a place with magical healing properties, a place where a hundred years ago tuberculosis patients traveled in droves, like gold prospectors in covered wagons, thinking the dry mountain air would cure them. If you had a creak in your knee or a head full of phlegm, you came west. New Mexico was the place where all of one's earthly problems would disappear—a spiritual and therapeutic epicenter. I tried not to consider the irony as my head throbbed relentlessly.

I turned into the cannery parking lot and saw Ellen's car before I saw her. Her new BMW, the second one she'd been given in her sixteenth year, was parked across the lot from a group of kids I didn't recognize. They were talking and laughing around a nucleus of lit cigarettes. Ellen wasn't standing with them, so I pulled up alongside her car. Then I saw her combat boots twitching on the sill of the open window. She lay alone in the backseat, staring blankly through her sunroof. I walked around to her top half.

"Hey, Ellen," I said as amiably as possible.

It took her an eon to crane her neck back far enough to see me. She even blinked in slow motion.

"Ah," she said, "if it isn't Hula Girl herself." That smarted. She'd always teased me for liking to hula-hoop, even before she got on drugs. That was just how she was. Superficially abrasive. Rough on the outside, soft on the inside. At least I hoped she was still soft somewhere in there.

"In the flesh," I said, determined not to let her get to me. There were more important battles to fight right now than the one for my ego. "Can I come in?"

"*May* I come in," Ellen corrected me, using her best imitation-mom voice. I guess drugs make some people sticklers for proper grammar. Or maybe, to her, I was some Goody Two-shoes with impeccable syntax. Well, I do read a lot of books. Another trait inherited from my favorite (and only) aunt.

I opened the passenger-side door and slid inside Ellen's car. She sat up slightly and lit a cigarette. The breeze whisked the smoke through all four open windows in turn.

"I need to talk to you," I said.

"Hit me," Ellen said in a faintly robotic tone. "Wait," she said with more gusto. "If we're going to talk for real, I need a cigarette."

"You already have one," I said, already exasperated. Ellen looked at the cigarette she held as if it were a number 2 pencil and she was about to take a test.

"So I do," she said, marveling. Her eyelids started settling into sleep position.

"Please, Ellen." I twisted my body further around so I could look her full in the face. All my muscles seemed to creak from the effort. Ellen peered at me through one eye only.

"We've been friends a long time," I said. "Since we were twelve. Like, when we both had braces and reputations for being super dorks. And what I'm about to tell you cannot— I repeat, cannot—leave this vehicle. I don't care if you're high. I don't care if you're, like, drunk on truth serum. That's the rule."

"Bitch, I don't even think *I* can leave this car right now, let alone smuggle your big, important secret with me." She sank even further into the seat cushion, if that were even possible. I'd never seen a car seat more closely resemble a patch of quicksand.

"Listen, Ellen," I said, "try to concentrate. Have you heard of MS? Multiple sclerosis?"

Her eyes rolled laterally from the sunroof cavity to the back of my seat. This was an improvement. Then her eyes began to close again. I snapped my fingers. "Please focus," I said.

"MS," she said. "Sure. When your brain starts attacking itself and you start having seizures and you can't hold your pee." Wow. She was like some kind of druggie savant. The mysterious meth phenom of Santa Fe. "Isn't that what your aunt had?" Had. This was the first time Ellen had acknowledged Karine's sickness. Her death. My aunt who'd been so kind to her when she'd visited from California last fall. My aunt who'd taken us both out for long, confidential chats over virgin margaritas. My eyes welled up.

"Yes," I said. "That's what Karine had." I quickly wiped my tears away. I didn't want to exhibit any weakness that Ellen could pounce on. But she was barely cognizant.

"I'm sleepy," she said.

"Because you're on a barrelful of drugs," I snapped.

"How insightful," she said. Then she giggled. "A barrel. Like fish. Or pickles." She tossed the remainder of the cigarette behind her head, and it sailed onto my nearby car, streaking ash across my rusty paint job. "Remind me why you called this meeting?" A note of irritation had crept into her voice. I had to move fast, before either she passed out or I lost my temper.

"I might be sick with it, too," I said. "I could have MS. Maybe the super-bad kind. Like what my aunt had."

Ellen was quiet. I fiddled with the metallic Mardi Gras necklaces snaking around her gear shift, not knowing how to interpret her silence.

"Sucks," she said eventually. Then she started laughing, a dry cackle that quickly advanced into hysterical territory. She started kicking her legs in the air like an upside-down insect trying to right itself. "Look, Lo, I'm hula-hooping upside down! I'm going to break your world record for dorkiness!" She laughed harder, but I soldiered on.

"I met this guy on Thursday," I said. "A sort of medicine man. He said that he could help me. Help us, I mean. Me and four friends. He knew I was sick before I even told him, Ellen. He seemed . . . wise. Soulful."

Now Ellen started laughing even harder, and I knew I was losing her. *Focus, Lo. You can still get through.*

"Look, Ellen. I know you don't believe in that shit, and I don't either. Not necessarily. But I don't have a choice at this point. I'm sort of at the end of my rope here. There's no cure for what I . . . might have. But this guy, Jay, said he could heal me and four friends. Four. And I've already got three." I decided to give her the optimistic number. "I just need one more."

She was nodding off again in the backseat.

"Don't you want help?" I said. "Don't you want to be free from . . . this? Your addictions?"

"*Pssssssssshhhhh,*" went Ellen, like she was a balloon letting out air. She seemed to have moved into some stratosphere where only hollow sounds made sense.

"Great," I said, as her dirtbag boyfriend, Mike, suddenly materialized in the parking lot and slid into the driver's seat.

"We're going for a ride, babe," he said. Ellen reached carelessly for his heinously tattooed arm—Was that a sexy Little Mermaid riding a motorcycle across his bicep? How could she even work the pedals?—and her fingers landed in the console's overflowing ashtray instead. A swing and a miss.

"You," Mike said to me, pressing one dirty finger into my left shoulder. "Out."

He smelled like burnt hot dogs. "My pleasure," I responded.

Ellen rolled over, revealing pink boy shorts under her sundress. I felt a sudden urge to cover her up, tuck her into bed, bring her a glass of milk, and read her a storybook—like we used to do with her little sister when I'd spend the night at the Davis mansion. I cracked open the car door and put one foot on the pavement, leaving my butt in the seat so Mike wouldn't drive away.

"Aren't you at least going to prop her up?" I said. "Make sure she's buckled?" Mike laughed and muttered something that sounded like "buckled to my dick." It took everything I had not to smack him.

"Strap yourself down, babe," he shouted into the rearview mirror at Ellen. "You're in for a bumpy ride." Then he stomped on the accelerator with the engine in neutral. He was either trying to scare me into jumping from the car completely, or his attempt at murdering me was foiled by forgetting how to drive a manual. I jumped out of the car and slammed the door behind me, and they sped away.

So much for Ellen. For a few minutes I stood seething next to the black skid marks that Mike had left behind.

"Yo!" shouted someone in the group of smokers at the other end of the parking lot. "You need a hit, girl?"

I shook my head and walked toward my car, bone-weary all of a sudden. I didn't need a hit. I needed Ellen. And she needed me, even if she didn't know it yet. I was still determined to convince her of our mutual necessity, before it was too late.

I pulled up to Thomas's house at four P.M. on the nose. I was planning to make three stops, so I was surprised to see not one but two boys waiting for me on the Dents' front stoop. Kit was with Thomas! After my initial glee, I was momentarily disappointed that I wouldn't have Thomas all to myself—which is of course why I chose to pick him up first—but then I reconciled myself to Kit's dour expression. This was a dream come true, and I knew it was a big step for him to join us.

They made their way to my car. Thomas's face didn't betray any of the extreme emotions from the airfield the day before.

"What's up, Lo?" Kit said.

"Hey!" I said brightly. "Does this mean you're coming with us?"

"I guess so, unfortunately. Kamara was a pretty good recruiter. Says I could use some help and shit. Plus, I'm crashing with him for a while, and I figured I'd better do what he says."

"Really?" I said. "You're staying here?"

"My mom and I aren't exactly getting along these days."

"I'm sorry," I said, "but I'm really glad you came." I squeezed Kit's hand in the backseat. I might have imagined it, but I felt that Thomas's blank eyes lingered a beat too long on my platonic gesture. I smiled at him in the front seat.

"Thanks, Thomas," I said. "This means a lot." It was pretty much the sweetest thing he could've done on my behalf.

(With the exception of falling madly in love with me. Or single-handedly curing my MS. My Severity. My Separation. *Focus, Lo.*)

Thomas shrugged his shoulders but was otherwise non-responsive to my gratitude. I shifted my car into gear.

"Next stop, Johnson residence," I said. Now I had Kit in addition to Thomas and Kaya. Only one point of Jay's star of burdens remained to be filled.

———

"Lo, didn't you say we need five people?" Kaya said as she climbed delicately into the backseat, checking first for foreign objects. "There are only four of us."

"I know," I said. "Ellen Davis is our fifth."

"No way," she said. And part of me was just as incredulous. But my estranged Agua friend was our only shot. I would beg and plead with her to join us. I would get down on my hands and knees if I had to. I would turn a blind eye to her fury. Whatever it took. This ritual could potentially save our lives.

"Well, we can probably find her shooting up heroin on the railroad tracks right now," Kit said. I glared at him. "Jesus, Lo," he said. "I was joking. Wait, unless she's actually on heroin. Last I heard it was meth. I can't begin to tell you how sick I am of rich kids who do hella drugs and expect everyone to feel sorry for them because they're so misunderstood. The world is dangerous enough without taking more risks."

"Sorry, Lo," Kaya said, "but I can't see Ellen consenting to do this with us." Or maybe she didn't *want* Ellen to do this with us. I remembered then that Ellen had at one point been the ringleader of Kaya's bullies in middle school. She was the one who'd nicknamed her "Kaya No-Feel-Um." I'd given Ellen hell for it at the time, and now I privately vowed to make sure that she played nice on this occasion. "How are you going to get her on board?"

"I'm still working on it," I said. "But I have an idea. And I'm going to need help from all of you."

———

Ten minutes later we were parked in front of Ellen's house.

"Okay, guys," I said. "You know what to do. Remember that I don't want to hurt her. And if she really puts up a fight, I guess we just have to let it go. But Ellen needs this. Just make sure that you stress it's for her own good."

"Roger, boss," Kit said. "Kidnapping is a go." Thomas nodded, then the boys hopped out of my car and jogged up Ellen's front walk, side by side.

"Are you sure this is a good idea?" Kaya said.

"Nope," I said. "Not by a long shot."

We waited in silence, listening for I don't know what from Ellen's house. Shouting? Gunfire? A wall-shaking recording of the Beatles' "Help!"? Or, god forbid, "Helter Skelter"?

"Oh my gosh," I said, suddenly breaking out of my anxious thoughts. "Kaya, I'm so sorry. I just realized that I never unrolled the painting you gave me. I've been so distracted by"—I gestured at the Davis mansion—"all this."

"It's okay. Not a big deal. Maybe I shouldn't have...."

But I had already reached into my glove compartment and withdrawn the small scroll that Kaya had given me the night before. It was a beautiful watercolor painting of a girl who looked like me, hula-hooping in a yard that looked like mine, being watched over by a woman who looked a lot like my aunt. And it took me right back to the April afternoon four years ago when Karine was visiting from California. She'd taken me thrift-store shopping and had bought me some of her favorite records, as well as two butterfly-emblazoned hula-hoops.

"But I don't know how to hula-hoop," I'd said in protest.

"Then you must learn immediately."

Our first lesson began promptly after we returned to my parents' house. Karine tossed a hoop over my head like a lasso, and eventually I got the hang of spinning it around my waist without looking like I was having a seizure.

"This isn't so hard," I said.

"Next I'm going to light them on fire."

"No you are *not*!"

"Don't worry," said Karine, laughing. "I'm not going to do it. That's for pros only. But listen, Consuelo: Fire can't burn you as long as you keep moving."

We stayed out there for hours, just playing at keeping those hoops alive. Whenever I got frustrated or tried to move my body too much, not letting the hoop's spiral do most of the work, Karine would say, "Find your gravity, *mija*. Just let it all float around you. Circle home."

"Kaya," I said, wiping my tears away from the unexpected memory. "Thank you. I love it."

"I remembered you telling me the story once," she said, "and I wanted to paint it. Long before I knew. . . ."

Just then the Davises' magisterial red front door was flung open with a bang. Thomas and Kit emerged, holding Ellen's kicking, screaming body between them. She was more animated than she'd been earlier in the parking lot, when she could barely lift her head from her chest. *Far* more animated. Like, Roadrunner animated. Whatever edge the Oxy had taken off was apparently back on.

I hastily rolled up the painting and placed it back in the glove compartment.

"No offense to your plan," Kaya said, "but that does *not* look like a person who wants to be helped."

As the two abductors and Ellen neared my car, I saw the cold look in Thomas's eyes as he wrestled with his prey. It was like he was on autopilot: no emotion whatsoever. Then I started making out the verbal content of Ellen's screams.

"Put me down, you bastards! There's nothing wrong with me! You might all be messed up and in need of magical wizard therapy or whatever, but I'm just fine!"

Kaya and I got out of the car to help. Ellen wore a long-sleeved shirt even though it was eighty degrees outside. When the boys put her down, she began to scratch vigorously at her arm over the cotton fabric. I grabbed her wrist and pulled up her sleeve. Red welts and deep scratches climbed her forearm.

"Then it's true?" I said, as Ellen shook me off. I'd read that meth addicts sometimes felt insatiable itches on their skin. "Do those marks mean what I think they mean?" For a moment I was indignant. What I wouldn't give to be in perfect health like her, and here she was sabotaging it with poison that some amateur chemist had concocted in a trailer park.

"Buzz off, Lo," she said.

"We're trying to save your life," Thomas said mechanically. Though the words might have been sincere, he looked totally apathetic, as if it didn't matter to him if Ellen was dead or alive. It distressed me to see him looking so blank under such dramatic circumstances, but I couldn't think about that now. With a full car, the ritual had a chance of succeeding. Thomas threw Ellen in the middle of the backseat and climbed in next to her.

"No way," she said. "You kidnap me *and* I have to ride bitch? Let me out immediately. Lo, he didn't even let me get my . . . bag."

"You don't need to bring anything," I said. I knew that she wanted her stash of whatever it was she was doing on a daily basis. But she had her tiny designer purse, and that would have to be enough for now. Ellen reached across Thomas's lap for the door handle, but I'd already hit the child locks.

"Great," Kit said. "Now there's no escape, and I have very little confidence in Lo's driving abilities. Everybody buckle up."

"You're all insane," Ellen said. "You trust Lo to whisk us away to happiness?"

"Ellen, shut your mouth. For once," Kaya said. I was shocked—Kaya never spoke a harsh word to anyone. Even Ellen was momentarily stupefied. "Some of us need to have hope in this quote unquote insane ritual. Keep in mind that Consuelo is trying to help you."

Ellen retrieved something from her purse, popped it into her mouth, and washed it down with a half-empty bottle of Gatorade she'd found on my car floor. I decided not to make an issue of it considering we'd just forcibly removed her from her home. Plus, her drugging days might soon be over. After she swallowed the pill, she crossed her arms over her chest and stared out the window in a huff. I was finally free to think about where we were headed.

8

THE SUN-FADED HIGHWAY LED STRAIGHT through our sub-urban deserts to the base of the Sangre de Cristo mountain range. Sunsets are always something of a miracle in New Mexico, and this evening's was no exception. The soft pink of the sky seemed to soften and tame the barren landscape, turning the parched terrain into an oasis. We were on our way out of town at last.

As I drove, my head started to throb. I rubbed the pressure points on my right temple, trying to soothe the ache. Kaya leaned forward to put her hand on my shoulder.

"Are you okay, Lo?" she said. It was remarkable that even though she'd never felt physical pain in her life, she was still attuned to mine.

"Thanks, Kaya. It's just a headache. I'll be fine."

All of my passengers seemed melancholy. Especially Thomas. He hadn't said a word since downtown Santa Fe had fallen from view behind us. He just stared out the window at the desert. I caught his eye in the rearview mirror, and he nodded at me. Or did he wink slightly? I immediately felt calmer. Maybe we were still connected after all.

Ellen had managed to trade seats with Kaya in the back and was now chain-smoking out the window.

"Must you do that?" Kit said. He was seated beside me, not through any great desire to be close to me but because his legs were the longest and he was tyrannical about the music selections. "You're giving lung cancer to everyone in the car." Ellen responded by blowing smoke into the front seat.

"Gross," Kit said. "Not to mention homicidal." He struggled to find something other than static on my crappy stereo. "How much further?"

Kit had already asked me to slow down and watch the road several times, even though I was concentrating fiercely. Okay, *once* I'd turned around to check on Thomas, but Kit had immediately barked at me, "If you do that one more time, I'm getting out of the car."

"Cheesus Christ," I said. "Sorry." It was like Kit really thought we were all on the verge of death. But I guess it made sense. After all, if the love of his life could die out of nowhere for no apparent reason, we were all vulnerable, at any time.

When I finally satisfied him with my ten-and-two grip on the steering wheel, Kit loosened up a bit. "Lo," he said. "Let's be real. What's the story with this so-called sacred ritual? I study the Native Americans. I don't get mixed up in fake Anglo wannabe shit. And I'm not giving this charlatan any money."

"Who is this *hombre* anyway?" Ellen said, lighting up another cigarette in the backseat. "How do you know he's not just luring us into the desert so he can rape and kill us?"

"He's authentic," I said. "He gave me a good vibe."

"Good vibes," Ellen said. "Great. Surf's up. Let's nobody harsh Lo's mellow by talking about rape and murder."

"That's right," Kit said, biting the tip of one of his fingernails and spitting it out the window. "If we don't die in a car crash on the way to this park—which no one has ever heard of, by the way—we'll most likely get slaughtered upon arrival."

"This man won't hurt you," said Thomas, who seemed to have awoken from his daydream behind me. His voice was severe, somehow laden with consequence.

"Oh yeah?" Ellen said. "What, like you're going to put the jungle moves on Jay Shaman?"

"Christ, Ellen," Kit said. "Have some respect. Thomas has been through hell and back. You and your spoiled-rich-girl routine are way out of your depth here."

"I'm just saying that you guys are being too trusting of Consuelo's freaky stranger."

"Okay, well, I agree with you there," Kit said.

"So what if we're trusting?" Kaya said. "It's cool to trust people sometimes. Consuelo has good judgment. If she doesn't think this guy is dangerous, I believe her." I reached around and squeezed her knee.

"Two hands on the wheel," growled Kit. "Anyway, Kaya, that's easy for someone who can't feel pain to say. The torture won't register. *You'll* be in la-la land. *We'll* be the ones screaming."

"You guys all have extremely dark imaginations," I said. "Just relax. Try to get into a spiritual mindset."

Ellen scoffed. "He's probably sharpening his machete as we speak," she said.

"In Liberia," Thomas said, "we made our victims dig their own graves before we shot them, so we could conserve our energy for more killing."

We spent the next few miles in silence.

———— \

We weren't exactly sure what we were looking for.

Jay had said that our destination of Pecos Park contained Pueblo ruins. I'd visited a handful of Pueblo Indian villages— both the kind that were actively inhabited and those that had been abandoned for ages— in the Santa Fe region, mostly on field trips in elementary and middle school. The dwellings reminded me of vast urban apartment complexes, with multiple stories and dozens of rooms. They were intricate communities, like beehives or anthills or the island of Manhattan.

"Are you sure this place exists?" Kit said. "Kaya is half Pueblo, and even she's never heard of Pecos Park."

"Well, in all fairness, I don't get out much," said Kaya.

"How'd you convince your mom to let you leave the house anyway?" I asked.

Kaya giggled shyly. "I told her you were taking me to watch a badminton tournament."

"You did not," said Ellen, with respect.

"I did. I figured she couldn't argue with shuttlecocks," said Kaya. "They're pretty harmless."

"Yeah," said Kit. "Badminton is only second to the NFL in causing traumatic brain injuries."

"Shut up, Kit," said Ellen. "Score one for Kaya. I should try that one out on my mom, not that she ever asks me where I'm going."

I was starting to feel as if we'd driven too far. The only landmarks along the road were cacti and scrub trees. Every once in a while we passed a larger tree that looked too thirsty even to cast shade.

Then we rounded a curve in the road, and I saw a cluster of green ahead.

"That must be it," I said, relieved.

The park entrance was next to a scrap metal yard that had seen better days. Totaled pickup trucks with missing tires sat on concrete blocks, waiting to be crushed and re-born as cutlery. The setting sun reflected off what little glass remained on the cars, casting an almost blinding glow in places. The vast, leveling uniformity of the sunset drew long, shapely shadows from the junked cars, evoking an organic landscape.

After I turned onto the dirt road, a black cat with one eye gouged out crossed our path. "An auspicious beginning," Ellen said. Then she took a swig from a small purple flask. I smelled whiskey.

"Where did that come from?" I said. "Are you supposed to be drinking that on those pills you took?"

"Is it any of your business?" she said.

Thomas glared at her.

"Just . . . please, Ellen. If you have any love—or even any

respect—left for me at all, at least try to take this seriously."

"Fine," she said, and stuffed the flask back in her purse.

I couldn't tell if we were still on the dirt road, or if the dirt road had simply blossomed into a dirt parking lot, so I just stopped the car, and we all climbed out. Though we'd moved away from the scrap metal, there was no real indication that we'd made it to a recreational zone. Eventually Ellen discovered a playground, but even that was in ruins. In some corners fescue grass seemed to be trying halfheartedly to grow through the sandy dirt, but the green plants had mostly given up. Everything was tangled roots and boulders that seemed to have been shaken loose from some distant, prehistoric cliff. There was no question that this "park" had been abandoned for years.

"It's starting to get dark," Kit said nervously as we strolled around the grounds, unsure what to do. "I don't like this. We should go." He crept closer to Thomas, who seemed on high alert.

"Jay said he'd be here at sundown," I said. "Give him a few more minutes."

"Sundown," Ellen said. "Of course. The witching hour for mass murderers."

"Forget this," Kit said. "I'll be in the car." He leaned his weight from sneaker to sneaker as if he could shuffle away his anxiety.

"Hold your horses, Kit," Thomas said gravely, and I smiled despite myself. He sounded like a cowboy in a Western movie. My very own Clint Eastwood, by way of Liberia. All he needed was a cowboy hat and badge.

I was still entertaining the image of Sheriff Thomas when I heard a low growl and saw a torch appear from the brush behind the collapsing jungle gym.

"Consuelo," Jay said as he stepped onto the crumbling playground surface across from us. "Hello, dear. I knew you'd make it."

Dakota trotted ahead of him and circled my feet, staying just beyond arm's length.

"Oh shit," said Kit, backing up. "That's . . . not a dog, Lo. That's a coyote. No sudden movements. Everybody, stay still."

Thomas slowly began inserting himself between me and Dakota.

"It's okay, guys," I said. "Hi, Jay. Hi, Dakota." Dakota whined in what I interpreted as a friendly fashion. I rubbed her between her ears and thought I heard Kit gasp. Jay smiled at the posse I'd assembled.

"Lordie," murmured Ellen, gazing at our strange, laid-back leader in his faded Fleetwood Mac T-shirt and cutoff cargo shorts. She seemed slightly dazzled by his general appearance.

"This guy's a total stoner," Kit whispered behind me. That wasn't exactly a compliment, but at least Kit wasn't accusing Jay of trying to take advantage of us by attempting to appear "authentic."

"Ha," I whispered back, amused by Kit's stubborn cynicism. "You probably thought he'd put on one of those cheap woven ponchos, stick a feather in his hair, do a war whoop, and call himself an Indian chief."

"Whatever," said Kit.

"And who are your friends, Lo?" Jay said, drawing closer to our group.

I nudged Kaya forward first, careful not to bruise her. "This is. . . ."

"Wait," Jay said kindly. "I changed my mind. Not here." He closed his eyes and licked his finger, then held it in the air as though gauging the wind, which was nonexistent. "There are fretful spirits here," he said. "Follow me."

We trailed behind him in a tight mass through the juniper bushes, as if we were kindergartners in some five-part buddy system. Now that it was dark, we could barely see ahead of us, but no one wanted to follow Jay too closely since the coyote at his side kept turning her head to stare at us with suspicion.

"Feel free to pet Dakota," Jay said cheerfully.

"No thanks," Ellen said. "I'm really more of a cat person." Jay turned to smile at her, and, to my surprise, Ellen smiled back. Maybe our guru had been a lion tamer in another life.

Only Thomas seemed sure of his footing in the dark. A branch cracked. Suddenly Thomas grabbed me, pushing me away from the noise, almost throwing me to the ground. Kaya shrieked and crouched defensively at the side of the trail. Kit and Ellen whirled around in alarm. Thomas's chest heaved, and the torch's flames shone on his sweating forehead, even though it was a cool night.

"Thomas," I said, unhurt but breathing hard against his torso. "Are you okay?"

"I. . . . Sorry, Lo," he said. "I don't know what happened. I just . . . reacted."

Kaya's lanky body had gone totally stiff. Ellen looked at her warily.

"Jesus, Thomas," she said. "Chill out." She offered Kaya her hand.

"It's all right," I said. Thomas's reaction was unexpected, but I knew it was instinctive. And protective of me.

"He'll be fine," Jay said authoritatively from up ahead. "It's just phantoms." For some reason, this explanation sounded like the most rational thing in the world.

Thomas slowly released me from his arms, but as we proceeded, he kept reaching around to brush my hand, as if he needed to reassure himself that I was still behind him.

We walked until we came to a thick stone disk on the ground. Jay led us to the middle of the circular slab and removed a smaller metal disk, about the size of a manhole cover, which looked as if it had been smelted by hand. A blast of cold, dank air emanated from the depths of the crypt.

Jay deftly lowered his body into the hole, and then dropped out of sight completely. We heard the echo when his feet hit the bottom of the chamber.

A wooden ladder appeared through the hole its top two rungs visible above ground. This was it. Time to decide. To ritual, or not to ritual. Jay was either luring us into a torture chamber, or we were on the verge of a momentous spiritual experience. I looked around for Dakota, but she had apparently wandered off.

"Hell no. I'm not going down there," Ellen said, as contrary and defiant as ever.

Ignoring her, I pulled away from Thomas's hand and then situated myself above the ladder.

"No," Thomas said. "Let me go first. I'm not afraid."

I'd wanted to set a good example for the others, but I was still nervous, and I let him lead the way. Kit reached down for Thomas's shoulder, but Thomas shook him off.

"It's cool, man," he said.

I was next. Down the rabbit hole I went.

As my eyes adjusted to the torch-lit darkness, I realized that we were in a Pueblo kiva. We hadn't been allowed to descend into these chambers on school trips because they were sacred, but I'd seen drawings of them. I hadn't noticed ruins of apartments above, and kivas were usually sunken hollows beneath housing. This kiva must be the only remaining structure of a razed, ancient village, perhaps overlooked for decades.

Okay, maybe not entirely overlooked. The Pueblo Indian artifacts that belonged here had clearly been picked clean from the floor long ago. Arrowheads and shards of ceramics had likely disappeared inside greedy coat pockets. Now the sacred space was littered only with cigarette butts and empty beer bottles that kids—most likely from Santa Fe High—had probably discarded over the years. Someone had sprayed DO THE COSMOS on the adobe wall in green paint, obscuring the petroglyphs engraved by native worshippers. Perhaps we were on consecrated ground, but it sort of felt as if we were squatting in some high schooler's basement drug den.

"Guys?" Ellen called from above. "Are you okay?"

"Everything cool down there?" Kit hollered after her through the hole.

"Very cool," I said, trying to sound confident. "Come on down."

As Kit and Ellen reluctantly descended, Jay busied himself preparing the central fire. He spread five colorful wool blankets at exact intervals around a ring of rocks, which was located directly under the entrance that doubled as a smoke hole. We stood around and watched as he chanted in low tones to himself. His voice, though soft, filled the chamber with a bewitching echo.

Kaya still had not come down, so I called to her. No response.

"I'll be right back," I announced and then climbed back up the ladder.

There, sitting on the stone disk with her arms wrapped tightly around her trembling knees, was my old friend. I had never seen her scared before, not even when we'd convinced ourselves that we were having Ouija board communications with dead serial killers. Kaya was always the tough, unflappable one when it came to otherworldly matters.

"I don't feel right about going down there," Kaya said. "In fact, I feel really weird all of a sudden. Like I shouldn't be here. I don't think Jay was lying about the phantoms."

"There's no such thing," I said. I felt more spooked now but was still determined to put on a brave face. "You've met with enough bad psychics to know that."

She smiled. "I guess so."

"Don't worry," I said, as she allowed me to hoist her up by the hand. "Nothing will happen to you while you're with me. I promise."

Then down we went.

Finally together in the kiva, the five of us milled about awkwardly for a few moments, unsure of the proper etiquette for sacred rituals. Only Thomas seemed somewhat secure in his surroundings.

"You act like you've done this before," said Kit.

"My grandmother in Liberia was a shaman," said Thomas. "She taught me not to fear enchantment. You just have to respect it."

We all went quiet again.

"Well, I think this is fucking weird," Ellen said, and I almost laughed. I could always rely on Ellen to say the most obvious thing that no one else dared say, and in the most profane way possible.

Jay smiled and gestured toward the fire. We took our seats on the five blankets and awaited further instruction.

"You know me as Jay," he said, "but here my sacred name is Walks with Coyotes. I will be your guide tonight. First I must purify the circle." He began gathering objects from his backpack.

Okay, that sounded reasonable. Like something a real shaman would say and do.

"Someone got an A in Shamanism 101," muttered Kit in a shaky voice. Thomas elbowed him lightly in the rib cage.

Jay/Walks with Coyotes took a leather pouch from his backpack, untied it, and placed it on a small blanket in front of him. With deliberate, dancelike movements, he picked up a ceramic vase and sipped from it. Then he spit the contents on Ellen's back.

"What the hell?" she shouted, jumping up almost to her feet. Again, I had to stifle my laughter.

"Sacred oil," Jay said. "Sit." Ellen sat, but her look of disgust remained. He took another deep swig from his bottle and lightly sprayed Kaya's back. She didn't flinch. When Jay was through spitting on us, he lit a smudge stick on fire and waved it over each of our heads.

"What are you doing, exactly?" Kit asked, trembling slightly as he pulled his damp shirt away from his spine.

"I'm expunging the phantoms and settling the spirits," Jay said. Just then, Ellen's cell phone went off, playing—inexplicably—the *Scooby Doo* theme song.

"I'll wait," Jay said patiently, mid-smudge.

"Whoops," Ellen said. "My bad."

"Cell phones *off*, people," I said. "Try to be respectful." Then, of course, my phone lit up with a text from Alex. Ellen snickered, and I hastily shut down the device.

Jay, satisfied that we'd extinguished all electronics, continued his fragrant circuit.

"I have created a safe environment," he said. "A place where you can unburden your hearts and freely draw out your souls. Tell me your names. And what you suffer." He turned to me first.

"I'm Consuelo," I said, hoping my voice didn't betray my anxiety. I crossed, then uncrossed, and then recrossed my legs. They were tingling, maybe falling asleep, but I couldn't tell if I was sitting wrong or if my symptoms were kicking in. *Focus, Lo.* "Hi, Jay. Um, I mean, hi, *Walks with Coyotes.* We've . . . um. . . met already."

"Welcome, Consuelo," Jay said. "Thank you for being here. It took great fortitude to take such a risk and to expose your friends to the same unknown elements."

I wouldn't have called it "fortitude." I would've called it "audacity," as I'm sure the others would as well. Audacity, or pure desperation.

"Now, please tell us all why you're here," Jay said.

"I'm sick," I said. "I have . . . I think I might have . . . an incurable disease that could debilitate me or . . . kill me, even, I guess. Maybe sooner rather than later." My tongue grew heavy, and I began to stammer. "I mean, I feel it in my bones. I know I have it . . . it's what killed my aunt Karine . . . it's in my brain . . . it's growing . . . I can feel it . . . I know it. . . ." My eyes were burning from the smoke.

"Hey," Ellen said with concern. "Catch your breath, girl."

"I'm sorry," I said, squeezing my knees to my chest.

"It's quite all right," Jay said. "You've been holding a lot in. Let your words carry away your pain. And what do you want to ask for from the spirit world?"

"To be healed," I said. I breathed into my stomach and tried to feel the oxygen coursing through my body. *TranquiLo.*

Jay nodded deeply. "Did you bring your fetish?" he asked.

"My what? Oh, right. The horse." I pulled the turquoise figurine from my pocket. I hadn't brought it to the ceremony on purpose, but like I said, I'd been carrying it around nonstop since Thursday night. The horse just seemed to belong with me.

"The horse is wild and powerful," Jay said, "but she is

also a force of unity. When the Spanish introduced the horse to the native people of this land, the new mode of transport strengthened bonds between tribes and even forged new ones. The horse is potent medicine for creating—and keeping—meaningful relationships."

Jay walked clockwise around the circle. I was relieved that my turn was over.

Jay stood before Ellen now. "What's your name?" he asked. "How are you suffering?"

"I'm Ellen Davis, and I'll cut to the chase. I like drugs. A lot. Probably too much, if we're being totally honest here. A long list of them. Does this work like Narcotics Anonymous or something? Do you want me to, like, acknowledge a higher power and do a twelve-step program?"

"Higher powers don't need your acknowledgment to exercise their order in the world, Ellen. They only need receptive vessels. Why are you here?"

"Because I can't sto—Because I can't escape. I don't know—because pills are too damn expensive. Because life is too long. Because everyone seems to be coping with who they are better than I am. I'd rather have what someone else is having, you know? Anybody else. These feelings are just too . . . hard. I want out of my brain." Ellen looked down, perhaps surprised that she'd admitted so much, and wiped a tear from her eye. I could barely believe it.

Jay handed her an object from his pouch. "The raccoon is strong, but she is deceptive. She wears many masks." Ellen took the small raccoon totem and jammed it into her jeans pocket without another word.

Jay then moved to Ellen's left. Kit.

"What is your—?" Jay started.

"I got this, dude. I'm Kit Calhoun. What I'm dealing with is grief. Maybe it's fear. I don't know." He pulled a hand through his short brown Mohawk. "I'm depressed and scared all the time. Because everyone I care about is going to die. I can't even talk to my mom anymore because . . . because she reminds me too much of what I've lost. What I'm still losing. I want that feeling to go away. Next?"

Jay nodded. "Death comes to us all," he said. "It does not need to be your enemy. The omnipresence of death can teach you how to live fully, gratefully." He reached into his pouch and withdrew another small animal. "The rabbit is constantly fearful. He doesn't understand that he invites predators with his apprehension. They sense his deep negative energy and come knocking." He placed the rabbit totem in Kit's hand.

Jay moved on.

"And what is your name?" Thomas was hunched over his own lap, his face hidden by his hoodie, his eyes lost in the fire.

"Thomas Kamara," he said quietly, without lifting his head. "At first I thought I came here so I could help someone. But what I . . . most want in the world . . . is to be relieved of the memories of the things that I've done. To erase the past."

Jay whispered something that sounded like a blessing into his hand, then handed Thomas a small object carved out of black stone. "The bear," he said. "He spends much of his life in hibernation because he has a great wealth of wisdom and experience to digest. But every bear knows when winter is over. You, too, must know when to come out of hiding."

Thomas squeezed the bear so hard that white showed on his knuckles. What was he seeing that made him fight himself so hard?

Kaya was last. The color in her face had deepened in the firelight, illuminating the facial scars that had never detracted from her beauty.

"I'm Kaya Johnson," she said. "I'm constitutionally incapable of feeling pain. I feel like I'm only living half a life. I want to feel pain."

"Of course," Jay said, handing her a totem. "Pain can be a wise teacher." *Or it could destroy you,* I thought, considering my disease. "I'm giving you the deer. She is a peaceful creature, a perceptive creature. An animal that senses everything, good and bad, and is gentler for it."

Kaya seemed mesmerized by the deer in her palm, looking upon it as if it were a rare jewel.

"Welcome to you all," Jay said.

Ellen toyed with her raccoon of polished granite. She'd sternly wiped the tears from her face, and her body was all tense again. "I feel like we're trick-or-treating in . . . purgatory or somewhere," she said.

Jay smiled. "No tricks, Ellen," he said, "though your totem is known to be nocturnal and a bit of a bandit."

"Great," Ellen said. "I'm miserable, and my spirit animal is demonic."

"Just because raccoons can be ferocious when scared or antagonized doesn't mean they're demonic."

"Oh, come on, Ellen," Kit said. "You're lucky. It's not like you're dealing with life or death. You can master your disease any time. Just stop. Doing. Drugs. Meanwhile, the rest of us are kind of screwed. Thomas can't go back in time and unfight his battles. I can't bring back Lucita. That's forever."

I leapt to Ellen's defense. "You don't know what you're talking about, Kit. Addiction goes really deep. It's not that easy to master."

"I don't know," Ellen said, brushing off Kit's words and mine. "I think I'd prefer to have a problem like Kaya's. Or Thomas's. I think part of the reason I maybe overdo it with all this stuff is because I don't want to feel anything. Not feeling anything seems like bliss."

"It doesn't exactly work like that," Kaya said. "I feel lots of things, just not in the way everyone else does. It doesn't mean I don't hurt. But, like, when Lo told me that she's been getting terrible headaches, I don't even know how to conceptualize that. I just feel stunted, you know. Stuck in this childish place."

"But, Kaya," I said. "Think of what you're asking for. For instance, you don't want what I have. This morning I collapsed in the shower because of the pain . . . I promise you don't want this."

"Even that sounds better than what I'm dealing with," Ellen said. "Sometimes I just want to bash my head against the wall to stop my thoughts."

"At least you guys *have* feelings," Thomas said. "Half the time I wonder if I still qualify as human. It's like all my emotions were burned out of me back in Liberia. Now I'm just a shell. A shell with nightmares. Feeling something—anything—sounds like a miracle."

"I want to go to a Weekends on Wednesday party for once," Kaya said. "I want to ride a bike. I want to cry when I skin my knee. I want a normal life."

"Normal life isn't all it's cracked up to be," Kit said. "Not when it can end at any moment."

Jay raised his arms above his head, and we went quiet.

"I hear your needs and your pain," he said. "And nothing is insurmountable as long as you keep toxins from creeping into your souls. Even when you feel weak or without agency, you'll discover that your internal fires are always burning. Now, keep in mind that this isn't some abracadabra, magician-sending-his-white-rabbits-forth-in-the-world kind of exercise. This is a sacred ceremony, the efficacy of which has been honed throughout many generations. We are dealing with human suffering, and it's not to be taken lightly. Tonight the magic begins. One week from this moment, you'll return to reverse the ritual."

Reverse the ritual? If the effects were going to be as salutary as Jay said, why would we reverse it?

"Burdens only have as much power as you grant them," Jay said. "They represent a disease, a disconnection. A lack of soulfulness. You can't allow them to separate you from the earth, or from each other. You will see that. You will start to understand."

I looked at my friends. In place of the four troubled faces I'd seen a few minutes ago were varying expressions of hope and reflection. Jay had inspired us all to tap into something we'd lost. Was it just a more positive attitude? Or something more concrete than that? I locked eyes with Kaya and smiled. Then, as if to taunt my hopefulness, a sharp pain shot down my arm.

Jay looked at me with compassion, even though I didn't think my face had given anything away. "It's impossible to take away human pain completely," he said. "But I can give you the tools you need to live in harmony with your suffering and with yourselves. When the ritual is complete, each of you will have a new perspective. Your jealousy will take a backseat to your gratitude. The things you previously thought defined you will no longer define you. You will remember who you really are. When you wake up in the morning you will truly know what it's like to walk a mile in someone else's shoes, and those shoes will bring you home."

This was all a bit too abstract for me. When was he going to get to the part about healing my disease?

The shaman pulled another leather pouch from his satchel and reached his hand in, withdrawing an ash-like powder. He held it over the fire and began chanting in a language I didn't recognize. Just then, I heard a scuttling behind me. A dark figure dashed through our circle, barely evading the central flames. A coyote. Dakota must have found a hidden entrance. Or was it possible that she'd been there the whole time? And in her mouth, I saw a skull. A small human skull. Jay threw his powder into the fire. I screamed.

Then the kiva went dark.

———

By the time Thomas got the fire started again, Jay was gone.
As was Dakota.

"Is everyone okay?" Kaya asked as she reflexively checked
her body for damage. Kit was clinging to his cell phone,
flashlight function engaged.

"Sure," Ellen said. "Except now I'm dying for some real
medicine. The kind that comes in a plastic bag. That 'ritual'
was such a joke. Whoever heard of a sacred burden-shedding
ceremony? And then trying to scare us like that by putting
out the fire? I don't care how smooth Jay is. He's obviously
an amateur."

"But the coyote?" I said. "The skull?"

"Huh?" Kit said. "A skull? That's not funny, Lo. Let's just
get out of here. I'm starting to feel claustrophobic."

Did I imagine the coyote altogether? I was too afraid to
ask. Perhaps hallucinations were another side effect of my
illness.

I looked around the kiva. I didn't see my own terror reflected on anyone else's face. They all looked either baffled
or embarrassed. For me?

"Wait," I said. "You guys agree with Kit? You don't think
the ritual did anything?"

"Look," Kit said, his tone gentler than usual. Great.
They thought I'd wasted all their time. Maybe I did. And
worse than that, I'd wasted their hope. "At least Jay . . . Does

Jumping Jacks with Coyotes, or whatever, didn't steal our wallets. Though we should probably get back to your car before he tries to hot-wire it."

"You're right," I said, feeling totally demoralized. "We should go."

On our dark walk back to the parking lot, Thomas put his arm around me and left it there for a brief moment. "Don't worry," he said. "It's not your fault. You tried."

"Thanks, Thomas." I wanted to sink into his shoulder. The experience had been so intense, so revealing for everyone, and now it was just stamped out, like our kiva fire.

Everyone was quiet as they piled into the car. They all fell asleep on the long drive home, leaving me alone with my thoughts. Meanwhile pain periodically shot down my arms, wrapping itself around my white knuckles like razor blades.

The ritual had been a failure. Maybe I deserved this pain. Maybe it was better that I stay sick and just learn how to cope with it. I shouldn't tamper with other people's lives. I contemplated throwing my horse totem out the window. It was worthless now.

I glanced in the rearview mirror. Ellen was asleep on Kaya's shoulder. She looked so peaceful when she wasn't high, smoking cigarettes, or getting drunk and scrappy. I thought again about tucking her into bed, singing her a lullaby.

"Are you okay, Lo?" Thomas said, breaking up my reverie. He sat beside me with his eyes closed, leaning his head against the windowpane.

"Oh," I said. "Hey. I thought you were sleeping." I unclenched my hands from the steering wheel. "I'm fine. Maybe just disappointed. Why?"

"I can feel the tension in your body."

"Is it that strong?" I said.

"Yes."

"You know, I used to be able to do that. Sense people. Except . . . well, it's dumb."

"Tell me," Thomas said, cracking one eye open.

"Well, I used to think that I could sense people's energies. That sounds really hokey, like I thought I could read auras or something. But you know how sometimes you can just sense if someone is happy or sad? Or nervous? Well, I sensed that, but it was a little different. Often it was . . . musical. It sounded just like a song."

"You said 'used to.' Do you not perceive people's songs anymore?"

"Not really," I said. "My own noises are too loud right now. It's as if some little girl has stationed herself inside my body and she's banging on pots and pans."

"Did you ever hear my song?"

I blushed. I couldn't lie to Thomas, and yet the truth was so embarrassing. When I used to pass him in the hallway, the Cat Stevens song "The Wind" would spring into my head unbidden. Sometimes I couldn't shake the melody for the rest of the day. I had to go home and listen repeatedly to the record Karine had bought me.

"Once or twice," I said. Thomas was quiet.

"Don't you want to know what it was?" I said.

"I don't think so," he said. "I probably wouldn't like it."

"No," I said. "It's good. It's one of my favorite songs."

"Really?"

"Really." I quietly started humming the tune. His whole body relaxed, and he leaned his head against the window once more. In his sleep I saw him smile. Suddenly I felt hopeful again. Maybe tomorrow would be brighter after all.

9

IT DIDN'T SEEM FAIR THAT, thanks to my alarm clock, my body was so used to jerking awake at seven A.M. that it was now physically incapable of sleeping in, even on a Sunday. A day that was made for sleeping in, despite what Mom says about church. Even God took a rest after he made the world, right? And I'd had a rough Saturday night.

I was still locked in my dream world as I shook off the covers. I'd been doing what? Kissing Thomas? We'd been together, but I couldn't remember where or why. Maybe something about a garden? No, a jungle. We'd walked through a jungle holding hands, and the tree canopy was so high and had sunk us so deeply in shadows that it was like being underwater. It had been unnerving. But also wonderful. Because I'd been alone with Thomas.

Then I heard Seymour scurrying back and forth on my windowsill as usual and felt the morning sun on my eyelids, and I remembered the real world soon enough. I reached for my fuzzy purple bathrobe and began walking in the direction of the only thing capable of decisively waking me from my dreams: a cold shower.

Bang bang bang!

I almost dropped to the ground in fright. When my aunt Karine used to jump around corners to scare me, she laughingly called this my "playing dead" stance. "Up, Apple!" she'd say, swinging me to my feet with my childhood nickname. "Up!"

Bang bang bang!

I whirled around to see Kit grinning in my window, Mohawk still all kinds of angular from sleep, fist poised to begin pounding again.

"Kit?" I said.

This blast from the past worked almost as well as a cold shower. In elementary and middle school, Kit used to tap on my window when he wanted to organize a neighborhood game of flashlight tag or capture the flag. What was he doing here now? Wait, was I wearing indecent pajamas? I looked down and was relieved to see my modest tank top and shorts combo under my open bathrobe.

Kit began tapping the beat to "It's a Hard-Knock Life." Was something different? Then I remembered the ceremony. Something radical must have happened overnight to supplant Kit's perpetual scowl with this giant, luminous smile. I'd forgotten what a cutie he could be when he was happy.

All in one movement, I rushed to the window and tried to lift the sill, a hustle that simultaneously made me trip and cause the window to slam down. Clumsy. I was glad Dad hadn't seen—I'd never hear the end of his teasing. He still ribbed me for the time I dropped a full bowl of mashed potatoes on the living room rug at Thanksgiving. We ate instant rice instead.

"Consuelo!" Kit said once I'd managed to open the window with more feminine grace. "Have you been outside yet?"

I shook my head, stunned into silence by his exuberance. This was not the same Kit who'd been in the kiva last night.

"It's seven A.M.," I said, smiling at him quizzically. "I'm just waking up. Clearly."

"I've been up for hours," Kit said. "I skated over from the Dents' house. Thomas wouldn't get out of bed so I came here to bother you. I was literally the only person on the road here this morning . . . the only one inhaling the . . . sky . . . the birds. . . . Except there's this one Mexican lady on Old Santa Fe Trail who sets up her table of flan and *pan de muerto* early, like at the break of dawn. Swear on my life, Lo, her flans smell exactly like sex."

I'd have to take his word for it.

"Man, Kit," I said. "How much coffee have you had? What's gotten into you?" Not that I necessarily disliked whatever it was. He seemed more like the boy I'd known the summer before high school, the one I'd laughed with in the swimming pool. The one I'd kissed.

"What got into me? This knockout *morning* got into me. Got into my blood, like a freaking transfusion. The sunlight got to me. Who knows, maybe underground magnets got to me. . . ." He was talking a mile a minute, but then he stopped abruptly.

"Lo," he said curiously. "Your hand."

I looked down and saw a large gash on top of my hand. It looked as if someone had gone overboard with a Halloween makeup kit, had substituted flesh-colored putty and red corn syrup for my actual flesh. But this was . . . real blood. My blood. My own skin torn apart. What the . . . ? How . . . ? Was this . . . was it the window? But I hadn't felt anything when I'd tripped. As I looked at the bleeding wound, I registered it mentally, but not physically. Was I still dreaming? I clenched my fist. Blood dripped onto the sleeve of my purple bathrobe, but it was still as if it was someone else's blood, someone else's hand.

"Kit," I said, "I can't feel it. I can't feel my hand." Oh no, oh no. My Sclerosis. Was this the next phase? Had I lost all feeling in my limbs? Had my nerves finally disintegrated completely? My phone rang softly on my dresser, but I ignored it. My body. I'd lost my body for good.

I began to cry, not caring that Kit was still there and could see everything. "Is this it?" I said. "The last stage before the disease takes over? I thought. . . . Jay said the ritual would make me better. . . ."

"Wait a second, Lo," Kit said calmly, like a scholar contemplating a philosophical quandary. "Let's think about this. There's something really weird going on. But the universe works in mysterious ways, right? This might not necessarily be bad."

I sniffled. I guess my nerves were pretty frazzled. *TranquiLo. For external use only. Call ahead to refill your prescription.*

"Come to think of it," I said, turning my gaze to Kit, "you're acting pretty unusual this morning, to state the obvious. When was the last time you knocked on my window? No, scratch that. When's the last time you were *happy*, and talking about the birds and the weather? At seven A.M.?"

Kit laughed. "Oh my god, you're *right*. This morning is the first time since Lucita's accident that I didn't wake up under a freaking little black storm cloud. I actually feel *good*. Maybe my antidepressants finally kicked in?"

I left the window open and stepped back, trying to think, while Kit started chattering again about the smells outside, the "bioluminescent energy" coming off the flowers. Then he began playfully chasing my mom's chickens around our aboveground pool, but I was too lost in thought to follow the movements of Pollo Hermano and company.

I wandered toward my desk to grab some tissues for my hand. My phone was still blowing up on the dresser, but I returned to the window, pressing paper against my wound to stanch the bleeding. I still felt nothing, even when I wiggled my fingers. Then it hit me. This couldn't be related to my sickness. I hadn't woken up with my usual aches and pains. No migraine. No stumbling out of bed with a doomsday feeling and tingling toes.

"Kit!" I shouted. He was cackling gleefully as he dashed around the yard in pursuit of Pollo Bronco, Mom's prized leghorn.

"Kit!" I shouted again, over the sound of the berserk clucking. He reluctantly left the hysterical hen and returned to his bleeding, petulant Juliet leaning against her windowsill.

"Kit," I whispered, with a growing amount of clarity. "Do you think that during the ritual we could have . . . somehow . . .

swapped? Our burdens? I don't feel at all like myself right now. In fact, I feel really, really . . . weird. Pinch me. Pull my hair. I feel nothing. I feel like. . . ."

Oh. I knew exactly who I felt like. Kit pinched my arm between his bitten fingernails. Nothing. We looked at each other with wide eyes.

"I feel like Kaya."

"Hm," Kit said. "Hell of a theory. I mean, if you got Kaya's . . . whatchamacallit . . . analgesia, then what did I get?" I thought for a second. It clearly wasn't Thomas's burden. Couldn't be my MS or Kaya's painlessness. That left only Ellen. Kit wasn't on drugs . . . but he did have a manic energy about him that seemed to seek and feed off external stimulation. Like chickens. Or sex flan.

"Ellen. You have Ellen's addiction," I said, suddenly convinced. But Kit was barely listening. He took off after the hens again, trying to corral them into my mom's herb garden.

"Oh my god," I said, knowing both that I was right and that this was not going to end well.

My phone buzzed again. I scrolled through my messages and saw Ellen's name over and over again, dozens of times.

where are you, she'd texted earlier in the morning.

Then, i feel like hell.

    what did you do to me?
    this was such a bad idea.
    call me as soon as you get this.

Crap. Something had happened to her too. I called her back, and she picked up on the first ring. The only word I could make out in her panicked speech was my name.

"Ellen," I said, interrupting her sobbing rant. "It's okay. Calm down. Kit is with me. Get in touch with Thomas and Kaya. Just pull yourself together and tell everybody to meet us at the Dents' balloon field ASAP. I have a pretty good idea what's going on."

———

I threw on my jeans and sneakers without the usual struggle and galloped to the kitchen with a bra balled up in my fist. "I'm taking off," I called to the parental sounds behind the bedroom and bathroom doors. "Love you guys!"

Kit was waiting for me in the driveway, skateboard in hand, grinning. Despite my initial moment of alarm, and despite how awful it had been to hear the distress in Ellen's voice . . . I actually felt pretty good. My body felt right again. It was in motion without hesitancy. Without Mysterious Symptoms. I wasn't in pain. My mind galloped. But did this mean that someone was feeling what I used to feel?

In my car Kit blasted music and danced in his seat, cajoling me to join in. Finally I relented, and it was actually kind of great. I hadn't listened to music that wholeheartedly since before I started feeling lousy all the time. For those brief, blissful moments of keeping time on the steering wheel while my torso abandoned itself to the beat, I let myself forget about Ellen and everyone else.

This was amazing! The ritual had worked, in its own way, and I really couldn't have hoped for a better outcome. I was already informed enough about Kaya's medical condition to know how to protect myself. But first I needed to make absolutely sure. I slammed the butt end of an empty iced tea bottle against my kneecap. I bit down hard on my lip. I even made Kit burn my finger with my car's cigarette lighter. Nothing registered. Then I remembered that my hand was still spouting blood through the tissues, staining my shirt and shorts, not to mention the interior of my car. I should probably clean that up before seeing the others.

I dug around in the glove compartment, pushing past the painting Kaya had given me, until I found a handful of fast-food napkins. Meanwhile Kit craned his head out the window, taking in the scenery. He kept gleefully pointing things out to me—squirrels pocketing nuts in trees, dogs reveling in their early morning walks—not the least bit concerned that he was forcing me to take my eyes off the road. I pressed the napkins to my hand, containing the blood flow and leaving shreds of paper stuck to my skin in the process. Still, I felt nothing. Only mild euphoria. I could do anything. I was sitting pretty not only where my illness was concerned, but I was also ecstatically above the laws of pain.

This was a miracle.

I couldn't wait to test out my new body.

10

OURS WERE THE ONLY FOUR cars in the Psalms Over Santa
Fe parking lot that morning, indicating that it wasn't
only Christian people but Christian balloons that took
Sundays off. Judging from the erratic angles and dis-
regarded white lines, everyone had parked in a hurry.
As Kit and I rushed toward the balloon hangar looking
for our friends, I almost began doing handsprings across
the airfield. I could have hula-hooped until I lifted off
the ground. The same field that had seemed barren and
ugly when I'd met Thomas on Friday now seemed lush
and inviting. Where I'd seen only death before, I now saw
life.

Finally we spotted them, huddled against the far side of
the hangar.

When Ellen caught sight of us, she stormed up to me with
arms crossed over her chest. She shook with what I could
only identify as fury. There was a rag doll quality to her
movements that I'd never seen before.

"You!" she screamed. "I'm *sick*. You made me *sick*."

"What?" I said, taking a step back, out of her line of fire.

Ellen gesticulated erratically, and that's when I noticed it. My turquoise horse. In *her* hand. "This is what I woke up with this morning," she said. "This . . . sick pony. And you know that Jay gave me the raccoon last night. That's what I took home from the ritual, anyway."

Kit reached into his pocket and pulled out Ellen's raccoon. And I was sure that when I went home, there would be a deer on my dresser, just as there would be new totems in Kaya's and Thomas's rooms.

"I've been on Google since six AM," Ellen continued. "I have every symptom of MS. The pins and needles. The dizziness. The blurred vision. You gave me your disease, Lo. You. Tricked. Me."

"Ellen," I said, "I'm so sorry. I had no idea that this would happen. Jay didn't say anything about a trade. . . ."

"Maybe you were just too fixated on getting *your* cure to listen." Ellen hurled the horse to the ground. Her eyes were bloodshot, and her whole body shook inside her silk pajamas.

"Ellen, please, just calm down for a second," I said. "I need to think. What's going on with everyone else?"

I looked at Kaya. She stared into the overcast sky, failing to register my presence. What on earth had the ritual given her?

"Oh, yeah," Ellen said. "Kaya here has been catatonic all morning. We haven't gotten two words out of her since she got here."

I looked at Kaya again. She was acting exactly like Thomas did when he withdrew from the world, and I put the pieces together. The bear. Oh no. This was bad. But at least she could feel pain now, right? Isn't that what she'd so desperately wanted?

"That leaves me," Thomas said solemnly. I'd been too caught up in Ellen's panic to acknowledge the lonely figure in a gray hoodie leaning against the white metal wall of the hangar. *The bed is checked for monsters / And the food for poison. / You are not looking hard enough, he says.*

"You," I said. I flashed back to my dream of us. Walking through the jungle, feeling his arm around me, the humidity from the treetops settling on my skin like morning dew. Then I was drawn back to the quick math of the present moment.

"It's Kit's," I said. "Kit's problem." The rabbit. Was Thomas . . . afraid now? Petrified of death? Thomas had never seemed to fear anything. Except his own memories, and I'd only just learned that recently. He was a warrior.

"What. The hell. Is going. *On*," Ellen said. I slowly bent to pick up the horse she'd thrown. She snatched it away.

"I think we all . . . swapped," I said. "I think that's what the ritual did. That's why you have my symptoms."

"Well, yeah," said Ellen. "That's becoming blatantly obvious. But *how*? And how do we swap back?"

Now Thomas definitely looked scared. Kit slapped him amiably on his back, making him jump, as if he thought his friend was about to punch him.

"Whoa, man," Kit said. "Sorry." Then he reached down and picked a purple flower from the field—probably the only wildflower for a mile. Kit presented it to Ellen as if it were a four-leaf clover, but she just scoffed at him, still in disbelief. He shrugged his shoulders and stuck the flower in his black T-shirt pocket like a prom corsage.

"Jesus, Lo!" Ellen screamed. "I was just trying to be *nice* when I told you I'd rather have MS last night! I'd never in a million years volunteer for this life!"

Thomas stepped toward me, taking note of the bloodstains on my pajamas.

"And you," he said, touching my hand and displaying the fresh blood on his fingers. "You clearly swapped with Kaya."

"It seems so," I said, trying not to let on how secretly pleased I was. Fresh terror washed over Thomas's face.

"Don't worry," I told him, hiding my lacerated hand. "It . . . doesn't hurt. I can't feel anything. Nothing like a flesh wound to start your day, right?" No one was amused.

"We have to find Jay," Ellen said. "Right now. We have to switch back. I can't be this sick, not even for a week. Lo, you yourself said that this disease can work quickly. What if I die before the ritual is reversed next Saturday?"

"Ellen, calm down," I said. "It's one week. You're not going to die. And it's not like taking on my burden temporarily is more dangerous than doing *meth*. Or washing down a bunch of pills with booze and then going for a drive around the block."

"At least I *chose* to do those things! I didn't sign up for this. None of us did."

"Ellen's right," Thomas said. "This whole . . . situation feels wrong. We need to find Jay."

"I . . . don't think he has a phone," I said. "He told me he lives in a cave."

"Glorious," said Ellen. "Perfect."

Kit had lifted a spider from a rock and was gazing at it in wonder, letting it crawl up his arm. "Check it out, guys," he said, giggling. "It tickles."

"Look," I said, ignoring him. "We just need to get through the week. Jay said the experience would ultimately be positive, right? For all of us. One week, and then we switch back. I know none of us exactly consented to this, but here we are. Now we're bound to one another, and we need to get through it together." I could get everyone through it. I had to. "One week." I turned to Ellen. "I repeat: It's not going to kill you."

"Easy for you to say," Ellen said. "You won the lottery here, as usual. I'm the one who has to suffer this week. Worse than before. When this ritual was supposed to make me feel better too, remember?"

"Ellen, I'll help you," I said. "I promise. I'll show you the medications you can take for pain. . . ."

"Ironic that you were the one who said all you wanted to do was get me off drugs, and now you're the one trying to push them back on me," Ellen said. "I thought I was supposed to be detoxing this week." She stopped, softening her voice. "It's so surreal, though. This morning I woke up with absolutely no desire to . . . self-medicate. It's like my head is revolting against being anything but clear."

"See?" I said. "It's not all bad."

"No, it sucks, actually. I feel like I'm . . . overflowing."

Before I could come up with a response, I saw that Kaya seemed to be noticing me for the first time. She looked me up and down, evaluating the drying blood on my tank top and the wound on my hand. Then she broke out of her stupor like a pack of wild horses.

She lunged for me, but before I could assess whether she meant to protect me or murder me, Thomas had restrained her. Kaya was not a violent person, except to herself. She was kind and gentle, like the doe that Jay had given her. But now she was practically growling through her teeth, swiping madly at me with her ravaged fingernails. If Thomas hadn't reacted so quickly, I had no doubt that she'd be tearing me apart. Sweet Kaya? It didn't make any sense. Why was she at war with me?

I realized that I hadn't moved a muscle when my body was under attack. It was as though my body had lost all fight-or-flight response. Was I simply in shock, or did I really think I was invincible?

Kaya collapsed to the ground through the sieve of Thomas's arms and began trembling in the fetal position.

"You don't know what they did to us," she said. "They mutilated our bodies. They scalped us."

"They?" I said. "Who is 'they'? Did someone try to hurt you, Kaya?"

Kaya was silent again, shivering on the ground. I wanted to gather her up in a hug, but her body language was still so forbidding. Thomas stood over her, looking as helpless as I felt.

"Thomas?" I said. "Do you know what she's talking about? Are these your memories?"

"No," said Thomas, his voice scared and defensive. "I never . . . did any of those things."

"They pried our eyes open and left us to burn in the sun," Kaya said. "Left us half buried in the desert until the wolves found us, ate us alive."

Ellen grabbed for Kit's arm and missed—he couldn't stand still, not even now.

"What? What desert?" I said softly, starting to get really frightened now. "Kaya, where are you right now?"

"I don't know what she's talking about," Thomas said. "It's like she's suffering from my trauma . . . but with different memories."

He knelt in front of Kaya and wrapped his arm around her. As much as I knew that it was unjustified, I felt a small pang of jealousy that I quickly tamped down. I guess I wasn't immune to all pain.

"It sounds like Indians," Kit said from further out in the field. All of us except Kaya, who was still curled up on the ground, looked at him in surprise. "Am I the only one who pays attention in Mrs. Laramie's class?" he said. "It sounds like Kaya's remembering the war for the West."

Kaya never talked much about her ancestry, but I knew right away that Kit was right. You couldn't live in the Southwest and not know at least a little something about Indian history. The scalpings and the mutilations; the slow deaths from exposure. The newcomers from Europe had set out to annihilate the people who'd made their home in the Americas for tens of thousands of years.

"You're saying she's remembering things that happened, like, two hundred years ago?" Ellen said.

"That's exactly what I'm saying," Kit said. "Think about it. Her people were traumatized for decades by Anglo incursion. So, there's that, and now she can feel pain for the first time. She's probably emotionally reexperiencing what her people went through. It's what Thomas said—she's expressing his trauma, only differently."

"But that's impossible," Ellen said.

"Says the girl who now has walking MS because of a horse figurine," Kit said. He began laughing gleefully. "What a crazy world."

Thomas coaxed Kaya to her feet.

"What's going on?" she said sleepily. "Did I fall? I'm so tired."

Everyone looked at me for a response. Did she really not remember what had just happened? Should I tell her that she'd maybe just tried to assault me while in some kind of mystical, time-traveling, body-swapping Indian trance? No, I decided to brush it off. It was better to minimize the unforeseen by-products of the swap. At least for now.

"You just . . . fainted," I said. Thomas gave me a disappointed look and turned away.

"Are you sure?" Kaya said. "I had this crazy vision that. . . . Never mind."

"This is so effed up," Ellen said.

"It'll be okay," I said, snapping into action mode to prevent Ellen's doubts from pervading the whole group. "We just need to help each other. Like, Ellen, whenever my headaches start up, it helps . . . or it used to help, to turn out the lights for a little while."

"Wonderful," Ellen said. "Thanks so much, doctor. I'll just suffer in the dark."

"And Thomas, maybe you can look after Kaya, since you have a better understanding of. . . ."

"I'll try," he said.

"I feel so different . . . ," Kaya murmured. She was rubbing the dusty thighs of her sweatpants with a look of wonder on her face.

Thomas looked from my face to my hand. "But who will look after you?" he said.

I wanted to say that I wouldn't need looking after. That my new "burden" made me immune to destruction. I wanted to say that everyone *but* me was at risk, that I was living in an earthly paradise.

"We'll all look after each other," I said. "We'll be okay. We just need to figure out what to do next."

11

"I HAVE AN IDEA," **KIT** said, now sitting cross-legged on the dusty airfield, as serene as a Buddhist monk. "We should all stick together, right? At least for the immediate future? So let's meet at Zozobra tonight."

I'd totally forgotten about Zozobra. The event was a favorite among the dramatic offerings of our city's annual Fiestas de Santa Fe. It was essentially a capital-A Arts event that involved publicly burning a giant action figure alive—a tradition that was founded way before the Burning Man festival in the Nevada desert made it trendy to burn a giant action figure alive. Historically it was an excuse for me and my Agua friends to get tipsy at a tailgate and then snuggle on blankets in front of a massive bonfire. Dad thought it was all an accident waiting to happen, but even Smoky the Bear couldn't fight the enthusiasm for the event of the season. Santa Fe had been burning that fifty-foot man (whose official name was Old Man Gloom) in effigy for almost a hundred years.

"Wait," I said. "I thought Zozobra wasn't until next weekend."

"They moved it up because of the wildfires," Kaya said. Weird—Dad hadn't mentioned that. Then again, I hadn't seen him much lately. He'd been working on the mountain around the clock.

"Okay," I said. Maybe it was too soon to tell, but it seemed as if the leadership role was perhaps beginning to suit me. "Tonight. That's a good plan, Kit. We all meet at Zozobra. Ellen, are you okay with that?"

"Will Jay be there?" she said.

"I don't know," I said. "It's possible. It seems like everyone in Santa Fe goes to Zozobra."

Ellen was about to respond when a howl rang out from somewhere, making me look to the edge of the hot-air balloon field, where a coyote stood, watching us intently. Was it Dakota? Was I hallucinating again?

"That's bizarre," Kit said, gazing in the same direction. "They usually don't come out in the daylight like that. Maybe it's a good sign? I bet Jay would say that's a good sign." So it hadn't just been me this time. Phew.

"Yeah, right," Ellen said. "Are you high? You have my burden, so I wouldn't be surprised. If a flock of vultures was circling our heads right now, you'd probably interpret that positively too."

"Lighten up, love," Kit said. "Your legs hurt? Here. Get on my back."

"No way." But Kit backed into her, caught her wrists, and flung her arms over his shoulders anyway. A second later she had been hoisted into a galloping piggyback ride across the airfield and toward her car in the parking lot. From a distance I couldn't tell if she was laughing or screaming. I guess Kit had a ride home.

"Kaya?" I said, starting to stroll away from the hangar with her and Thomas. "Are you cool with going to Zozobra tonight?"

"Hm?" she said, scratching intently at a bug bite on her forearm. "Oh yeah. Zozobra. That's fine. My mom owes me an outing." Blood smeared across her mocha skin from her bug bite. "Wow," she said, and kept scratching. I wasn't sure if I should interfere.

"Can I give you a ride home?" I said.

"No thanks," she said. "I have my car. Was just leaving. I've got some errands to run." Suddenly she looked a little mischievous. "You should stay here and see if Thomas needs anything. It looks like Psalms is opening up."

Sure enough, Mr. Dent was waving at us from the balloon hangar at our backs. Though he was probably curious as to why Thomas was there with two girls on a Sunday morning, he thankfully didn't come over to investigate.

We said goodbye to Kaya, who headed toward her car at a fast trot. Only Thomas and I remained.

"Are you okay?" I said. "With everything?" Together we watched a church bus pull into the parking lot, the people hot off a sermon and ready to take to the air.

"Actually, no," he said, staring at the passengers getting off the bus. "My shift's about to start. I'm supposed to take all those people up in a balloon in about ten minutes. That means igniting an extremely combustible gas burner, untying rope anchors, and launching us all into space in a glorified

Easter basket. It all just seems so stupid and unsound. What if something happens? What if someone gets hurt? And for what? So a handful of humans can pretend they're attached to a cloud for a couple of hours? They could just wait on the ground and get rained on."

I smiled. "They'd have to wait a long time. We're in the middle of a drought." He shrugged. "Listen," I said, "you've done this so many times before. You know how to keep people safe."

"No. No, I don't. Many people have . . . fallen . . . because of me."

"Whatever happened when you were a kid isn't going to affect the fact that you're strong, and brave, and *good,* and you know what you're doing. I was in a balloon with you, remember? You're a good pilot."

"I just don't know anymore," he said. "I start picturing the bad things that could happen, and I. . . ."

"I understand," I said. "Just try to ride out the anxiety. In a way it shows . . . progress. You know, that you care. Can I do something to help?"

"Will you just stay with me for a while? Help me set up? I think I can get Charlie to cover for me in the air as long as I do the prep work."

"No problem," I said. "Where do I start?"

———

When I pulled away from Psalms Over Santa Fe an hour later, I took one last look in the rearview mirror. The coyote hadn't moved. It still stood there at the edge of the field, seeming to scrutinize my departure.

For the first time in a long time, Kit and I were on the same page. I agreed with his conclusion: This seemed like a good omen indeed.

12

I DIDN'T LIKE THE WAY I'd left things with Ellen.

I texted her to see if she'd gone home after our meeting at the Psalms airfield. no, she eventually wrote back. the tracks. She didn't exactly invite me to join her, but within ten minutes I was downtown at our old hangout next to the Santa Fe Railroad.

Ellen was sitting on the boulder where we'd all scratched our names freshman year. Alex. Juanita. Luis. Brett. Even Kit's name was there, though I couldn't remember ever seeing him at the tracks. Ellen's name was carved the deepest, as if she thought she might disappear without that hold on the rock.

She sat with her legs dangling over our inscriptions, spinning an unlit cigarette between her fingers. Her eyes were still red and puffy. Exhausted. I sat down next to her. No trains in either direction.

"Remember how we used to come here?" she said, without meeting my searching gaze.

"Yeah." I scanned the bright, industrial horizon beyond the tracks for signs of life. Two years ago Ellen used to round up me and various other Agua characters to chill in this same spot at night if there wasn't a party or something going on. It was just a place to be, though you'd think we could've come up with a better location, at least somewhere that served late-night tacos.

"Though frankly, Ellen," I said, no longer afraid of her unpredictable wrath, "I never understood why this was your favorite spot. When I wasn't scared that we'd get caught drinking here, I worried that someone would have one too many beers and stumble onto the tracks when a train was passing."

"Yeah, well, I should be so lucky."

"Please don't say things like that."

"Okay, fine," she said defiantly. "You want to know why I was always dragging you guys out here? Because I liked to fantasize about jumping one of those trains and getting the hell out of town. Out of the Land of Entrapment. It didn't even matter where. I just needed to escape. And then, sometime last year, I figured out a much easier way to go about doing that."

Ellen and I used to sit alone together at those impromptu train track parties and daydream about leaving Santa Fe. Our town was so quiet, so hippie-dippy, so far from *everything*. I wanted to smell the ocean. Ellen wanted to be anonymous. But the difference was that I was content to wait until graduation to make my move, while Ellen's desire to flee was much more urgent. Unstoppable. A freight train.

"Escape from what?" I said gently.

"This. My life."

"Come on, Ellen. Is it really that bad?"

"Jesus, Lo. You're so naïve sometimes. You don't know what it feels like to see your father—the guy who unceremoniously abandoned you, FYI—stumbling drunk down the middle of the street on a weekday afternoon. And you have to pretend you don't recognize him because you're with your friends and you're mortified. And you don't know what it's like to have a mother who constantly buys you things because she thinks it's an adequate substitute for spending time with you, loving you. Hell, even knowing what your favorite color is."

"Pumpkin," I said automatically, remembering that Ellen had told me that once in middle school art class. For a second she smiled. Then her face fell again like a stone.

"Lo, you don't know what it's like to just . . . want to erase yourself. Completely."

That shut me up. Had I really been that ignorant of Ellen's problems? I just thought she'd been rebelling. Fairly normal teenage stuff. I hadn't known that she was hiding so much.

Her gaze was still fixed on me. Then, as if I were the one who needed comforting, she reached out and put her hand tenderly on my back.

"Listen, Lo. I'm not blaming you for having nice parents and ridiculous backyard chickens and a charmed life in general. I'm really not. The more well-adjusted people in the world, the better, right? And I know you've suffered your own hardships lately. I'm just saying that you can't understand. And now *this*. Your—no offense—*asshole* of a disease is forcing me to be . . . present in my body in a way I haven't been in over a year. It's like, I knew how to deal with my emotional pain. That was easy. Vodka, pills, cigarettes, weed . . . the other thing. . . ."

"Meth."

"It was just a few times. I'm not a total idiot."

"I know you're not. You're really effing smart." She turned her head away. "You *are*, Ellen. Remember in eighth grade when you got into a debate about global warming with Mr. Henry? You totally schooled him. I think he went straight home after teaching biology and bought an electric car. I thought you were the coolest girl I'd ever met."

"Anyway," she said, "yesterday I could self-medicate all my feelings, but now that isn't an option. And not only that but I'm dealing with all this physical pain too. It's like now both my mind *and* my body are revolting against me."

"I'm so sorry, Ellen," I said. And I meant it. "I would take it back from you if I could." Did I mean that?

She scoffed and removed her hand from my back. "Yeah, right. Are you sure? Or are you just fooling yourself?"

"Why are you so angry with me? You think I've never felt pain? Grief? I was just trying to *help* us. Heal us. I had no idea that we'd all be swapping like this. I was just as misled by Jay as you were!"

Ellen sighed and threw her unlit cigarette onto the tracks. I wondered if she could give me back my disease through some kind of vengeful osmosis. After all, weirder things have happened, especially in New Mexico.

"I know," she said. "What happened is *all* of our faults. We were all playing with fire. Imagine thinking that our problems would just disappear because some dude spit on our backs and then ran a glorified group therapy session."

An approaching train's whistle blew in the distance.

"Ellen," I said, "I know that part of you still wants to get on a train and leave, and I know that you're pissed off. Mostly at yourself." She flinched. "Wait, listen. Maybe this week is an opportunity to face whatever it is inside you that leads you to do all this super-unhealthy stuff. It might feel like a dark place to go, but can you try just looking at it openly instead of fighting it? Maybe you'll be surprised. You're tough as nails—everybody knows that—but it's okay to be sad sometimes. It's okay to hurt. I'll help you. I'm here for you. And plus, a lot of people would be really heartbroken if you disappeared. You keep us on our toes. You're like . . . thunder and lightning and the rainbow all wrapped into one." Ellen dismissed my praise with a skeptical laugh.

"I'll try," she said eventually. "It's just that I feel so . . . defeated most of the time. Before I even begin. And it makes me lash out at everyone and push them away."

"I know," I said. "And it's okay. But let's try to do something about it."

"Thanks, Lo. To tell you the truth, I'm sort of looking forward to spending time with you this week. I've been . . . lonely."

I leaned my head against her shoulder. "No more."

Our cell phones buzzed simultaneously with a group text from Kit, telling us that we were all going to dress up

for zozobra. *way* up. black tie, he wrote. think prom.
no arguments. see you in a few hours. xokit.

"Can you believe him?" Ellen laughed. "He's, like, loony tunes all of a sudden. I'm kind of digging it."

She shifted her leg to reveal the remainder of Kit's engraving on the rock: ♡'s Lucita

"I am too," I said. "I haven't seen this side of him for a long time. But of course it's been there all along, just . . . buried."

"It gives me hope," Ellen said.

"Me too."

Just as the whistle had promised, a train rumbled past and drowned out our voices. I put my arm around Ellen. For a few minutes we just sat in silence, on the rock inscribed with our names and our memories, watching the metal train cars pass by, headed to parts unknown.

13

EVERY YEAR, AS PART OF the Zozobra tradition, we stuff the giant wooden man with our burdens before we burn him. In the weeks leading up to the festival you're supposed to write down your problems on little slips of paper and submit them to the festival organizers. Then, on the big night, your problems go up in smoke. The idea is that the fire eats up all your gloom. You burn your burdens in effigy and keep your fingers crossed that they disappear in real life too.

I know the ceremony is purely symbolic—mostly just a way of attracting tourists to Santa Fe—but it's also fun, and I actually get excited about it every year. I try not to think that gloom must have been built into the fabric of our city if every year there's an event organized to take it away.

In loyal adherence to Kit's instructions, I decided to wear my prom dress from last year, when a senior named Cale Hannigan had invited me to be his date. I'd felt pretty then, even though I was nervous to attend prom with someone older (and in the closet, it turned out). But tonight I felt beautiful.

My floor-length gown was asymmetrical, with one strap over my right shoulder. It was grayish-purple, which I was told brought out the green in my eyes. It hugged my figure all the way down to my knees, and then flared out like a mermaid's tail. It was sort of hard to drive a dirty station wagon in such a fancy number, but I made do.

I hadn't seen Kaya since she'd left the airfield in a hurry that morning. I was still feeling uneasy about her episode, so I told her that I'd pick her up at her house and we'd drive to Zozobra together.

I was running late due to lingering at the tracks with Ellen, but Kaya wasn't out front when I pulled up. Once again, Mrs. Johnson answered when I knocked on the door, stumbling slightly in my silver heels. Good thing I hadn't honked the horn.

"I still don't understand why you kids are dressing up for Zozobra," Mrs. Johnson said. "Last I checked it was a casual event, not a debutante ball."

"We just thought it would be fun," I said. "Something different. And plus, we're celebrating."

"Celebrating what?"

"Well . . . today sort of marks a new start."

"What do you mean?"

"Just . . ." I stammered, trying to dig myself out of this hole.

"Hi, Lo," a barely audible voice said above me. Hallelujah, I was saved. Kaya descended the stairs gingerly, arms folded across her chest. Her strapless empire-waist black gown grazed the rug, even though she was wearing heels.

"Wow, Kaya," I said. "I feel like I'm watching one of those slow-motion scenes from a romcom. You look amazing. That *dress* is amazing."

"It's my mom's," she said, crossing the foyer. Mrs. Johnson began fussing with Kaya's earrings.

"Are you sure you want to wear the silver ones?" she said. "You have comfy plastic ones that would look just as good."

"These are fine, Mom," Kaya said. "I promise I'll be careful. The day I manage to injure myself with an earring is the same day I get my female license revoked."

"All right, then. You'll be home by nine?" Mrs. Johnson said.

"Is . . . ten okay?" Kaya's mother frowned. "Mom, you promised you'd give me some breathing room."

"I know I did, baby. It's just hard. Okay, ten. Or earlier. And stay away from the fire. *Far* away. The head of the Kiwanis Club is a notorious drunk. I wouldn't trust him with matches, let alone lighter fluid and fifty feet of ultra-flammable tinder."

"Don't worry, Mom. The fire will look like candlelight from where we're sitting. Love you."

"I love you too, baby. Be careful."

I was happy to see Kaya in such a normal state after what had happened at the balloon field, but the minute we got in my car, she became sullen and quiet. She stared vacantly out the window as I unsuccessfully tried to make her laugh by telling her about the gymnastic maneuvers I'd had to make in order to fasten the zipper of my gown without any help— or without spraining any ankles (at least as far as I knew).

But I wasn't breaking through. I decided to take a more direct approach.

"So. How's it going?" I said. "Do you feel any better since this morning?"

"I don't know if 'better' is the word. I feel different. I feel heavier." She was slow getting her words out, as if they too were heavy.

"How do you mean?" I said. She was quiet for a moment.

"When you first proposed this experiment," she said finally, "I sort of thought it was another one of your whims, like when we were kids and you started the séance club."

Ah yes, the Santa Fe Séance Club. I'd almost forgotten. The SFSC met two times total and hadn't managed to recruit any members besides a younger neighbor girl who used to worship me and Kaya. But when Mrs. Johnson got wind of it she quickly pronounced our membership activities "satanic," and our association fizzled out.

"Ha," I said. "I thought *you* launched the Séance Club."

"Okay," Kaya said, "maybe we were mutually inspired. Remember how we tried to contact Judy Garland at our inaugural meeting? 'Come back, Dorothy!'"

"Because, you know, if Judy Garland came back from the dead we'd clearly be the first people she'd want to talk to."

"Right," Kaya said. She bit her top lip. And then her bottom lip. And then her tongue. "Anyway. I didn't really expect this ritual thing to *work*. I kind of just wanted to . . . well, you know. I don't get out much. Lo, it's so weird to be vulnerable physically. It's what I said I wanted, but I'm not sure how I feel about it yet. This afternoon I shaved my legs for the first time. Mom had never let me have a razor before, but I drove to the pharmacy so I could buy one on the way back from the airfield."

"I thought you might be up to something," I said.

"And of course I cut myself shaving. Like, immediately. First pass of the razor. Like my shinbones were magnets. But when I felt the pain—at least what I can only assume was pain—I started crying and then I couldn't stop. I wasn't sure if I was crying from happiness or sadness or what. It was the first time the blood in my body had ever mingled with . . . a feeling. You know? Something that wasn't just . . . numbness." She pulled up the black chiffon of her dress and pointed at her shin. "Look, ninja Band-Aids."

"Cool," I said, at a loss for words. For some reason I couldn't reconcile Kaya's half dozen ninja Band-Aids with her report of uncontrollable crying.

"I guess I don't really have a context for physical pain," Kaya said. "Like, I've seen movies and stuff where people get shot in the stomach and double over, but I couldn't begin to fathom their actual suffering until now."

"Just like I could never imagine what you were experiencing by *not* feeling pain."

"Yeah. I guess I'd never really thought about it the way everyone else seems to. I didn't think I had something that anyone else could ever *want*. Like when I got all those letters after that article came out. People saying things like how dare I whine about my incredible gift. Guys saying they wanted to father my 'bionic' children. I was just . . . mystified. And now it's so strange to see you enjoying my condition."

"What?" I felt like I'd been caught shoplifting or something. "That's not true. . . ."

"Come on, Lo. You've always had a terrible poker face. You obviously like the results of the trade. I'm not mad at you. I haven't seen you look so happy in a long time. Not since the summer, anyway. I guess before your aunt got sick."

My aunt. I hadn't thought of Karine all day. Noticing this made me feel guilty, but also . . . lightened. "Yeah," I conceded. "I guess you're right."

"But Lo, I don't think you totally understand what you've gotten yourself into. I don't think you understand that what you've got right now is dangerous. I know my mom can be a pain in the ass, but she's probably right to overthink everything I do."

Suddenly, I desperately wanted to change the subject. "Don't worry about me," I said. "Hey, what exactly happened this morning? When you said you had a vision? You were really . . . out of it for a few minutes. Kit said you might've been having . . . flashbacks or something?"

"I guess that's what you'd call them," Kaya said. "I saw things that happened a long time ago. I can feel pain now, but so far it's always . . . associated with these images of my people. Even the shaving cuts. In the shower I closed my eyes and saw a young Pueblo girl running bare-legged through thick and spiny underbrush . . . like she was trying to get away from something." She tugged hard at her earring. "I dunno. I guess you wouldn't understand."

"Because I'm not Native American?"

"Because you have a bright life ahead of you. And your ancestors haven't been decimated. So you can't comprehend what it's like to know in your bones and to see in your dreams how your whole family's future was stolen, long ago."

I thought of the entire Indian villages of women and children that were massacred here, of Apache warriors fighting losing battles against superior firepower on the frontier, and about how I only knew about these things secondhand from American history class.

"I can at least try," I said. "Like Kit tries." Kaya turned away to gaze out the window again.

"I don't want to talk about it anymore."

"Okay," I said, but I was bummed that she wasn't letting me in.

"Jeez, I never would have guessed how much high heels hurt." Now it was Kaya changing the subject. "Is it normal for straps to dig into your skin like this?" She held up her foot so I could see the blisters forming behind her ankle.

"Unfortunately, yes," I said. "Comes with the territory. Beauty is pain, my dear."

We arrived at Fort Marcy Park just as the pre-Zozobra entertainment was reaching a crescendo. The place was packed. Local artists hoisted papier-mâché dragons aloft, and children carried glowing white balloons that from a distance looked like UFOs. The night air swam with the smells of fresh tacos, fry bread, and tamales. Indian women sold anise-flavored bizcochito cookies in little paper funnels. Families of all shades and sizes spread out on red-and-black Navajo blankets, while hippies drummed in circles at the margins of the crowd—either under the influence of psychedelic mushrooms or the magic in the air. Then there were the Kiwanis Club sponsorship tables to remind us that nothing is ever *that* cool, even when you're setting fire to things.

Kaya and I walked the periphery of the park to Kit's meeting place. Kaya's heels started sinking into the irrigated park grounds, so I knelt down and undid her sandal straps.

"Hey, you should undo yours too," she said. "You might not realize how much they're biting into you." Sure enough, my skin was crisscrossed with red welts, so we walked barefoot through the grass as the sky darkened around us.

"Ah," she said. "That's way better." I took her word for it.

A troupe of Hopi dancers made a clearing in the crowd. I recognized a girl from school, Mary Falling Leaf, among them, but she looked completely different in this setting. She wore a white ceremonial dress covered in tiny bells, and as she danced solemnly to a drum accompaniment, she jingled in perfect tandem with the rest of her troupe. I tried to catch her eye, but couldn't. She was carried away by the music. I knew that feeling.

Our boys were easy to spot in their black suits. I'd never seen Thomas wear anything other than a T-shirt and Levi's, but tonight he looked like an African dignitary, maybe even a prince. Kit didn't look half bad either. He'd even smoothed back his Mohawk with hair gel. He was busy arranging grapes, cheddar cheese, and Oreo cookies on a gray picnic blanket when Kaya and I strolled up with our metallic heels in our hands.

"No Ellen?" Kit said, looking disappointed.

"She's driving herself," I said. "But what are we? Shredded taco meat? How about a 'You look beautiful, girls'?"

"Girls," Kit said, dropping to his knees and seizing our hands in high dramatic fashion, "you look ravishing tonight."

"That's more like it," I said. Kit kissed our hands and stood. Thomas rolled his eyes and glanced nervously toward the Zozobra proceedings, skipping over me entirely. Maybe my dress didn't highlight my eyes after all.

"So why did you want everyone to dress up anyway?" Kaya said, settling down on the blanket and smoothing her dress around her.

"Lucita and I did this same thing last year," Kit said cheerfully. "I just wanted to relive the memory."

"Oh," Kaya said. She fiddled with her earring. Before that morning, I'd never heard Kit talk about Lucita without despair in his voice, if at all. Now it seemed he wanted to talk about her ardently, and at every opportunity.

"Lucita liked to turn little, everyday occasions into events," he said. "Sacred ceremonies. Speaking of which, would you ladies consider joining me and Mr. Kamara for the second annual Zozobra Cookie Gala, commencing now?"

"Our pleasure," I said and sat beside Kaya on the blanket.

The festival atmosphere was infectious. Even Kaya and Thomas appeared less sulky the more cookies we ate. Still kind of sulky, though. I didn't know why I always felt as though I had to start from square one with Thomas every time we saw each other, even if we were just passing in the hallway and I tried to smile at him. I never knew from minute to minute what kind of signal he was going to emit in my direction—real warmth or just smoke. But I was determined to have fun. Determined not to think of Ellen's pain. Determined not to think of Lucita's death, or of my aunt. . . .

"Save any cookies for me?" Ellen said, sneaking up behind us. I was relieved that she'd made it to the festival and quickly tugged her down to blanket level. She wore high-top Converses with her black minidress and easily made herself comfortable.

"Any sign of Jay?" she said.

"No," I said. "Just the usual Fiestas crowd. Sorry." But the truth was, I'd forgotten to look for him.

Kit tried to tackle Ellen playfully, but she kicked him off.

"Geez, Kit," she said, clearly irked or in pain, and I felt guilty once again. "Try to stay in your own body, *por favor.*"

A group of drunken college-age kids walked by our blanket. One of the girls wore a bikini top and carried a hula-hoop. When she accidentally tripped over the hoop, she cursed and then kept walking, leaving it on the ground. I leapt to my bare feet and grabbed it.

Settling it around my hips, I began doing every trick I knew, including revolving the hoop around my neck and arms. My dress allowed a surprising range of movement, especially when I hiked it around my knees.

"Okay, my go, McDonough," Kit said, joining me in the grass. We took turns spinning the hoop around our appendages and then tossing it back and forth in the dark.

"Wait a sec," I said to Kit, exhausted from laughing at the stunts he kept trying to pull off. "There's something I've always wanted to try but was too scared. My aunt used to do it."

I found three paper napkins in the picnic basket and wrapped them around the circumference of the hoop at regular intervals.

"Ellen, do you have a lighter?" She groped around in her purse until she came up with one.

I stepped into the hula-hoop, then lit the napkins on fire. They didn't burn long while the momentum of my hips carried the hoop around my waist. That was partly because paper burned fast, and partly because I was suddenly soaked in cold water. Thomas, without warning, had emptied a full bottle of water on my torso.

"Thomas!" I said. I dropped the extinguished hoop and took stock of my damaged gown.

"Sorry, Lo." He looked down at the empty bottle as if surprised at himself. "I just saw it ending badly. Because you wouldn't be able to . . . you know."

Kaya looked away. I wondered how many times she'd burned herself without realizing it.

"It's all right," I said. I really didn't care about the dress. I was still high on endorphins from having danced with a burning hula-hoop. Maybe I could be as brave and adventurous as Aunt Karine after all.

"Speaking of ending badly," Kit said, "look what I brought." He opened his backpack to reveal boxes and boxes of Fourth of July sparklers.

"Whoa, Kit," Ellen said. "What did you do, rob a fireworks stand?"

"Maybe," he said. "Couldn't let Old Man Gloom have all the fun." Kit was so gung ho about everything, it was starting to make me slightly nervous. Thomas looked as anxious as I felt when Kit lit his first sparkler and began darting around the picnic blanket, raining fire on everything. We exchanged a glance.

"Okay, Kit, that's enough," Thomas said. But Kit just waved at least three lit sparklers in each hand at us, then started running in faster and tighter circles around the blanket. And he was beginning to stumble a little.

Suddenly, Kaya bounded to her feet and joined Kit, as if just remembering that certain activities were no longer off limits.

"I don't think that's a good idea," said Thomas, but before he could stop her, Kaya was running around the blanket as well, grabbing sparklers out of Kit's hands. They were already halfway burned away, and Kaya seemed determined to see them fizzle down to her fingertips. Then, abruptly, she went still and stared into the small fires burning in her hands. She looked like a goddess admiring a universe of her own design.

"Lights," she said, the darkness in her voice the total opposite of what sputtered merrily on the ends of the sparklers. "All the lights will go out," she said, trancelike. "All the people." Her eyes darted around the park, as if she were being hunted.

Thomas gently removed the charred remnants from Kaya's hands and then stubbed them out under his shoe. She seemed to calm down the moment Thomas placed his hand on her shoulder.

"It's okay, Kaya," he said. "Let's just sit down and let Kit do his thing. I'll pour you some lemonade."

Kit scampered off to flirt with two freshman girls from school, while Kaya lay down on the blanket beside Ellen, looking into the Southwestern night sky. Thomas and I joined them, the tops of our heads all touching. We tried to identify shapes in the clouds of smoke.

"It's a shame we can't see all the stars tonight," I said.

"I never had much to say about the stars," Thomas said.

"What about you, Kaya?" I said, feeling her drifting away again.

"They never had much to say to me," she said. "Until tonight."

I lifted myself onto my elbows to ask what they were telling her and immediately saw strange movement at the edge of the park woods. A coyote? But then my attention was diverted, and all I could focus on was the central spectacle. At a distance, the wooden man was finally burning. Dancers emerged at his feet, their bodies lit by the glow of destruction. My body began to pulse to the beat of drumming and chanting. A fifty-foot torch stretched into the night sky. Scraps of scalded paper floated down from a great height, some of the edges still glowing red, and I imagined what the fragments of words might say. House . . . cancer . . . child . . . *corazon*. Anonymous burdens falling from the sky. Would the night carry away everyone's gloom? I hoped that soon the whole park would feel as free as I did.

I heard a howl at the edge of the forest. Then the howling was absorbed by the sound of crackling wood. Even the wild animals had come to see the spectacle. Why not? It was theirs too.

A dozen blankets away I saw an Indian man who, as he danced, seemed to turn into a bird with a twenty-foot wingspan. The shapes around him kept changing, but he was always at the center, controlling the movement.

"You guys, look," I said, pointing toward the metamorphosing figure. "Let's get closer."

Thomas said he wanted to stay on the blanket and watch the fire.

"Me too," said Ellen, with an eye on Kit, who was still talking to the freshman girls. I pulled Kaya to her feet, and we walked barefoot to where the Native American man in buckskin ceremonial garb was manipulating at least a dozen small, interlocking hoops with his legs and arms, transforming himself into hybrid creatures in the process. First he was a bird, then a bear, then a coyote. On either side of him a line of musicians pounded on drums.

"What's he doing?" I said, enthralled. I'd never known that hoops could have so much life in them.

"Native American hoop dance," said Kit, who'd approached us from behind.

"I didn't know that was a thing," I said.

"Well, they don't exactly sell these hoops at Toys "R" Us." Kit hadn't lost his sardonic edge after all. "This man is telling stories through dance."

"Wow," I said. "It looks like he's holding up the whole world."

The man concentrated all the hoops around his head and then held them aloft in a perfect globe.

"What does it mean?" I murmured.

"The circle of life," Kit said. "The hoop represents the connection between spirit and matter."

Behind the hoop dancer the wooden man still burned, and I thought about what it must be like to fly over such a fire, as my father and his crew did almost every day from their airplanes. I imagined being up there too, but instead of extinguishing the flames, I was admiring them. Letting history do its exhaustive work, letting it burn itself out, until not only the problems but all its beauty, all its people, were gone. The dancer threw his hooped world over his head, into orbit. I turned to go before he caught it safely in his hands.

"Let's get back to the blanket," I said, suddenly feeling a touch dispirited. "And to Thomas and Ellen. It's starting to get cold, and we should stay together."

14

WE RECONVENED ON OUR LITTLE plot of Zozobra. Thomas invited me to rest my head in his lap, which I gratefully did. I shivered, and he laid his jacket over me. Kaya sat on the blanket in silent thought, watching the faraway man burn down to his toes. Kit was zipping around again, and I was so distracted by his antics and the warmth of Thomas's lap that it took me a couple of minutes to realize that Ellen was missing. If I should've been looking out for anyone, it was the girl who'd taken on my burden, and she'd disappeared.

The drums and chanting amplified from the Zozobra stage as the festival organizers cheered on the burning man. Kit gave a whoop.

"Let's have it! Burn, baby, burn!"

Then I spotted Ellen. She was about five blankets away, crouched next to a little girl in a floral sundress.

"Hey, look." I grabbed Thomas's arm, and we hustled over. The girl Ellen was talking to was probably seven or eight years old, and she looked terrified. As we got closer, I realized that Ellen was not talking to her in the soothing maternal voice befitting interaction with a lost child. She was nearly shouting at her. Thomas and I stopped short, shocked, when we heard what she was saying.

"Listen to me." Ellen was crouched down, at eye level with the little girl. "Just listen. You're not listening. I know you're scared now, but that's nothing compared to what it's going to be like if you don't listen."

Ellen rubbed her temples, and I could tell from her posture and pained expression that she was in the midst of an acute migraine. The pain was inflecting everything she said, making her words sharper.

"But you might still be okay if you just listen. Maybe. Being a teenager sucks, and you're going to suffer, but don't start doing drugs, because they only make things worse. They only make it harder to fix yourself. They might even make it impossible. Do you hear me? Are you listening?"

I knelt down beside Ellen and wrapped my arm around her waist. "Ellen," I said, "you're scaring this little girl. Do you know her?"

"Where's my mommy?" the girl cried.

"She needs to be protected," Ellen said, shaking me off. "When I was her age, I wish someone had talked to me about *real* life and how shitty it is. Then maybe I could've been prepared. I could've been stronger. I wish I'd had someone like me around to tell *me* not to end up the way I ended up."

"Ellen," I said. "She's too young to understand. And she's lost. And scared."

"Come here, sweetheart," Thomas said, placing his hands on the girl's trembling shoulders. "We'll find your parents."

Just then an agitated woman approached and snatched

the girl away. "What are you doing with my daughter? Sophia, are you okay?" She looked up at us. "Did you do something to her?" She seemed to address this last question specifically to Thomas, and I bristled on his behalf.

Thomas and I apologized for Ellen. We brought her back to the blanket and set her down next to Kaya, and I rubbed her back until her breathing slowed.

"What happened?" Kit said.

"Lost girl," I said.

On the other side of the blanket, Thomas seemed upset. "Don't take it personally," I said. "That lady was just really worried."

"Sure," Thomas said. He was preoccupied for a moment before speaking again. "Will you take a walk with me? I need some distance from this fire. I feel like I'm overheating. Are you?" He put his hand on my forehead.

"I'm okay," I said. "But yes, a walk sounds great." Kit promised he'd stay with Ellen and Kaya, so Thomas and I wandered away from the crowd.

"You weren't burned by any of those sparklers, were you?" he said.

"Nope. I was careful."

"I'm not sure if we should've come here," he said. "It all feels too dangerous."

Near the edge of the forest, people were beginning to pack up their blankets and go home.

"Everyone's doing pretty well under the circumstances," I said. "At least I think they are. But I definitely fell asleep on the job back there with Ellen. It's weird—I've only ever seen her that intense when she's been high, but this time it was *my* symptoms feeding the intensity. It made me think about how I must have appeared to everyone else these past few months."

"Quieter," Thomas said immediately. "More thoughtful."

"Oh," I said. True to form, I didn't really have a response to that. "Can I confess something?"

"Of course."

"I, um . . . read something of yours once."

"Read something?"

"A poem. About the fire back home. And feeling like static. A few weeks ago I was waiting for the school counselor in her office—I guess I was really desperate to talk to someone about . . . everything—and I saw a piece of paper on her desk with your name on it. And so I read it. And . . . took a picture of it with my cell phone so I could read it again. I'm sorry."

Thomas was quiet, and I assumed the worst. "So how was your talk with Ms. Vega?" he said eventually.

"I left before she got back. I'm a total chicken. You?"

"I've never had much luck with therapists. I had to see a few when I first got here because of all this legal stuff. I'd usually just sit there on the couch and wait in silence for the hour to be over. But Ms. Vega . . . instead of getting frustrated with me for being so unexpressive, she suggested I write poetry. So that's what I've been doing, for better or worse. I'm sorry you had to see my crude efforts."

"No, I loved it," I said. "For me, you captured . . . that distance, you know? Between where your body is and where your mind is. It's really painful to feel separated like that. Sort of alien to yourself."

"Okay, now it's my turn to confess something."

"Shoot," I said.

"I'm especially nervous about you this week, Lo. This painlessness puts you in a particularly fragile state. You must exercise precaution." (Because Thomas learned English from antiquated textbooks along with Hollywood action movies and underground comics, his diction was sometimes overly formal. Not all the time, but when it did happen, I found it pretty adorable.)

"But I feel the exact opposite of fragile right now," I said.

"I get that. But listen. It's like . . . imagine if all of a sudden, you don't know yourself. You don't even know what it's like to live in your own skin. You might snap. You might hurt someone else, or yourself, without realizing it. When people are given power—or even weakness—beyond what they're used to, there can be a major disconnect between that and who they thought they were. They can get totally lost. They can create irreparable damage."

"You're thinking of something specific."

"Yeah, I guess I am. The warlords back in Liberia. When they were given power, it dominated them. It completely overtook their humanity."

"Their souls," I said.

"Yes, their souls." We were quiet for a moment.

"Please promise me," he said finally.

"What? That I won't sell my soul to Satan? I promise."

"That you'll try to stay centered. Not go around being a

daredevil or anything. Okay?"

"Okay," I said. "Cross my heart."

"Good. When I was in the war, I also felt invincible. But you know what? I was just a kid, pretending to be omnipotent. I see that now. You'll see it too."

"You're probably right," I said.

But I wasn't entirely convinced.

Look under my bed again, new mom, new dad.
Find my brown parents burning.
Because I see them, and others with their matchsticks.
And most nights I am with them.
Not here with you.
Not here with me.

I wrapped Thomas's coat tighter around me, hiding the many places on my naked arms where the sparklers had burned me.

15

ON MONDAY, I COULDN'T BELIEVE IT.

Not only was Ellen eating lunch in the courtyard—and actually *eating*, no less—instead of hiding out in the bathroom doing god knows what or skipping school in favor of Meth-Head Mike's company, she actually seemed to be having fun.

She was sitting on the concrete circumference of Agua de Water with Alex and Juanita. Smiling. Laughing. She looked like a different person. I'd completely forgotten how her eyes shone when she was happy because it had been so long since I'd seen her looking anything other than remote or angry. Her skin was clearer, and her designer clothes didn't seem to swallow her as much. She definitely exuded health.

I trotted up to my friends and put down my backpack. All September I had hardly been able to wait to throw it down because the straps bit into my shoulders with the weight of textbooks, but today, of course, I felt zero discomfort.

"So, *chicas*," Ellen said, "where's Weekends on Wednesdays this week?" Alex and Juanita exchanged an anxious glance and then looked to me for support.

"About that . . . ," Juanita said. Oh, crap. I'd forgotten about the intervention we'd planned last week.

"You guys," I said, "maybe it's not such a good time." But Ellen had already lost her sunny expression. I had no idea what to say next, and Alex took over for me.

"Listen, Ellen," she said, adopting a maternal tone. "You know we love you. Always have and always will. And it's *because* we love you that . . ."

"We don't think you should go to the party this week," Juanita blurted. "In fact, we think it's a really bad idea."

"What?" Ellen said, genuinely dumbfounded. Even after the swap, she still didn't seem to know how unruly her bad habits had gotten.

"You've been acting like a beast," Juanita said. "You've been out of control, Ellen. *Especially* at parties. I'm glad you're acting civilized today—believe me, it's a breath of fresh air—but whatever you've been up to in your free time has kind of turned you into a nightmare. Of, like, Carrie proportions. Post–pig's blood Carrie."

"Yeah, I get it," Ellen said. Her face crumpled from all this so-called tough love, and Juanita hesitated.

"Lo," she said, "can you back me up on this?"

I wanted Alex and Juanita to know that I wasn't betraying our decision to confront Ellen about her problem, but at the same time Ellen's problem was sort of obsolete now. She was on to new things. Now she possessed *my* demon.

Before I could say anything, Ellen opened her mouth to speak. I was expecting the worst—normally she'd go totally ballistic whenever she felt threatened or insecure—but amazingly, her voice was calm and even.

"I get why you guys are worried," she said. She serenely intertwined her fingers in her lap and made sustained eye contact first with Alex, then Juanita. "I know that it comes from a good place. Really. And I appreciate it more than you know. But I'm a lot better now, and I promise that going to the party won't be a problem. Plus"—and here she looked to me for complicity—"I talked to Lo about it over the weekend. She promised that she'd be my date to the party and make sure that I behave myself. She swore on her heart. Didn't you, Lo?"

I nodded sheepishly. But I didn't really understand why Ellen wanted to go to Weekends anyway, where we all huddled around a keg as if it were a campfire.

"See?" Ellen said. "I'll be fine. All good."

Alex and Juanita didn't look convinced, but they also didn't seem to have the wherewithal to argue with Ellen's earnest promises.

"Okay," Alex said. "Just be careful. Like we said, we don't want anything to happen to you."

Suddenly, Ellen winced as if she'd been stabbed, then quickly recovered before Alex and Juanita noticed anything. I could tell that it wasn't a reaction to Alex's words; she was having a muscle spasm. School was one thing, but I wondered how Ellen would cope with her symptoms in a more concentrated social situation. Like a party.

"Now if you'll excuse me," Ellen said, "I have to finish my homework before English class." She headed toward the library with a limp so subtle I was surely the only one who noticed it.

"You're really going to look after her on Wednesday night?" Alex said. I looked away from Ellen's melancholy, retreating figure. *Focus, Lo.*

"Yeah," I said. "Really. I think she's turned a corner. And more than anything she needs her friends right now. I won't let her leave my sight. Promise."

"You're sure?" Alex said. "You know the party's at Jason's house, right? You might be distracted by your ex's cute little butt."

"Gross, Alex. You know I don't share your flagrant butt fetish." I smiled. "Anyway, Jason and I are *long* over. Definitely just friends. Plus I'm . . . sort of interested in someone else."

"No way!" Juanita said. "Who? I can't believe you've been holding out. Please don't say it's Luis. He'd probably drop me in a heartbeat if he thought you were interested."

"No, he wouldn't, you coconut," I said. Juanita's insecurity streak never ceased to baffle me. "And it's *not* Luis. It's still too early to know if it's anything. I don't want to jinx it." I resisted the urge to gush, afraid that if I started talking about Thomas, I might reveal everything.

"You bad girl," said Alex. "So you think this is for real?"

"I don't know," I said. "I hope so." I stood up and tossed a quarter in the fountain, wishing for another trip in the hot-air balloon with Thomas. But if we went up again, I'm not sure I'd ever want to come down.

16

BY THE TIME SCHOOL WAS out, I was beyond tired. Still way better than going blind or breaking down from a migraine, but I hadn't anticipated how mentally exhausting it would be to avoid getting injured constantly.

I couldn't sprint down the hallway when I was late for class, because what if I stumbled and broke my ankle without realizing it? I couldn't risk slamming my locker door shut, because what if my hand inadvertently got caught, the way it had in my bedroom window? And I had to get in and out of my desk chairs very gingerly as I went from class to class. What if someone had left a pencil on the seat and I impaled myself? I had waking nightmares of sitting on knives and razor blades. But even though I was beat from all the vigilance, I'd promised Thomas that I'd be careful, so I moved delicately through my day.

When I finally dragged myself up my driveway that afternoon, eager to crash on the couch where nothing could hurt me, I heard a skateboard around the back of the house. I approached on the side garden path, past my bedroom window and the chattering chicken coop.

"Kit?" I called. "Is that you?" My previously bereaved neighbor was now doing kickflips on the cement patio that surrounded our aboveground swimming pool, and I was unexpectedly thrilled to see him. His smile was like a shot in the arm.

"Hey, Lo," he said. "I came looking for you, and your mom let me in. She said I could skate or take a swim while I waited. Cool?"

"Of course," I said. "But you know, if that pool were four feet lower I'd point out that what you're doing was dangerous."

"Oh, it might *still* be dangerous. Have you seen how much air I'm getting? I might rocket into your pool. I'm like a New Mexican jumping bean."

"Hi, Consuelo."

I started and turned around at the sound of the new voice. Kaya stepped gracefully through the patio doorway and pushed the glass shut behind her.

"Kaya!" I said. The last time Kaya was at my house was in eighth grade, and that was only because my parents had convinced me to invite her to my birthday party. Of course barely anyone but me had talked to her, and I'm sure she'd had a terrible time, but Mom's conscience was clean because she'd tried. And at least Kaya had returned home in one piece.

"Kit wanted to teach me how to skateboard while we waited," Kaya said, "but it's still so hot out—your mom said we should take a swim instead."

"That's cool. Do you need to borrow a suit?"

"Kit, um, ran next door to get me one. He still has one of Lucita's old suits. And it fits."

Was my pang of jealousy directed toward Kaya or Kit's dead ex-girlfriend? My friends used to tell me that Lucita and I looked sort of alike. Because the pigments of our eyes and hair were totally different, not to mention the color of our skin, I dismissed the comparison. It wasn't until I saw Lucita's photo above her obituary in the *New Mexican* that I first noticed the similarities in our features. I couldn't stop staring at her face. In that photo, we could have been sisters—or at least cousins. Our noses and lips were almost the same. The way we always cocked our heads slightly when we knew that someone was looking at us. I wondered if I reminded Kit of Lucita. Or if gorgeous Native American Kaya struck a familiar nerve as well.

Standing next to the chicken pen, Kaya took off her shirt, revealing an unconscionably beautiful body. In Lucita's red bikini, she was stunning. The scars and bruises that blighted her torso weren't enough to play down her curvy, perfect form. Who knew she was hiding that figure under her loose-fitting jeans and sweatshirts?

Apparently not Kit. I tried to signal him to stop staring before he made Kaya uncomfortable.

Then, as she took off her shorts, my awe at her centerfold measurements turned to shock. At first it looked as if the fronts of her legs were dyed or tattooed black, or that the flesh on her shins was infected with gangrene or dark scabs. Then I realized that every centimeter of Kaya's legs was covered with ink drawings.

"Whoa," Kit said, trying, like me, to contend with her body.

"Your legs," I said, feeling timid. "Can I . . . ? Is it all right if I look more closely?"

Kaya shrugged and took a seat on a lounge chair. She leaned back, closed her eyes, and wiggled her naked toes in the sun. The drawings looped all the way down to her feet.

I could barely take in the range of images depicted in ink: Scenes of Indian warriors battling uniformed soldiers on horseback, tableaus of men shooting arrows into herds of buffalo, Navajo hogans burning. Pictures of dead chieftains, slaughtered families, razed orchards and cornfields—all interwoven with the scars that crisscrossed Kaya's legs. She stood up and walked to the edge of the pool.

"Kaya, stop," I said, still somewhat dazed by the surreal landscapes on her body. She looked so beautiful. "You can't go in. All the pictures will wash off."

"It's okay," she said. "I can always draw them again. The scenes are in my head. They're like photographs. Or movies." Then she climbed the ladder and slipped into the water.

Kit and I looked at each other warily as a small gray cloud formed in Kaya's wake. "I'm worried," he said.

"So am I."

We stood there in silence for a few minutes, watching Kaya swim the meager circumference of the pool over and over again, the storm of ink still trailing her.

"So you and Thomas, huh?" Kit said abruptly, clearly unable to keep his frenetic mind from wandering, even from this incredible sight. I looked away from the pool, startled, and felt my cheeks redden.

"What do you mean? Did he . . . say something to you?"

Kit gave me a knowing look. "Not exactly."

"Oh. Well. Nothing's going on. I don't think." But if I'd been a little braver, and a little more sure of what I wanted, maybe something could have happened at Zozobra the night before. At times it had taken all I had not to kiss him. "Is that why you came over?" I said. "To ask me about Thomas?"

"I quit taking my antidepressants," Kit said. Again, no segue. His mind moved too fast for me to try to keep up with his stream of consciousness.

"How long have you been on them?" I said.

"My parents put me on them last year. After Lucita. But I don't need them anymore."

"That's good," I said. "I'm glad that you're happier." Kit nodded proudly. ("Happier" might have been the wrong word to use. He was like a human disco ball. Definitely a hard boy to figure out.) I wanted to delve deeper. "I guess, though, that I don't entirely understand how Ellen's addiction translated to you. You seem to be doing better than any of us. Don't get me wrong—I . . . we all think it's great. But . . . can you explain it?"

"I think I'm just seeing life for the first time. And really living it moment to moment. It feels like a drug because it's fresh and illicit somehow. You know, like it feels so good it must be wrong."

I smiled. "You're not going to get in trouble for enjoying the world again."

"That's a relief. Because I'm ecstatic." There was still something eerie about all this. Like Kit didn't seem willing to acknowledge darkness along with the light.

"But don't you worry that you might lose this new state of mind?" I said. "I mean, I feel better too, but I'm still scared that it will all come crashing down in less than a week. That being healed is an illusion."

"You mean if we swap back on Saturday?" *Yes*, I thought, but I still hoped we'd never have to switch back.

"Or if we just lose our new ... gifts," I said. "Somehow."

"I don't think Ellen would define what she gave me as a 'gift,'" Kit said. "And neither would Kaya for you."

"That's the weird thing about it. These burdens seem to be transformed, depending on who has them. Depending on our pasts or maybe ... our attitudes."

"Yeah, well, you certainly seem to be thriving with Kaya's condition."

"You think? I mean, yeah. I can't really argue with you there. I'm tired from all the tiptoeing around, for sure, but physically I feel amazing. And you. . . . Don't take this the wrong way, but you're like a dying houseplant that's finally been given sunlight and water."

"And, like, a million-dollar ceramic pot."

"Exactly," I said. "But Kaya, meanwhile. . . ."

We looked to the pool. Kaya had stopped swimming in circuits and was now treading water, watching us intently.

"What are you guys talking about?" she said.

For some reason I wanted to shield her from the concern I felt. Though I was no longer intimidated by Ellen, Kaya somehow made me feel very small. There was something . . . I don't know . . . *formidable* about her since the ritual. Something deep that I couldn't access.

"We were just saying that it's time for your first skateboarding lesson," Kit said.

Kaya climbed out of the pool, toweled off, and put on her shorts. "I'm ready," she said. "My mom would *never* let me try this."

Kit handed her a helmet.

"No thanks," she said. I looked at her warily. "Don't baby me, Lo. I get enough of that at home. I'll be careful."

I didn't like this at all, but she was right. She wasn't a child anymore. I didn't feel that it was my place to stop her.

On Kaya's first attempt, the skateboard flew out from under her, and she crashed to the concrete patio, landing hard on her side. I rushed to help her up, but she just smiled up at me widely and rubbed her elbow.

"I guess I have a high pain threshold," she said. "Who knew? Hey, do either of you guys have a bike I can borrow?"

"Absolutely," Kit said. *Here we go again*, I thought.

Kit and I retrieved three bikes from our respective garages and went to the street. Kaya immediately took off ahead of us, toward the center of town. As I struggled to catch up, Kaya lifted her arms from the handlebars and stretched them to her sides. I hadn't even known that she could ride a bike. Her posture was strong, like she believed she'd never fall. She flew by adobe houses, galleries with art spilling practically to the sidewalk, and butterfly bushes planted along the empty road.

"Wait up!" I shouted.

She finally stopped at an intersection, and Kit and I pulled up beside her. I noticed that my calf was greasy and bleeding from getting scraped by the gears.

"With the wind in my hair," Kaya said, grinning ear to ear, "it feels almost like riding a horse."

"I didn't know you rode horses," I said.

"I've been breaking in stallions since I was a little girl," she said. "Just not in this lifetime."

KIT SLAPPED A COLORFUL FLIER down on the picnic table.

On Tuesday afternoon I was eating lunch in the court-yard with Thomas, Kaya, and Ellen, when Kit's incendiary arrival made Thomas jump and spill his seltzer.

"Whoa," Ellen said, mopping up the liquid with the sleeve of her flannel shirt. "Skittish much?"

"What's that?" Kaya said, picking up the flier.

"*That* is what we're all doing after school today," Kit said.

"A rodeo?" Ellen said. Kit straddled the bench beside her.

"A rodeo. Lucita and I always talked about going but never made it. We can all drive together. It's going to be awesome. And look, Jack Dynamite will be there. He's supposed to be the best bronco rider in the state—a direct descendant of Geronimo."

"Yeah, right," Ellen said. "That's what they all say."

Kaya glared at her.

"His horse, Lady Rattlesnake, is supposed to be the devil incarnate," Kit said.

"Count me out," Thomas said.

"You're coming," Kit said. "Remember how you dragged me to the kiva? This is your payback, *hombre*."

"What about you, Lo?" Kaya said.

I'd always wanted to see a rodeo. And it just seemed like the sort of thing I should be doing now that I had my health back—and then some. But I was hung up on the fact that Kit seemed to be re-creating his history with Lucita. They'd picnicked together at Zozobra in their finery. He'd wanted to teach her how to skateboard. And now the rodeo. . . . *Focus, Lo.*

"I think it sounds fun," I said. But Thomas still seemed reluctant. "Plus," I said, squeezing his arm, "you have to admit that it's a better idea than the matching tattoos Kit suggested we get this morning."

"Just little ones," Kit said. "On the butt or something."

"A rodeo's too risky," Thomas said.

"The world is risky, man," Kit said. "But you've got to jump in full force. Seize the day, soldier. Besides, how much trouble can we get ourselves into? It's just a bunch of ponies running around doing pony stuff."

"Let's do it," Kaya said. "After all, I'm descended from Geronimo too. Jack Dynamite and I are probably first cousins." She gave Ellen a challenging look, which she ignored.

"Fine," Ellen said. "But someone is buying my cotton candy. And we'd better get good seats, because my legs feel shaky and I don't think I can stand up for long, no matter how good the show is."

"No problem," Kit said. "I'll make sure we get the best seats in the house." He leaned into Ellen's shoulder. "And I will be personally responsible for your cotton candy."

We met in the parking lot after school. I'd volunteered my station wagon because it was the biggest of our fleet and I didn't mind driving. Kit also wanted to drive, but when we put it to a vote, I won by a landslide.

"I didn't even know you *had* a car," Ellen said.

"It's mostly been gathering dust," Kit said, "but last night I took it for a starlight spin, and damn, that baby can fly. You should let me drive your Beemer sometime."

"That'll be the day," she said.

Once we were outside town, I glanced in the rearview mirror and saw Thomas staring anxiously out the window.

"Please don't overthink it, Thomas. It's not like we're going swimming with sharks or something. Just try to have a good time, okay?"

"As long as we stay out of harm's way," Thomas said.

"We're not *riding* in the rodeo, silly," I said. "Just watching."

"If you say so."

Our words were drowned out when Kit reached forward from the backseat and cranked the Rolling Stones on the stereo. *Beggars Banquet* blared, and we sang along with Mick. Even Thomas joined in eventually, though he only knew the words to "Sympathy for the Devil."

———

We drove, music still blasting, but my attention now stolen by the miles of open road ahead of me. I always used to get a little nauseated when people rhapsodized about the New Mexico landscape. I'd never been one to appreciate its arid beauty. But now, as we drove across the desert, I couldn't fill my eyes enough. I zeroed in on the delicate greens and yellows, the subdued palette that hid so much life underneath. Winging down the faded highway toward our destination, I felt as if everything, as far as my eye could see, was mine. The surrounding desert and the mesas and the mountains all belonged to me, in a way. All I had to do was plant my flag. The future was my manifest destiny.

I turned down the volume on the stereo. "Look how much land there is," I gushed.

"I know," Kit said. "Hallelujah. Land for years. Enough for everybody."

"I bet Jay and Dakota are out there somewhere," I said. "Just walking along, doing shaman slash coyote stuff."

"Hell yeah they are," Kit said. "You know what I think about a lot?"

"Girls?" Ellen said. "Skateboarding? Doritos taco shells from Taco Bell?"

"No, but related," he said, reaching over to tug Ellen's triple-pierced earlobe. "I think about the difficulty of negotiating these deserts on foot. But for centuries—before Lewis and Clark and all the white explorers our greedy government paid to come out here and stake its claim—that's what the Indians did. They didn't have horses in the New World until the Spanish introduced them in the early 1700s. And then there was no turning back. Can you imagine *walking* across this land, carrying everything you own?"

Last week I couldn't, but this week I could. I could walk to California. I could hike across the Sierra Nevada in the dead of winter. What was frostbite? What was muscle ache? What was sunburn? I touched the deer totem I'd tied around my neck, wishing it was still a stallion, then stepped on the gas pedal to pass another car on the two-lane highway.

"Please slow down," Thomas said from the backseat.

"No, don't," Kaya said. "I like the speed."

"Hey," Kit said. "Here's a fun fact. Before the U.S. declared war on the Navajo, back when our backstabbing government was still pretending to honor the treaties it made, the American army used to socialize with the Diné tribes surrounding Fort Fauntleroy. The Navajo would actually come to the fort to eat food and trade stuff with the soldiers. They'd drink and gamble together. This is 1861, right. Start of the Civil War. So they're all hanging out, Americans and Navajo, getting along like wildfire, and to amuse themselves, they start placing bets on whose horses can run the fastest. They set up this big race with an army guy's undefeated horse on the American side, and a prized pony, rumored to belong to the great warrior Manuelito, on the Navajo side."

"Oh yeah, I've heard of Manuelito," I said. "Total badass."

"Right. Major stud. You'd like him, Ellen. He was like Mike, but the exact opposite."

Ellen rolled her eyes, but I could tell she was somewhat embarrassed now by her association with Meth-Head Mike.

"So anyway," Kit said, "as soon as he left the starting line, the Navajo rider went awry, like totally out of bounds, and lost the race. The Indians demanded a rematch. They said the Navajo bridle had been tampered with. Of course the Americans denied it. Everyone started arguing, playing the blame game. Then a gun detonated from the fort. A soldier had shot at an Indian. And this seemed to give license to the rest of the soldiers to shoot at Indians. Anarchy broke out immediately. The unarmed Navajo scattered, but not fast enough. It was a total slaughter. Women and children trying to escape were gunned down one by one by the Americans. I don't think their horses competed much after that."

The conclusion to this story was met with several moments of silence, due (at least on my part) to the unnerving fact that the upbeat tone of Kit's voice didn't at all reflect the facts he'd related. And he used to dissolve into pure emotion whenever he gave an oral report like this in history class. He began drumming his hands on his lap.

"That's a grim story," Ellen said.

"You're a grim story," Kit said. Ellen gave him the finger. "Anyway, it's par for the course. Welcome to *real* Native American history."

I noticed Thomas fidgeting in the backseat.

"What's the matter?" I said.

"Nothing," he said. "I can just see it, is all. I've seen similar things back home."

———

In the dirt parking lot outside New Mexico's oldest rodeo grounds, fans tailgated with coolers of beer. Mini grills sizzled near the beds of pickup trucks, cooking hot dogs and corn on the cob wrapped in aluminum foil. One carload of buxom women wore T-shirts that read BUCKLE BUNNIES.

"Rodeo groupies," Kit said. He punched me lightly on the arm. "That will be you someday."

"Try rodeo *rider*," I said. My fearless future stretched out before me like the land we'd just crossed to get here.

Cowboys and Indians in stark white shirts and stiff new blue jeans swarmed the rodeo grounds. For a second I even thought I saw Dr. Osborn, then squealed and quickly hid my face behind Thomas. Under the rusted rodeo structure, Anglo tourists took pictures of brown-skinned children as if they were scenery. Everyone's shoes and boots kicked up dust, so our bare skin was instantly filmed in a fine, glittering silt. Kit bought cotton candy for Ellen and for two beautiful little Mexican girls standing nearby in party dresses the same color as the candy floss. "*Gracias*," they said. Their parents didn't look happy about the gift at first, but Kit quickly charmed them. "*Pero son tan bonita*," he said, "*que se merecen toda la felicidad.*"

"What did you say to them?" I asked him.

"That their daughters were angels. That they reminded me of someone." Lucita seemed to be a living presence around him.

On our way to the bleachers, we stopped outside a corral and watched the cowboys prepare their animals for sporting events: oiling saddles, tightening girths, and brushing their horses to a high polish.

"Kaya," I said, "do you remember when we used to play with plastic horses as kids? Before we got into all that esoteric stuff? I forgot how much I loved them. They're so . . . regal."

"Power personified," she said, staring.

People were beginning to take their seats. While Kit and I wanted to get as close to the action as possible, Thomas shied away, but I grabbed him by the shirtsleeve and dragged him along.

"Come on," I said. "You're going to love this."

Meanwhile, Ellen sulked in our wake. Her facial expression—sick and miserable, as if she wanted to throw up not just the contents of her stomach but of her entire life—made me vaguely remember what real pain felt like.

I tried to feel what she might be feeling—she was carrying my burden, after all. But I could only get so far. It was like trying to recall a psychedelic drug experience or something. How could I remember pain when I no longer felt it? When all I wanted was to never feel it again? But the slump of Ellen's body hinted at something I'd lost, a nightmare I'd awoken from. I felt guilty for turning away from her, but I just really wanted to enjoy myself while I could.

Kit found us seats together in the rickety metal bleachers, right next to the main arena. But even after we sat down, Thomas remained nervous, rolling and unrolling his program in the seat.

"Don't worry," I teased him. "The bulls can't jump the fence."

"No, but you can," he said.

"Oh, please," I said. "I'm quite happy right here." I linked elbows with Kaya. "Aren't you?" I said to her. "Or should we see if there's an amateur event we can compete in tonight?" She was quiet. I felt like I was annoying everybody but Kit, and that was only because right now it was impossible to get on his hyperactive cheerleader nerves. He squeezed in between me and Kaya, spilling popcorn on us in the process.

Soon the fanatical announcer drowned out everything else. "Welcome, cowhands and sheep wranglers!" the voice boomed through the gargantuan speakers that might have been antiques. "Welcome to the greatest show west of the Rio Grande, where you'll see barrel racing, saddle bronco riding, steer wrestling, and more . . . !"

Bucking broncos exploded across the arena, and cowboy after cowboy waved his hat at the cheering crowd. The cowboy introduced as Jack Dynamite was riding a particularly feisty filly, Lady Rattlesnake, whom the announcer indeed dubbed the "devil incarnate." (To me she just looked . . . in control.) A camera zoomed in on Mr. Dynamite and broadcast his rugged features onto the staticky big screen.

"Ooooh," Ellen said, pointing at the vintage Jumbotron. "Kit, you didn't tell me that your Geronimo wannabe was so good-looking." Kit shrugged nonchalantly.

"Whatever," he said. "Too bad he can't control his horse."

"I'd like to see *you* try," Ellen said.

Then out came the mutton busters. These hilarious little kids lay facedown on furry sheep that dashed to and fro as if they'd had one too many cups of *cafe con leche*. Together the children and sheep pairs ran around the ring in circles, the frenzied sheep doing a poor job of trying to shake their small but tenacious passengers. The sheep's wooly, natural saddles actually looked pretty comfortable—no wonder the young shepherds hung on so tightly.

"That kid's my favorite," I said, pointing out a little boy whose glasses were steamed up with anxiety.

"He's a champion," Kit said, and then the kid promptly fell off his sheep.

"Not his fault! You totally jinxed him, Kit." We began concocting scenarios for why little kids might need to wrangle sheep. They couldn't sleep and needed something to count. They had to get to the bouncy castle on time. They needed a place to put all their barrettes.

Yet as much as Kit sparked and flared and cracked me up, he was mostly just distracting me from how much I wanted to talk to Thomas. I wanted to see the boy who'd opened up to me in the balloon, but today's cagey version of Thomas looked right past me. It seemed I wasn't on his emotional radar anymore. I wanted to ask him to bite my lip and pinch my flesh in order to draw out the pain I couldn't feel, but instead I simply listened to Kit rant jubilantly. I was captive to Kit's ardor, and to Thomas's listless beauty.

He is still fighting his enemies.
From that bed.
Full stomach.
Unarmed.
Oceans away. . . .

Finally it was time for the main event. I leaned over to nudge Ellen in excitement, hoping that she was no longer miffed with me, but she and Kaya were gone.

"They went to the bathroom," Thomas said somewhat punitively. "Ellen didn't feel well."

How did I miss that? Should I follow them to the bathroom? They hadn't invited me. Probably on purpose.

With a big collective cheer from the audience, the real show started, and the excitement washed over me again like a drug.

From the moment the first bull shot out of the gate, I was enthralled. The creature was massive. Like an angry elephant, with herculean power. His hindquarters looked as if they were attached to a taut spring, and he flung his rear legs around with such force, I thought they might detach from his body. I could practically feel each rider's whiplash as he hung on for dear life—the cowboys could only manage to stay on their bulls for four, five, six seconds, short spurts of time that probably ticked away like hours while they clung to that unbridled mass of energy. Seeing it in person, I couldn't believe this sport even existed. It was like watching men wrestle with gods or their own fates.

Inevitably the rider hit the dust, and then it was *get out of Dodge fast or be killed*. The bull never settled immediately, but kept kicking and bucking, kept drilling the ring and looking for vengeance. Twice I saw all the weight of a bull's rear legs descend toward the prone body of his cowboy adversary. Just when I thought the riders were about to be crushed, the rodeo clowns did their thing, distracting the bulls from the vulnerable bodies in the dirt. Those horns were deadly, and the bulls badly wanted to impale someone with them.

"Wow," I said. "Go hard or go home."

"Yeah, no kidding," Kit said.

Thomas sat stone-faced and despondent between us. "Lighten up, Thomas," I said. "These guys know what they're doing. Here, have some popcorn." I tried to put a piece of popcorn in his mouth, but he refused.

"I want to go," he said.

"Soon," I said. "It's almost over." Now I *actually* felt terrible about dragging Thomas to the rodeo, and worse still for enjoying it so much. I wondered if he would've had fun if we'd come here together a week ago, just us, like on a date. And P.S., why hadn't Kaya and Ellen come back yet?

The last bull-and-rider pair was announced. The bull was named Beetlejuice, and his rider was a novice cowboy, a guy not much older than us. According to the hypermanic MC, it was the rider's first major rodeo. He put on a brave, determined face, which we saw in the fuzzy monitor before he and the bull were released from their gate.

Almost immediately, Beetlejuice hurled the cowboy from his back, and his arm got caught in the rope harness. He dangled off the flank of the outraged beast, the bull's legs bucking too powerfully and erratically for the clowns to approach. Finally the rider untangled his forearm and hit the ground, but I could see that he was injured. Barely able to move, let alone scramble to safety, he watched the bull in horror. The animal lowered his head for a decisive charge, as if he were out for revenge. We stood up in the bleachers and held our breath; my muscles flexed as if they wanted to do something other than just watch, helpless.

Suddenly a new rodeo clown leapt over the fence and into the ring. The clown was white, and he was dressed like a child's idea of an Indian chief. He waved a fake tomahawk in the air in an effort to draw the bull's attention from the fallen cowboy. While his gaudy feathered headdress only did just enough to catch the animal's eye, it totally absorbed Kaya, who was finally making her way back to our seats with Ellen.

"Do you see that?" Kaya said to no one in particular, her voice laden with fury.

"Unbelievable," Kit said.

"A real Native American would respect the bull," Kaya said. "Don't these idiots know that we're all connected? This is barbaric. You all can stay, but I'm leaving." She stormed off the bleachers and made her way toward the exits.

"Wait," Thomas said. "I'm coming with you." Kit, Ellen, and I exchanged glances and then gathered our things to go. I stole one last look at the ring, just to make sure the young cowboy had made it out safely (he had, thanks to the offensive "Indian"), then hustled after the group.

But before I saw my friends ahead of me, I heard screaming. I stopped short. Parents began snatching their children from the main, dusty rodeo concourse, and many others ducked beneath the scaffolding of the bleachers. It took me only seconds to realize what the commotion was all about. A horse was loose in the rodeo grounds. It was Lady Rattlesnake, that gorgeous animal. The chorus of "Sympathy for the Devil" flashed unbidden through my mind.

The horse bucked and cantered dangerously close to spectators, who ran for cover behind refreshment stands. Several cowboys tried to get near enough to throw a lasso around her neck, but they weren't having any luck. Then Rattlesnake leveled her muzzle toward a little boy who stood, frozen, near the exit to the restrooms. The horse snorted and pawed the ground purposefully, then charged directly at the boy.

Without thinking, I ran into the horse's path. A rodeo clown would've tried to distract the enraged horse from the periphery, but I stepped directly between Rattlesnake and the boy she seemed dead set on trampling. I was powerful too. The horse tried to veer around me, but I moved with her, and instead of stomping me to death, she dug in her hooves and braked. A cowboy ran up to us with a rope and threw it over Rattlesnake's head, shoving me out of the way. I landed flat on my butt in the dirt, and only then did I realize I had a giant smile on my face.

"Consuelo!" Thomas shouted from somewhere. But I didn't look toward his voice. I was mesmerized by Jack Dynamite, the cowboy who'd restrained Rattlesnake. He handed off the horse to rodeo authorities and then helped me to my feet.

"You could've been killed," Jack said.

Then Thomas's arms were around me. "Consuelo. I thought you were a goner. You can't pull stunts like that. You can't...."

"What happened?" Ellen said. She and the others had joined Thomas and were all standing around me now.

"Nothing," I said. My adrenaline was pumping, and I felt that if we stayed any longer I might do something crazy. Well, crazier. "Let's go."

Kit tried to put his hands on the snorting horse being led away, as if he wanted to be a part of whatever it was I'd started.

"Don't touch him, kid," Jack Dynamite said.

"Jeez," Kit said as we walked toward the parking lot. "What an asshole."

"Grow up," Ellen said. She made her way for the exits, and Kit tripped after her.

Kaya was quiet, but as we walked I thought I saw her scanning my body for bleeding and signs of bones out of place. Thomas gripped my hand tightly.

"I'm fine, you guys," I said. "Seriously. That was fun. Let's do it again next week. After we get our matching tattoos."

18

I DROPPED OFF KAYA FIRST, then Ellen. I'd planned to take Kit to Thomas's house, but he told me that he'd moved back in with his parents, so I took him home after dropping off Ellen at her mansion, where all the windows were dark, as usual. Of course it made the most sense for me to drop off Thomas before Kit, then head back to my neighborhood, but thankfully everyone seemed too preoccupied to note my byzantine driving decisions.

Finally, Thomas and I were alone in the car.

"You feel like coming over for a little bit?" he said halfway between Kit's house and his.

"Sure," I said, trying to sound calm even though my heart was racing like one of those rodeo sheep. "I, um, heard you have a trampoline." He smiled.

"Word gets around."

Ten minutes later he was jumping in circles around his younger siblings. As much as I wanted to show off my front flips, I'd been duly chastened by the look Thomas had given me when I'd tried to mount, so I stood on the tramp's metal circumference, just watching.

"I don't think so, Lo," he'd said, tugging on the back pocket of my jeans. I hadn't argued. He was probably right to be protective. Also, I sort of owed him some downtime after the rodeo.

It was fun to watch him with his kid brothers and sisters. Though he'd told me in the balloon that they should be scared of him, I didn't see any evidence of that. He was so good with them. Dreamy and thoughtful, but he could also put his own perpetual state of apprehension aside to do silly things to make the children happy.

"Bounce us!" they shouted. And he did, inexhaustibly, but never too high.

I was surprised that happiness came so easily to Thomas's siblings, to be honest. The Dents had universally adopted or fostered children with complicated backgrounds. One girl had cerebral palsy. One boy was full-blooded Native American whose mother had committed suicide on the rez. One was born into a brothel in South Korea, and another had been adopted from one of those anemic Russian orphanages.

I often speculated about what it must be like to have so much painful experience in one household. And yet when I saw all those Dent kids climbing into a minivan in the Costco parking lot, or going out for ice cream in the Plaza, or crammed into a single pew at St. Francis, they all looked pretty content. Especially now, as I watched their joyful heads spring up and down, shouting for their big brother to bounce them.

Thomas jumped off the trampoline, panting.

"Those kids wear me out." He grinned. "Every time." His dimples were showing again. His smiles were so rare, and I wanted to melt into this one. He stared at me for a moment as if he wanted to say something, then he abruptly dropped and rolled underneath the trampoline. His younger siblings continued to bounce above his head. When the biggest child—a boy named Matthew—jumped, he came within a foot or two of Thomas's face. I knelt down onto the grass and then crawled on my elbows like an infantryman into Thomas's shifting chamber.

"So what are we doing here exactly?" I asked over the sounds of rusty springs and children squealing.

"Sometimes I just like to lie here while they jump." I flipped onto my back so I could see what he was seeing. We watched the children depress dark pools over our heads. "Careful," he said. "Stay low."

"It's kind of cool down here," I said.

"Yeah," he said. "I think I like it because . . . I don't know. I guess I don't feel threatened here. In a way, from here I can see death approaching. I can't be surprised. And I can do nothing to stop the inevitable. If I sat up, I could break my neck. . . ."

"Don't sit up," I said. "Please. Stay in the trenches."

A particularly chubby sibling bounced over Thomas's face.

"Fire in the hole," he said, and I laughed.

Mrs. Dent opened the back door. "Bedtime for anyone not in high school!" she shouted. "Thomas, you've got thirty more minutes."

"Good night, guys," I said to the kids as they all crawled under the trampoline to give Thomas kisses on the cheek or wrestle him with hugs.

And then we were alone. I realized that even though Thomas and I had spent the entire afternoon together, we hadn't really interacted at all. I'd been too busy laughing with Kit and dodging angry broncos. He'd been too edgy from the rodeo events. Now it was getting dark, and Thomas felt infinitely far away.

"Let's get back on the tramp," he said. He sounded slightly awkward all of a sudden, which was unusual for him. "So we can see the stars."

"Are you sure I'm allowed up?" I said.

"Well, it depends. Only if you follow the rules."

"Which are?"

"One, no jumping."

"Gotcha. And two?"

Thomas looked at me with exaggerated seriousness. "No hopping."

"Okay. What about tramping? Can I do that?"

"Absolutely not. What do you think this is? A plaything?"

"Fine. I'll abide by those rules."

He helped me onto the black nylon fabric, making sure I didn't snag any body parts on the metal springs.

Once we were on our backs, Thomas scratched his fingertips across the surface of the trampoline without looking at me or saying anything.

"Is something the matter?" I said.

"I'm sorry to be so moody all the time," he said. "I'm not

like Kit right now. Or . . . you. It's hard for me to feel . . . solid, you know? Things have been all up and down since Sunday morning. I've been remembering more from my past. All these intense memories I thought I'd left behind. I've been thinking they shouldn't just be exclusive to my poetry. Maybe I should talk about them too. But . . . not to Ms. Vega. To you." He rolled over onto his side, facing away from me. "But you probably don't want to know."

"I do," I said, pulling him back and looking him in the eye. "You have no idea how much."

"I'm like a broken record. I'm sorry to keep burdening you with this stuff. It's just that . . . you're easy to talk to. In that way you remind me of my little brother, Henri. In Liberia. Or at least, being with you makes me think of him. And these past few days, I can recall details from my past without being floored by them. I recognize them as memories without having to relive them, like I'm actually there. And for the first time, I guess I want to . . . share the things that happened. With someone I trust. With a friend." Thomas squeezed his eyes shut for a moment, as if he was worried I would reject him.

"That's great," I said. "Huge. I'm proud of you, Thomas. And I would be honored to hear your stories." His stiff posture began to relax.

"Kit told me something interesting the other day," he said. "Did you know that before the Apache went to war, they did rituals to protect themselves from bullets? Back in Africa, when the militia recruited me and other kids for battle, the chief told us to drink this sour-tasting concoction that would make us omnipotent. 'Drink the potion and you won't feel pain,' he said. 'Drink the potion and you'll never die.' We were just boys. We didn't appreciate danger. We'd lost our families. We believed him entirely." For some reason this made me think of Ellen.

"Omnipotent," I said eventually, running my finger over the trampoline mesh, wishing it were Thomas's skin. "You know, that's kind of how I feel now. Since the ritual. Like I drank some superhero potion. Except it's actually sort of true in my case. If there were a war, I'd be on the front lines because no bullet could hurt me."

"Maybe," Thomas said. "But you would still die."

"Aren't you at least grateful that you survived the war?" I said, then immediately felt that it was the wrong thing to say. "Maybe not the potion, but *something* protected you out there. From death, I mean."

Thomas fingered the scar on his neck. "Sometimes I wish I'd been murdered with my parents that day in Liberia. At least their terror was short-lived. I hope they saw me and my little brother running away from the fire. I hope they died believing that we'd escaped the carnage, even though it's not true."

"You did escape," I said. "You're lying on a trampoline under the stars in Santa Fe. You're here with me."

Thomas threaded his fingers through my hair and tugged my head closer to his. His eyes were bright and fervent, even in the dark. "I can't protect my friends," he said. "And it feels terrible. Last night I lay awake, paralyzed by fear. I heard noises everywhere. I envisioned prowlers, banditos.

Rustling or wind, footsteps or dogs barking, they all meant the same thing. Imminent death. I convinced myself that soldiers were coming on a raid. It all felt so real. I imagined people attacking me, the Dents, Kit . . . you. And the worst part is all the attackers were versions of myself."

I draped an arm across his chest and nestled my chin on his strong shoulder. We lay like that for a long time.

"You're still not afraid of me?" he said finally. Maybe he was still a killer, but now I was starting to understand how someone could career headlong into battle. The adrenaline washed over you, and before you knew what was happening you were in the center of it all.

"No," I said. "Especially when you give me access, when you tell me things. But I guess . . . maybe I don't understand one thing."

"What's that?"

"How a person could just . . . stop feeling altogether."

"I've thought about that a lot too. I think that certain emotions can compromise you when you're at war. If you stop to mourn the dead, or even to breathe in what you've done, you'll be dead as well. Your brain goes to a primitive region, one inaccessible to feelings beyond pure anger and pure fear. Your brain is reduced to two impulses: fight or flight. Kill or be killed. No room for more delicate feelings. No room for a soul. All you're thinking about is how to maneuver your body in space so it will survive."

"That's sort of how I felt when I was sick," I said. "In the worst moments. When I just wanted to avoid pain. It was hard to care about anything else. At least care like I used to."

Thomas nodded. "One of the strangest outcomes of this whole crazy Jay situation is that I suddenly feel this flood of emotion," he said. "All those things I wasn't able to feel before . . . like love, for instance. . . . They're back now. I feel almost like I did when I was really young, before the war, but now with all these horrible experiences between me and the good heart I once had."

"It's *still* good," I said.

"I don't know. It's so weird to be worried for people again. It's scary and overwhelming to feel this . . . affection for my friends. I thought I'd lost that forever."

"I know. I love our weird little family." And like Thomas, I felt responsible for all its members.

We went quiet for a while, thinking and looking at the stars. I marveled at the worldwide wheel of fortune that had brought Thomas to my town and me to this trampoline. If there hadn't been a second civil war in Liberia, if Thomas had never picked up a gun—or whatever crimes he'd perpetrated in Africa—if I'd never gotten sick, the two of us would never be lying beside each other right now.

Circle home, Lo.

"Thomas," I said, "can I ask you something?"

"Shoot." Hearing him copy my speech patterns made me grin involuntarily in the dark.

"Well, I . . ." *I want to kiss you? I think I'm falling in love with you?* Suddenly I felt almost frightened by the intensity of the moment, and I wanted to neutralize it. "Not to change the subject," I said, "but I . . . um . . . don't think it's such a good idea for Ellen to go to Weekends on

Wednesdays tomorrow. Or for any of us to go, for that matter. MS symptoms can spring up out of nowhere, but so can flashbacks, borderline psychotic episodes, relapses, et cetera. All of our current excess baggage. What do you think?"

"Actually," he said, "I think we *should* go to the party, all of us together. As long as we're there watching over one another like we promised, it'll be fine. Together we're safe. Like right now."

"Wow," I said. "I was positive you were going to say we should all stay home and, like, take bubble baths instead. Are you sure?"

"Am I that much of a killjoy?"

"Not at all! Someone's gotta look out for the rest of us crazies. And you're right. I think. Let's just go to the party."

"Kit will be happy, anyway."

"Is he ever *not* happy these days?"

"Kit." Thomas sighed. "The Kit I know puts up a punk rock exterior, but that boy is emo to the core. His heart is like flypaper. Do you have that here? For the bugs? Anyway, it's like any girl can come along and stick to Kit. He trusts, loves, and so is left open and vulnerable to getting his heart broken again and again."

"I resent being compared to a fly," I said, smiling.

"Butterfly," Thomas said. "Anyway, I get why you two got together. Not that I want you to get together again. But I understand. You and Kit are sort of similar. The way you're both so . . . open. To feeling. To experience. Even if it hurts you in the end."

"He's your best friend here, huh?" I said, not wanting to think about experiences that could hurt me in the end. Thomas nodded.

"I have to confess something," he said. "Today, watching you two at the rodeo, I felt a little jealous."

"Jealous? Why?"

"You two have a connection. You have history. If you want to be with him. . . . I mean, I just want you to be happy."

"Kit's my friend, Thomas. I'm glad that he's in a good place right now. But my heart is . . . elsewhere."

"Do you know what drew me to Kit in the first place?" Thomas said after a pause.

"What?" I asked.

"He's interested in justice. That's one of the reasons I was able to reconcile my participation in the war as a kid. I wanted to avenge the deaths of my parents. I thought I could. But soon the idea of justice was wiped out. There was no such thing as true justice when everyone was just trying to retaliate and destroy each other. But Kit still believes in it. Like how he wants to make things right with the Indians. And now, sometimes, it's a comfort to be near him, just to hear his faith that wrongs can be corrected. Because a long time ago, when I thought I'd lost my soul, I stopped believing that they could."

"Wrongs *can* be corrected," I said. "People can start all over again on any given breath."

Thomas pulled his hoodie over his head and blinked. His eyelashes were long. He smelled of lilac and metal.

"In Liberia they already locked up everyone they're going to lock up," he said. "I wish they'd locked up people like me. At least then I would know for certain whether I was good or bad."

"You're good," I said. "I know that you're good." I wanted to touch him, to run my finger down the scar on his neck, to try to feel his pain by proxy. "You were a victim, Thomas. You did what you had to do to survive." Just as I had done what I had to do, by enlisting four others in my dubious experiment.

"I know," he said. "Intellectually I know that. But since the ritual, now that I can see my actions at one remove, I hate myself for them. I don't experience the trauma firsthand, like I used to, but the memories are still vivid. I see myself with knives, guns, playing with people's *lives*, Consuelo. And now that I can experience emotion again, I can imagine what my victims felt. It's like now I'm able to empathize with their fear as they faced me, a killer. It's . . . agony."

"You need to forgive yourself," I said. "Maybe your burden isn't the trauma so much as the weight of your conscience."

"No offense to Jay and his coyote, but I don't think this world contains enough magic to ease my conscience. To make me . . . better."

"Then maybe it's not magic that you need," I said. "Maybe you just need time."

Thomas softly touched my cheek. "Maybe," he said, ignoring the stars and looking into my eyes. "Maybe I can still feel a little magic."

Then, I couldn't help it. I kissed him.

I was done holding back, done restraining myself, done being nervous and shy. My body was invincible, ecstatic, and it knew exactly what it wanted. It wanted to feel warm against Thomas's skin.

"How did you know?" he whispered after a moment, pulling back and cupping my cheek.

"Know what?" I said.

"That this was my wish."

Then our lips were melted insolubly together, like glaciers turned to liquid, swirling through the oceans that had once separated us, and the spirit of his body was fused into mine, and we were connected, gathered in the same currents of wind and water, lightly bouncing on a trampoline under the vast universe of sky that bound us all. I tasted blood, but I didn't know if it was mine or Thomas's. Who had bit whom? It didn't matter. Our souls, for a few blessed moments, were one.

———

In bed that night I touched my body. I wondered if I could still feel true pleasure. Or true happiness. Because without knowing the opposite sensation, I was no longer sure. The positive and negative felt like two sides of a coin, and lacking one or the other, I was broke, penniless, with nothing left to wish on.

I rose from my bed and opened my window wide. I wanted to feel the wind between my fingers, to turn my hand into a weather vane. I wanted to feel a song coursing through my veins. But I only felt numbness. I returned to my bed so I could dream about Thomas, so together we could inhabit a world where it was safe to feel everything.

19

THE WEEKENDS ON WEDNESDAYS PARTY was at Jason Sibley's palatial desert mansion for the second week in a row. Jason hosted a lot of these parties because he essentially lived alone with the housekeeper ever since his dad had started his post-divorce dating life. The Sibley estate included a pool and a casita behind the main house, with boulders placed artfully all over the backyard. Mr. Sibley, a prestigious art dealer who always said I was the spitting image of the painter George Romney's *Lady Hamilton as Circe*—a painting I kept meaning to look up—had probably ordered them special from a catalogue.

The five of us drove there together that night. As soon as I came to a stop in the Sibley driveway, Kit tore off alone, heading straight for the scene in the backyard. Thomas and I entered the house first, with Kaya and Ellen lagging behind. We warily scanned the crowd, which was already drunk and rambunctious at nine P.M., due to excessively celebrating that evening's SFHS basketball victory over Santa Fe Prep. The boys who stumbled drunk across the room were doing a far better imitation of my former symptoms than I could approximate.

"Lo!" Juanita screamed as she barreled tipsily out of the kitchen with Alex hot on her heels. "You made it! *Gracias a Dios.*"

"Hey, *hermanas,*" I said.

To my right, Ellen and Kaya had been staring at an abstract painting on the wall, but they turned now to face the two chatty Aguas.

"Hi, Ellen," Alex said cautiously, as if she were saying hello to a loose jungle cat. She tugged me by the elbow toward the couch. I shot Thomas a helpless, apologetic look over my shoulder as I was led away.

"Are you sure she's okay?" Alex said in a loud, conspiratorial whisper.

"Ellen?" I said. For a second I thought she might be referring to Kaya, who'd never been to one of these parties before, as far as I knew.

"No, Mrs. Butterworth. Of course Ellen!" Juanita said. Just then our school mascot charged by in his buffalo costume with the ginormous head removed, shouting something about vodka shots. "I know you said it was okay, but . . . see? Temptation everywhere."

"I know you're worried," I said, thinking I could use a shot myself, "but Ellen is fine. Does she seem high to you?"

"Actually," Alex said, glancing around the room, "I don't see her anywhere." *Crud.* No Thomas either. Or Kaya. I hadn't even been at the party five minutes and I had already misplaced my sacred charges.

"Be right back," I said to the girls. "And see if you can flag down that drunken buffalo for me." I walked through the main room, out the broad patio doors, and into the back-yard. No matter how rich people are in Santa Fe, their yards still look freshly bulldozed. People here don't landscape with oak trees and carp ponds; they landscape with rocks and cacti.

Jason had set up a bar next to the pool and was personally manning the blender. And there was Ellen, standing pa-tiently behind a couple of sophomore girls who were waiting for drinks. When Jason saw Ellen he told the sophomores to hold on a minute. "VIP," he said. "Step aside." Ellen ap-proached the table edge.

"You're just the lady I've been waiting for," said my ex, whose lips had felt rubbery when we'd kissed and who didn't know how to make conversation beyond the subjects of movies, sports, and the best Mexican food in town. Not that those aren't important subjects.

"I've got something special for you," he said to Ellen. "Your favorite. In case you want to do your karaoke version of 'Livin' on a Prayer' again later." He poured a generous dose of tequila into a red plastic cup. I started to intervene, but before I could stop Jason from fulfilling his host duties, Ellen spoke up.

"No thanks. Do you have any ginger ale?"

Jason looked disappointed that his trusty wild child was turning down party favors. But he poured her some soda anyway and then summoned back the younger girls, who eagerly accepted tequila shots and sliced limes—though I didn't know how they could drink anything through their constant giggling.

I put my arm around Ellen, who now stood looking rather forlorn at the edge of the pool.

"You had me worried for a second, when I saw you at the bar."

"Wow," she said. "That felt weird. I wasn't sure that I could do it."

"Is that why you wanted to come tonight?" I said. "To test yourself?"

"Maybe. I still can't believe I turned down *tequila*. If there was any doubt left at all, it's gone now. I'm definitely sick."

"Or getting better?" I countered.

We walked around the pool to find the others. Kit wasn't drinking either; he was too busy practicing handstands in the irrigated part of the grass with Lacy Campbell, a petite junior, and a couple of her friends. When I walked up, Lacy was happily holding Kit's ankles as he balanced upside down.

"Hey, Lo!" he said, his face slowly turning pink as the blood rushed to his head. "What's up, Ellen?" Ellen shot Lacy a dirty look and then sauntered back toward the house.

"Don't be jelly!" Kit called at her back. She flipped him the bird.

"Hey, Kit," I said. "Good form. Have you seen the others?"

"Let's see," he said, dropping to earth when Lacy let go of his legs. "Thomas was lurking around here somewhere. That's probably who you're looking for, huh?" He gave me a significant wink.

"Sure," I said, almost definitely blushing. "But Kaya too."

"Yeah, right," Kit said. "I'm onto you, Lo. You have a one-track mind these days. Kamara round-the-clock. But if you must keep up appearances, I think Kaya's around here somewhere too."

I pulled Kit aside so his spotter wouldn't overhear. "How's she doing?"

"Oh, you know. Parties are stressful. You don't know whether to do Jell-O shots or eat pot brownies."

"I'm serious, Kit."

"I know you are. I'm just . . . I'm not sure how Kaya's doing. She seemed a little anxious when she came by a minute ago. I guess we should probably try to smoke her out. Find her, I mean. Not, you know, haha."

"Let me know if you see her before I do."

"Will do," he said. "I'm on the case. Just let me do a couple more handstands first. These girls need a show."

A show. I wondered how much of Kit's happy-go-lucky attitude was an act and how much of it was real. I watched him do a handspring in the grass. Athletes materialized out of nowhere to high-five him. Luis arrived holding Jason's adorable Chihuahua, Knick-Knack—the two starting *K*'s were pronounced, of course—and Kit was suddenly on the ground, rubbing the dog's belly and getting bathed in licks. It seemed like half the party was gathered around Kit, egging him on. This was the first time that most of them had interacted after-hours with my usually sullen neighbor, and they were clearly surprised and pleased by how cool he turned out to be. But I guess I'd always known.

Then I saw Thomas and momentarily forgot all about Kit. More precisely, before I saw his face, I saw the long scar on his neck. He was wearing a button-down tonight. No hoodie.

He sat alone on a bench at the edge of the pool patio, drinking a bottle of expensive iced tea, watching the Agua crowd as they set up an unsanctioned fireworks display in the Sibleys' barren backyard.

"Hi," I said, walking up to him. I grinned despite myself. So did he, and I wondered if he was also remembering last night's kiss on the trampoline. Maybe he was also tingling a little bit at the memory.

"Are those meatheads following safety protocol?" I said, gesturing toward Luis, Brett, and the basketball players surrounded by shrieking freshman girls eager to worship them and their pyrotechnics. Alex and Juanita stood at a safe distance from the installation, barking orders, with hefty drinks in their hands.

"Just barely," Thomas said. "You know how kids are these days with their fireworks."

"I'll be sure not to let my dad get wind of it. He might unleash the full muscle of the Forest Service on Juanita."

"Your dad actually hired me as his proxy. I'm satellite fire marshal tonight. Officially."

"Oh, really?" I said. "I thought that was my job. Isn't it inherited through bloodlines?"

"It was, but I fired you because you were so slow getting here. Meanwhile I've already seen three or four safety violations."

"You're pretty strict," I said. "I'll be careful not to violate any of your rules."

"You can violate me all you want." Thomas laughed. "Right now, in that dress, you're what's known as 'above the law.'" He winked at me, and I felt my cheeks grow hot with pleasure. Finally he was noticing my outfit. I'd probably put more thought into it tonight than I had into my Zozobra prom attire. Short white sundress with barely there straps, and boots with little kitten heels. I smiled shyly. It felt good to flirt with Thomas as regular teenagers, and not as members of the Damaged Persons Club. Then I heard an electric guitar riff coming from the casita. A band was setting up on a small stage inside. I squinted my eyes toward the music. With mild shock it hit me that I recognized the guys on stage.

"Oh my gosh," I said. "I actually know this band. Hijos de Juan! I heard them play once downtown. With my aunt."

"The one who passed away?" Thomas said tenderly. "You know, you've never really told me about her."

"I will," I said. "Just not right now. You guys would have liked each other." Then I spaced out just as I used to space out from my symptoms. But this time I credited wholly different reasons for my distraction. *Circle home, Lo.*

———

It was two years ago in the spring when we'd had a freak snowstorm in Santa Fe. I'd just gotten home from school when Karine rushed into the house with snowflakes still sparkling in her hair. She was visiting from California.

"Darling!" she said. "Consuelo, my dear little blizzard of a niece, we are going dancing tonight."

After promising my parents at least a dozen times that she'd have me home by ten, Karine took me to a little underground bar off the Plaza. "Follow my lead," she whispered, quickly glancing at the band listings outside as we approached the stairwell. The snow was still falling, though it now refused to stick to anything but our eyelashes.

"No way," said the bouncer after looking me up and down. "How old is she?" Even though I wore a bit of makeup (applied in the car) and wore my most dignified accessories (gold hoop earrings and a beaded headband), and even though I was wrapping up my first day of high school, in retrospect I probably didn't look a day over twelve. That's the curse of having reddish blonde hair.

"Young," said Karine. "Clearly. But she's with me, Sam. And if she doesn't get in to see Hijos de Juan tonight, her life will be *over*. Like, end-of-the-world over. Apocalypse. You know how kids are. Everything is so dramatic. She's got the lead singer's poster on the wall and everything."

"That's right," I said, taking the cue. "I *love* this band. They're, like, the ultimate. They're so freaking awesome. Hijos de . . ."

"Juan," whispered Karine.

"Right," I said. "De Juan." I raised my voice to a high-pitched, teenage squeal and began jumping up and down like a deranged rabbit. "If I could just get one autograph tonight, I will die happy. Pretty please, sir?"

"Fine," said the bouncer, waving us downstairs. "But no drinking."

Although I didn't become a superfan that night, I did end up dancing to the band for their entire two-hour set. Hijos de Juan—whose name, Karine found out, derived from the fact that the three brothers in the band all shared a *padre* named Juan—played loud, raucous, western swing that was impossible to sit still to. Karine, true to her word, did not let me anywhere near the bar, or near any men, for that matter. Instead she never left my side on the dance floor. Laughing and spinning me around and teasing me about all the love letters I'd supposedly written to the youngest Hijo, the *"bebe de Juan,"* she had never been so perfect. She embodied the unexpected, like weather that strikes in its undesignated season, so you just open your eyes in wonder, reluctant to blink away the snowflakes.

———

In Jason's backyard, the band was starting to play for real.

"Hey," I said to Thomas, shaking myself out of the past. "You don't want to dance, do you?"

"I suppose I could," he said. "Though it's been a long time."

"Show me what you got."

Soon Thomas and I were barefoot in the casita, unembarrassed to spin each other around and display our goofiest moves as Hijos played. More people joined us on the dance floor, and two songs later we had the whole party out there. I guess being unburdened was contagious. Thomas dipped me, and I felt pure bliss. I stretched out my arms and felt life flood my limbs. Thomas wrapped both his arms around my waist and pulled me closer.

But our routine was suddenly cut short. "Everybody back!" I heard Jason shout from the gravel behind the pool. Thomas and I ran out the wide casita doors to see what was going on. The Agua crowd darted for cover as their fireworks exploded, sounding like repeated volleys of gunshot. The kids responsible squealed in delight and mock fear. For a moment their faces took on the glow of the fireworks' bright rainbow colors, then they were enveloped in smoke.

"Holy hell," I said as the pyrotechnics concluded. "Was that really necessary?" Then I turned around. "Thomas, are you okay?" His breathing was panicked, and he clutched his chest. I looked down at my body, half expecting to have been impaled by a rocket. But I was intact.

"Thomas," I said. "You're hyperventilating." I'd never seen his eyes so wide. He nodded as if registering my voice, but he didn't calm down. I gripped his hand, still sweaty from the dancing. "It's okay, it was only fireworks. If you don't calm down and breathe, you're going to faint."

I knew this because at sleepovers Kaya and I used to induce fainting fits by breathing as rapidly as possible until our brains, starved for oxygen, shut down briefly. Maybe not the most responsible game, but it was such a rush. And I always made sure Kaya landed on something soft, like on a bed or in my arms. God, Kaya. Where was she anyway? No, it's okay, this was just a party. She could take care of herself. *Focus, Lo.*

Thomas still looked like he was about to pass out. "Inhale to the count of four," I said. "You can do this, Thomas. Focus.

Ready?" He nodded. "One, two, three, four. Now hold it. Now exhale until the count of five. Good, now repeat."

I watched his abdomen expand and contract under his shirt. I led him toward some fold-out chairs on the grass outside the tent.

"Is everybody . . . ?" He struggled to get the words out.

"Everyone is okay," I said. "No one is hurt. We're all safe." He relaxed somewhat, and I rubbed his back. "You're doing great," I said. "Keep going. Keep breathing."

"*There* you guys are," Ellen said, followed closely by Kit and Kaya. "Thomas, are you all right?" He nodded.

"Will you guys keep an eye on him for a minute?" I said. "I have to go to the bathroom."

20

I WENT UPSTAIRS TO ONE of the Sibley guest bathrooms, where I was pretty sure no one would find me. I was supposed to be strong and brave for Thomas, and here I was falling apart.

I'd never told anyone this, but last summer I'd kept my bedroom door closed. I didn't know how to watch Karine waste away. I couldn't witness her physical anguish. Which took place away from her home in California, away from all the places and people she knew best. Away from the San Francisco streets where she performed her hoop routines, and away from the little makeshift shrines in her apartment where she kept all her special things. She seemed to be not only sick but in exile, and I couldn't stand the tragedy of it. Neither could my mother. She did a lot of praying in the hallway between our bedrooms. And then the hospice people came with their soft eyes and brochures full of stock photos of sunsets.

One gorgeous Saturday afternoon in mid-July, Karine called for me. I was listening to Bob Dylan's *Desire* album while pretending to take a nap, but I timidly crept into her room when I heard her voice ring out across the hall. She asked if I wouldn't mind brushing her hair. Mortality was impossible, but hair I could manage.

I raised my aunt's rented hospital bed so I had better leverage and used the ribbons to secure the auburn braids I twisted in my fingers.

"You used to do my hair when you were little," she said softly. "Do you remember?" Of course I did. When I was three or so and Karine had just graduated from Berkeley, she used to come visit us in Sebastopol on the weekends. I thought she was the most beautiful, most magnificent woman in the world, and it was a privilege to play with her hair. I'm sure I inadvertently yanked out many a clump of it with my combs meant for baby dolls, but she never complained.

Those were happier, greener times. When Karine's life was just starting out. When we could smell the Pacific from our back porch. When I barely knew what death was.

But then my aunt lay in a rented hospital bed in Santa Fe and couldn't grip a brush because her muscles were so shot. When I was done, I wanted to unravel the braids and start all over again, ad infinitum, so her hair would remain in my hands and her vivacious body across the hall. What did she feel about dying? What did she dream about? Did she pity herself? Did she regret anything? Did she wish she could go back and do things differently? I so wanted to ask her, but I was afraid of the answers. I could only squeeze her tight and dash away again before the tears started. And a week later she was dead. And then buried in the ground. And then I was sick. Sick with the full knowledge that MS runs in families. McDonough Scourge. McDonough Sacrifice.

I wasn't able to be close—really close—to Aunt Karine while she was dying. Dying was a distant planet back then. But now I understood what she'd been going through while I was sequestering myself in my room, essentially abandoning her. Now I could relate. And it killed me to think that I'd done nothing to help her or to ease her pain. Especially since I knew that I would do just about anything to ease my own.

———

There was a knock at the door. "Lo, are you in there?" I recognized Kaya's voice. How long had I been in the bathroom? I unlocked the door.

"I've been looking all over for you," Kaya said. She sat beside me on the bench next to the shower. "Have you been crying?"

I started to nod, but burst into fresh tears instead. "I stupidly got it into my head that because I couldn't feel physical pain, I was absolved from all pain. But outside, I was remembering my aunt, and then when Thomas couldn't breathe.... I was so scared, Kaya."

"Consuelo, just because you're not hurting in the same ways anymore doesn't mean you're cured."

"Why not?" I sniffled. "Isn't that how it should work?"

"Our lives are a lot deeper than we know. They don't stop at skin and bone. All those creepy games we used to play together? We were always looking for some greater reality.

Something mystical beyond ourselves. But now I think we could have put down the cards and the candles and everything and just listened to what our souls were trying to tell us. They're right there, underneath our burdens and our problems and our complaints, clamoring to get out and speak."

"What do you mean?"

"I'm not sure I understand it completely either. Yet. Do you remember that day on the playground when I knocked out my tooth? I didn't feel anything, of course, but you got a toothache in the same place where I would've had one. *That's* what we should have been examining instead of our horoscopes. The mysterious connections between us."

"I found your tooth in the sand when I was playing a few days later," I said. "I still have it. Oh god, I've never told anyone that before. You can have it back if you want."

"It's okay," Kaya said. "Keep it. Consider it a relic. You know, like with the saints with their old yellow teeth and bones and hair." We both laughed.

"I'll make a . . . whatchamacallit . . . a reliquary for it," I said.

Kaya grabbed my hands tight. "Consuelo, can I be honest with you for a second?"

"That's sort of been the order of the day."

"I'm so grateful that you allowed me to be part of this. Although Thomas's burden hasn't, like, displaced my one true self, I feel like it's woken me up in a lot of ways. Taking on Thomas's trauma has allowed me to access some deeper part of me, some part that goes beyond *me*, even, and is connected to my people. I know it sounds a little bananas, but a few times since the ritual I've gotten this feeling that I'm not even *in* my body anymore. I'm just living on an intensely spiritual level."

"Wow," I said, not sure how else to respond. "That sounds really . . . extreme. Are you sure you can handle it?"

"Oh, definitely," said Kaya. "I was talking to Ellen about it yesterday at the rodeo. How special this is. How lucky I am."

"But the flashbacks?"

Kaya's face darkened. "They're awful. Dreadful, actually. My mom had always shielded me from the truth about my ancestors, so I'm seeing a lot of these things for the first time."

"It's super heavy, Kaya, what you're dealing with. Maybe we should find someone else who knows about this stuff, someone you can talk to. . . ."

"No," she said harshly. "I'll be fine. This is my path."

"Okay," I said, feeling like I was going to start crying again.

"Look," Kaya said, softening, "I'm sorry that I had to get all high priestess on you, but what I was trying to say is that you need to remember that pain is a part of life. Just because you can't feel it in your bones twenty-four/seven doesn't mean it's not there. And it's not all bad, Lo. I can feel the pain of my people, but I can also feel the earth. I am grounded to my soul again. To everyone's. Connected."

"I wish I could feel all of that," I said. "Right now I just feel sad. And alone." If I was no longer sick in body, what was wrong with me? Maybe I was sick in spirit.

"You're not alone. You've got me, and Ellen, and Kit. And you've got Thomas—"

"Is he doing okay outside?" I interrupted. "He seemed stable when I left. . . ."

"He's fine. Just had a scare, is all. He'll recover. You have a universe of people who love you, Lo."

"Thanks, Kaya. And if you don't mind *me* getting all Pollyanna on *you*, it's been wonderful to be with you these past few days. To be together again, like old times."

"That makes two of us," she said. "Now let's get back to the party."

We returned to the backyard to find the others still huddled together. As soon as I saw Thomas, I ran over and flung my arms around him. He was breathing regularly now and even had a drink in his hand. I didn't realize quite how terrified I'd been for him until I was leaning against his chest, inhaling his smells and nuzzling against his scar. The band was still playing.

"Anybody feel like dancing?" Kit said.

"You must be joking," Ellen said. "I've got pins and needles everywhere."

"That's okay. We'll just slow dance. Come on." Kit pulled Ellen toward the casita.

"You too, Kaya," I said, feeling like myself again. "Let's go."

Minutes later we were all on the dance floor. Kit stayed true to his promise to slow dance, even though the band only played fast songs, but he still managed to dip Ellen somewhat extravagantly at least twenty times. She didn't complain. Thomas took turns twirling me and Kaya around the dance floor. I knew that if Karine had been there, he would have twirled her too. Alex and Juanita kept trying to pull me aside for details about Thomas, but I wanted to keep moving. Soon the whole Agua crowd was right there with us, singing along and shouting out requests. Considering our states of mind just the week before, it was hard to believe that the five of us could all be so free and happy, so uninhibited, and all dancing at once, but I guess when we joined together and finally opened up, we made more than a star: We made music.

21

ON THURSDAY MORNING I WOKE up before dawn, even before the chickens and Seymour's usual dance across the window screen. I remembered the night before and felt peaceful— triumphant even—and decided to go for a walk before school.

Suddenly I loved September in Santa Fe. The air was so crisp and clear that I was no longer perturbed by its lack of Pacific breezes. I stepped outside my house to find dried chili peppers hanging in bunches from our front porch like shriveled red bananas. The first hints of an ethereal sunrise outlined their crimson forms. Over the Airstream trailer in my neighbor's yard, an American flag flew fast and lofty.

From my house I could cut across the railroad tracks and onto the hiking trails that led through the desert, toward the Tinderbox. I'd never done this alone and wasn't sure if my parents would be thrilled about it, but the landscape called to me.

I hadn't seen another human being for about a mile when I noticed two figures materializing through the cacti like ghosts. As they got closer I recognized them. Jay and Dakota.

As usual, the coyote trotted up to me first, then the man she walked with.

"Fancy meeting you here," Jay said. "Are you thinking of joining the ranks of the cave people after all?"

"Nah," I said. "Just enjoying the morning glow. We've all been wondering when you might show up."

"I have a lot of faith in you kids, Consuelo. You don't need any interference from me this week. I don't perform rituals for just anyone. Only for people who know how to honor the sacred within themselves. So how is everybody doing?"

"Well, to be honest . . . everyone was a little surprised about what . . . transpired after the ritual. Maybe—just maybe—you could have warned us about the side effects of the totem ceremony before we went through with it."

"I told you that it was powerful medicine, dear. You don't always know how it's going to affect different people. But it's always absorbed in the way it needs to be. Is everyone safe?"

"I think so. Last night we all went to this party at a friend's house. And it was good. We've become . . . close."

"I'm glad to hear that. Personal growth and transformation don't have to estrange you from others."

"I had this one moment at the party when I was remembering my aunt Karine, who . . . anyway, I was definitely sad. But Kaya helped me through it."

"Kaya has experienced many dark nights in her lifetime."

"Yes," I said. "I guess we all have."

"Did you ever talk to Karine about her own dark nights?"

"No. I think I was too . . . wrapped up in my own grief."

"I knew your aunt, Consuelo," Jay said.

That was the last thing I'd expected him to say.

"You knew Karine?" I said. But yes. Of course he'd known her. A vague recollection came to mind: a smell in the hallway, a coyote howling in the backyard one night, a quiet presence at the rear of the church when we had the funeral. No wonder I'd felt so comfortable with Jay. He was already familiar.

"I met her years ago," he said, "on one of her first visits to Santa Fe. She and I were immediately drawn to each other. We felt the earth in similar ways. We stayed in touch over the years, mostly through letters. She wrote beautifully about the ocean, the stars over California, the people she met on the street. About you. She was sensitive to the keys and colors of things. I came to your house when she was dying, and we spoke about spiritual matters that interested her. We talked for hours about the afterlife."

Yes, that all definitely sounded like Karine. I struggled to take in this disclosure.

"She asked me to look after you, Consuelo," Jay said. "Everyone needs a teacher, a guide, and yours left too soon. Karine knew that you would take her death the hardest. She was the perfect example of someone whose soul remained intact even though she was suffering from an illness that took possession of her body. Someone had to translate her life into a lesson. And for what it's worth, to me, she seemed strong—maybe even happy—at the end. Though who can really know a soul in its final movements in the waking world? You were the one full of sorrow."

"I let her down," I said. "I didn't help her or comfort her. At the end, you know. At the end I did nothing but stand back and watch her die."

"But you did do something," Jay said. "In her waning months, she told me she liked to listen to your movements. She felt your energy from across the hall."

"My energy is evil," I said, surprising myself. "It's a loud, obnoxious song. It's sick. It just hurts people. I'm not sunshine and light like Karine was. I'm all broken inside."

"You are more like her than you know," Jay said. I didn't believe this for a second. This statement, more than any other, made me doubt him. More so than on the day we met, when he was just some crazy coyote man from the Tinderbox.

"Souls aren't just some *thing* that you can wear around your neck or put in a box," he said. "Souls are an activity, a dynamic essence that you add to life."

"Can you . . . help me live like her?" I asked.

"You already are."

Overwhelmed, I sat in the sand and caressed Dakota's fur. I felt like a human cactus.

"Let me tell you something," Jay continued. "When Karine died, I took to the woods. I missed her terribly. I loved her. She was brave and honest and sublime. Her soul shone through everything she did. So when she left this world, I left it too, for a while. I fasted. I burned the items that reminded me of her. My grief was bottomless." I knew the feeling. But I hadn't prayed or fasted. Instead I'd inherited her disease. It was as if my body wanted to remain as close to Karine as possible.

"And now?" I said, as Dakota licked my palm.

"Now I don't feel so sad anymore," he said. "I also did a swap. Like you and your friends. Except I conducted the ceremony myself, out here in the wild. And instead of swapping burdens with other people, I swapped with the mountains, I swapped with the valleys. They could absorb the pain of Karine's death. They could take it when I couldn't. And now I carry the peace of the land with me. The timeless peace that can withstand every tragedy."

That sounded nice: to exchange a hurting, human heart for the resilient earth.

"Kaya said something like that to me last night," I said. "About what she's been experiencing since the ritual. Do you think she also carries the peace of the land now?"

Jay was silent for a moment. "Kaya cannot be a mountain," he said. "Because she is a volcano."

I shivered.

Jay went on. "As for your new condition, it's important that you don't get carried away by the thrill and novelty of it all. I know this is a rare and magical experience, but you still have responsibilities. Even when it's difficult, an awakening is always a gift you must treasure, in yourselves and in each other. You must nurture each other's souls. Keep up the good work, but do remember to tread lightly and protect one another always."

"You've got nothing to worry about," I said. "I already made the mistake once of neglecting someone I love when life . . . and death got too hard. I won't do it again."

Jay gave me a hug that felt like a beam of light through my body. I'm sure I must have imagined it, but I seemed to smell my aunt in the wilds of his hair. He whistled for Dakota.

"See you Saturday," he said over his shoulder as he walked toward the rising sun.

22

THOMAS MET ME AT MY locker after school let out.

"Are you free this afternoon?" he said. I smiled.

"I was planning to ask you the same thing." Jason's party had ended on a high note, so I didn't necessarily regret that Thomas and I hadn't gotten to spend much time alone together. But now I wanted to talk about our kiss, or the future we might have after Saturday. Or maybe it was too soon for future talk? Maybe I just wanted to kiss some more.

"What do you want to do?" I said.

"I've been thinking about my little brother," he said, scooping up my backpack. We began walking down the corridor toward the parking lot. "Henri. Until now I've been too . . . I don't know. Ashamed, I guess, to contact him. He saw me do so many terrible things. But I know that he's living with our aunt and uncle in Monrovia, and his birthday is coming up. Do you think you could come downtown with me and help me pick out a present for him?"

"I'd love to," I said.

When we arrived at the Plaza, the historic soul of our fair city, it was more crowded than usual. The tourists were in full tourist mode, obliviously gumming up the sidewalks as they stopped to moon over every psychedelic wolf T-shirt and shapeless cowhide jacket in the shop windows. In a frenzy of frying, vendors served greasy tacos and tamales to long lines of customers who probably couldn't handle the spices. Even the street performers seemed to be firing on all cylinders as they out-juggled and out-saxophoned each other. And amidst all the chaos, Native Americans sat cross-legged and quiet under the awning of the Palace of the Governors, selling their handcrafted silver and turquoise jewelry spread down a long row of traditional Navajo blankets.

"I came Christmas shopping here once," I said as Thomas and I walked under the awning, pretending to admire the time-honored craftsmanship but really savoring the life experience on every seller's face. "And I started talking to this old Indian woman selling her handwoven blankets. I'd been eyeballing this beautiful red-and-black one, thinking that my mom might like it, when the woman pointed to a flaw in the pattern. She told me that every blanket the Navajo make has a flaw built in. Did you know that?" Thomas shook his head. "She said something like 'Imperfection leaves room for the spirit, for the creator to enter.' It stuck with me."

Thomas knelt and ran his finger thoughtfully along the wool fabric of a blanket. "I wonder if that's true for humans too," he said. "That our imperfections and our problems are how we stay open to something greater than ourselves. That embracing our burdens is actually how we grow and become our best and truest selves."

"Problems can definitely, like, kindle something in you," I said. "You just have to be willing to pay attention without . . . I don't know. Freaking out? Is there a better way to say that?"

"Probably not," said Thomas, smiling. I told him about my encounter with Jay that morning. "Wow," he said. "Do you think we'll see him again before Saturday?"

"I don't know. But he'd fit in perfectly with these Santa Fe eccentrics."

"For real," Thomas said.

In the Plaza's too-green grass, adult neo-hippies played hacky sack and strummed guitars for spare change. The horns of mariachi bands erupted at every corner. Preteen boys skateboarded around the Plaza's central Civil War monument, harassing passersby. The monument's controversial inscription read: TO THE HEROES WHO HAVE FALLEN IN THE VARIOUS BATTLES WITH SAVAGE INDIANS IN THE TERRITORY OF NEW MEXICO. Evidently the rock had been carved before the era of political correctness. At least someone had scratched out the word "savage."

For his brother's birthday present, Thomas decided on a little oil painting from a street artist. It depicted a young Indian boy on horseback, naked from the waist up, pulling taut the arrow in his bow.

"Henri would like this," he said. He playfully twisted the deer totem around my neck. "He always wanted to ride a horse."

After Thomas completed his errand, we wandered down Old Santa Fe Trail. "Trail" was a bit of a misnomer now that the road was paved and resembled any other gift-shop-lined route in the vicinity, but this was the same historic route that had been used by tradesmen, trappers, and missionaries for several hundred years. I'd seen photographs of exhausted travelers from the East Coast finally arriving at their destination in the center of town, having evaded Indian attacks, rattlesnake bites, starvation, dehydration, hypothermia, and every other variety of disaster to make it to the great capital city, as if they'd beaten some kind of epic frontier video game.

Many of the storefronts still looked the same as they had well over a century ago. The adventurers of yore had drunk beer in these saloons and slept in these hotels. And at one point or another they had probably all passed through the city's cathedrals and intoned desperate prayers. Even now, just past the reliquaries, there was a book in St. Francis where people wrote down their wishes. My mother had once shown me the inscriptions: "Please, God, take away my infertility." "Pray for the soul of my dead father." "May the hungry children be fed." I don't know why it took a book of burdens, all with different penmanship, to drive home the fact that *everyone* has obstacles to overcome.

I steered us left toward Canyon Road, a quaint street where art galleries sold larger works, the kind that couldn't be contained inside the shops off the Plaza. We stopped to admire a cherry tree strung with rosaries that rattled like wind chimes. A bench sat empty next to a bronze, life-size statue of a horse.

"Let's sit here," I said, but Thomas was one step ahead of me. At my side, he unwrapped the painting in his lap, and we both stared at it. "You made a good choice," I said. "I love how sure of himself that boy is. How centered."

"Me too," Thomas said. "Lately I've been reading a lot about the Indian warriors."

"Kit's influence, I imagine," I said.

"He might have loaned me some books. Anyway, they make me sort of . . . envious. After going to war, these young warriors got to return to their villages and pueblos as heroes. They were celebrated in their communities. Even if they were just boys. Like I was. But I returned to Monrovia as a pariah. Worse, actually. I was not allowed to return. I was sent away. At the time I thought I was a warrior, but I was just a killer. And a fool. I was a trained beast. There was nothing noble in my actions. Now, in my dreams, I see these young Indian men riding their horses across the mesa, like this one in the painting, and I gun them down. . . . It's dehumanizing. Consuelo, I'm afraid that I stopped being a real person during my year in the bush. I'm not sure if I can ever retrieve my soul. Not completely."

I gripped his hand in mine. "Imagine if a war like Liberia's had come to that hypothetical Indian boy's village. Imagine if he'd been kidnapped, brainwashed like you. If he'd been taken from his family and his friends. If he'd been given a machine gun and had been told that it was basically a toy. He would've done the same things that you did. He would've met your same fate. People are the same everywhere, none better or worse. They just grow up in different circumstances."

"I don't know," Thomas said.

"What would you tell that Indian boy in the picture if all that had happened to him? To give up? What if it was

Henri?"

"I'd never tell Henri that, no matter what he'd done." He reached into his hoodie pocket, where I knew he kept his rabbit totem. My eyes wandered upward.

"Look, Thomas!" I said. "Is that one of yours?" A white balloon was crossing the sky over St. Francis Cathedral. The pink-rimmed, sunset clouds behind it made me think of paradise.

"Yep," Thomas said, smiling.

"You know the artist Georgia O'Keeffe, right?" I asked. "She lived in the desert north of here. I once read a book about her. She said that if she painted a particular mountain often enough, God would give it to her. Maybe it's like that with you. Maybe if you go into heaven often enough, like in one of your balloons, God will give it to you."

"I don't need a balloon to feel like I'm in heaven," Thomas said.

Then he kissed me. I didn't taste blood this time, only elevation and our combined weightlessness. It was as if we were in the sky again.

"Why do you like me?" I asked him, pulling my lips away reluctantly. "I'm just normal. There was nothing special about me until I got sick."

"You're wrong," he said. "You're the opposite of war, the antidote to war. You are peace. You're the opposite of scorched earth. You plant seeds wherever you go. It's so subtle you don't realize you're doing it. You leave a trail of small ideas, small affection, that grows and grows until it touches everyone. Heals everyone."

"I *wish*. I wish I had that much power."

"It's not power, exactly. It's energy. Remember when I first started school here two years ago? You spoke to me like a human being. It was the first time I felt normal here."

"But you're not 'normal.' You're special. And I knew that right away. Before I even read your poem. Maybe that day at Agua you weren't responding to my treating you like an average student so much as . . . you were just glad to be recognized as whole. And unique."

My phone rang in my purse. Kit.

"I should probably get this," I said, hitting ACCEPT.

"Are you with Thomas?" he said before I could even say hello.

"Yes."

"Good. I need to talk to you guys. Where are you?"

Fifteen minutes later we met Kit in a coffee shop off the Plaza.

"Kaya asked me to go with her into the Sangre de Cristo Mountains tomorrow," he said. "She told me there's something she needs to do there, some sort of ceremony to communicate with her ancestors, and she needs my support. She was pretty intense about it, and I know that we made a pact to protect each other and stick together, so I just wanted to let you know. . . ."

"Thanks, Kit," I said. "For telling us. Kaya should go up the mountain, if that's really what she wants. The rest of us have gotten to follow our whims this week. But if she's going, we're all going."

"You too, Thomas?"

"I'm with Lo," he said. "I'm not crazy about going up the

mountain when all I hear are wildfire warnings. But Kaya wouldn't ask unless it was important. Let's do it. Let's go together."

"All right!" Kit said. "Camping trip. We'll blow off school tomorrow and climb a mother-effing mountain. And you know we have to spend the night up there—tomorrow is the last day of the swap. Or so Jay said. It will be like a farewell party for our adopted burdens. I'll tell Ellen. We'll all meet at my house at eight tomorrow morning." He elbowed Thomas lightly in the ribs. "And don't forget your two-person sleeping bag."

23

I HAD NIGHTMARES THAT NIGHT. Dreams that my father's lungs were turning black, dreams that Thomas was an Indian warrior shot off his horse, dreams that I got so swept up in a song that I danced myself right off a cliff.

But somehow I woke up happy. And at seven thirty Friday morning, I still entered the kitchen feeling wide-awake and excited about the camping trip. I'd packed my overnight gear in my book bag so my parents wouldn't be suspicious, and planned to call them later and tell them I was spending the night at Kaya's so they wouldn't worry.

The kitchen smelled like burning wood, because my dad wore his work clothes. I cherish his characteristic fragrance, even though I've never told him so. Flaming piñon trees notoriously smell of incense, so being around Dad is sometimes like being dragged to one of my mother's high Catholic masses, where the heady aromas are often the only redeeming features of the service. I inhaled the sweet smoke as I plopped down at the kitchen table and poured myself a glass of orange juice.

"*Buenos días*, McDonoughs," I said brightly to my parents. "*Habla desayunos?*"

"I don't know about a three-course breakfast," Mom said, "but we definitely speak cold cereal."

"A bilingual household is better than nothing," I said. Mom gave my shoulder a brief squeeze as she walked to the fridge. She still wore her nursing scrubs from working the night shift at the hospital, and I suddenly wondered about the people she'd touched, those she'd helped to heal.

"How you feeling, hon?" Dad asked from the sink.

"Hunky-dory, Daddy-o," I said. "Same as always." This week I was carefully avoiding all domestic discussions on the subject of my mercurial body.

Dad set a cereal bowl in front of me, and I started cracking up. A fat green chili sat on top of my steaming oatmeal like a maraschino cherry on an ice cream sundae. "Don't you think the day is a little young, Dad?"

"Never," he said, taking his seat across from me and rolling up the sleeves of his uniform. He dug his spoon into a matching bowl. "Think of all the vitamin C you're about to consume. Forget the orange juice, Lo. New Mexico chilis beat Tropicana any day as part of a balanced diet. On three. Ready? One, two. . . ."

Dad and I had an ongoing contest to see who could maintain poise the longest when eating habañero peppers. I took a deep breath and began chewing on the count of three.

"You think that being sick is going to mess up my game?" I said. "Fat chance." Mom sat down with a bowl of ungarnished oatmeal and proceeded to sprinkle brown sugar on top.

"How *reasonable* people get a healthy start," she said.

"So, you're up awfully early this morning," Dad said as his eyes began to water from the habañeros. "Trying to get a jump on the chickens?" He tried to act casual as he reached for his glass of water, but I was onto him. His whole body was rigid with effort. I could tell he knew that I knew, but he remained committed to the ruse. When his forehead broke out in a sweat from the chili, he began whistling "You Are My Sunshine."

"Is it early?" I said innocently, dabbing my lips with a napkin, not feeling the usual burning sensation enveloping my mouth. I might actually win this time. "I'm catching a ride to school with Kit Calhoun."

"I thought his mode of transportation was exclusively skateboard," Dad said.

"Yeah, well, he's more comfortable behind the wheel these days. What's up with you? Do you have work today?"

"Just have to finish getting the blaze on the mountain under control. Should be today or tomorrow."

"Please be careful, Dad."

"I always am. I firmly abide by something your aunt used to say. 'Fire can't burn you as long as you keep moving.'"

"And she was right. Just make sure the fire doesn't move faster than you."

"Sure thing, boss."

Dad and I smiled at each other as matching chili tears dripped down our cheeks. I could still have the telltale reaction to the peppers, even though I didn't feel the pain.

"Tie," I said, winking at him. "Gotta run. Great breakfast, *padre*, though a *pequeño* mild."

"Glad to see you're brushing up on your Spanish, sweetheart," Dad said. "Be sure to commend your teacher for me. *Hace calor!*" He ran for the sink for a water refill.

I docked my mostly full bowl of oatmeal on the counter under a tin can Jesus and kissed my parents goodbye. I wanted to leave before I felt too guilty for lying to them about skipping school and confessed everything.

———

I threw my backpack in the trunk of Kit's car. I was the last one of our group to arrive at his house and the most eager to leave. With the exception of Kaya, anyway, who'd been watching for me in the driveway when I walked over. Even though we'd been hanging out all week, I felt that camping was going to be our biggest and best outing yet. Spending the night with Thomas on the mountain? *Fantástico*.

"Let's do this," I said. "Before Thomas decides it's too dangerous." I gave Thomas a kiss on the cheek so he knew I was teasing, and Kit smiled approvingly at my little display.

On the way out of town, Ellen insisted we stop for breakfast at Cocina de Carlos.

"It's the best roadside Mexican stand in the state," she said. "My appetite has come back with a vengeance this week, and I'm taking a sick, sick pleasure in food. I think these chorizo breakfast burritos might qualify as a drug."

"Careful, Lo," Kaya said, as I prepared to take a huge bite of my steaming egg burrito. "They're hot. I've burned my mouth on them before without realizing it."

"Thanks, Kaya," I said, blowing lightly on my breakfast.

"Speaking of burning," Thomas said, "aren't there still wildfires on the mountain? Maybe we should just camp out at the KOA near the river."

"No," Kaya said. "There's something I have to show you. We're going up. All the way up." She was acting more impassioned than she'd been even in the last few days, but we weren't worried about it that morning, considering that she was our leader. It took some intensity to reach a summit. We had no idea that she was the last person we should have allowed to be in charge.

"Kaya!" I said, suddenly remembering something. "Didn't you have a birthday party planned for tonight?"

"I canceled it," she said. "I'd rather do this."

"When's your birthday?" Ellen asked.

"Tomorrow."

"No way," Ellen said. "Well, we'll have to do something tonight to celebrate. Damn. Did anyone pack candles, by chance? A layer cake?"

"I might have a sparkler or two left," Kit said.

"It's really okay," Kaya said. "I'd prefer not to do anything this year. Birthdays all sort of blend together, you know." Not for me. I hadn't had *that* many.

"Can we at least play a birthday game of truth or dare?" Kit asked. "In Kaya's honor?" Ellen stuck out her tongue at him.

"Keep dreaming, Kit," she said, smiling coyly.

Shortly after passing the site of our ritual in Pecos Park, Kaya directed us off the main road to a deserted parking lot at the timbered base of the mountain.

"Whoa," Ellen said, gazing up the rocky, overgrown trail issuing from the edge of the lot. "It looks steep."

"Do you think you can make it?" I said.

"Yeah. I feel okay for now."

"Well, tell me if you start hurting or something," I said. "We can stop."

"Good thing you haven't been smoking cigarettes this week," Kit said to Ellen, swinging his backpack over his shoulder.

"I haven't been doing a lot of things this week," Ellen said, as we started up the trail, Kaya first. "And I don't know if it's Lo's wack symptoms talking or what, but I really don't miss them."

"So . . . are you saying that, if given the choice, from a purely hypothetical standpoint, I mean, you wouldn't want to switch back tomorrow?" I asked, testing the waters, even though I was pretty sure I knew—and wouldn't like—her answer.

"Are you kidding? I can't *wait* until we switch back tomorrow. But not for the same reasons as a few days ago. Now I feel way more equipped to conquer my old habits. Even if everything is reversed, I just can't go from *this* back to . . . that."

"What's 'this'?" I asked.

"I don't know. Like, allowing myself to feel stuff again? Even when it sucks? I might be shaky this week, but I still feel more like myself than I have for the last year or so. After the ritual, if I feel tempted by pills or . . . whatever again, I can see myself going to get some help."

"You mean, like therapy?" I asked.

"Yeah," Ellen said. "I guess. And maybe some kind of outpatient treatment or something. If my mom can buy me a brand-new car after I drunkenly crash mine, she can certainly pay for me to get sober. I know what I need now, and I just have to tell her, because otherwise she's clueless." Ellen held a branch aside until everyone passed, then let it fly back into the empty path. "I'm sick of feeling sorry for myself."

"Atta girl," Kit said, stopping to high-five her.

"Thanks, Kit," Ellen said, blushing a bit.

The higher we climbed, the more triumphant I felt. Here were five people who'd never hung out together before last Saturday, and now we were taking the world—or at least one of its peaks—by storm. Though I still had some nervous energy I didn't know what to do with, I felt pretty good. Proud even. Of myself and of my friends.

Thomas seemed especially to enjoy the mountain air. After several miles, he hadn't even broken a sweat.

"This reminds me of when I used to take walks in the hills with my little brother," he said. "Before the war."

"Lucita and I hiked around here once or twice," Kit said. "She hiked barefoot, if you can believe that. Said it gave her better traction. Plus it was a lot quieter, so we didn't scare off the animals. We used to see the deer even before they saw us." He reached down to help Ellen negotiate a large rock in the path. For a second I didn't think she was going to accept his hand, but then she took it gratefully.

"Do you smell something, Lo?" Ellen said at my back. "Like smoke?"

"I don't smell anything," Kit said.

"Don't worry," I said. "The fire's almost under control."

Ahead of us on the path, Thomas turned around and smiled broadly at us, eyes shining. Then his face changed. He became deadly serious. He held up his hand for us to stop walking and then pointed to something behind us.

We all turned to look. Kaya was trailing us by several hundred yards. She walked slowly, as if in a trance. How long had it been since she'd said anything? Maybe twenty minutes? We'd all been giddily chatting away and hadn't noticed her dismal silence or her retreat to the back of the group.

"Kaya?" I said. "Are you okay?" She didn't answer. She just kept walking robotically, lost in her own dark world. As if by instinct, we looked to Thomas for guidance.

"We need to be careful," he said. "If we push her, she could snap. Let's just keep a close eye on her." We stood aside as Kaya passed us without acknowledging our presence. We exchanged glances as she began to speed up. Then she veered off the trail at a jog.

We struggled to keep up with her, following her through the thickening underbrush. In a short time we reached a ravine. It was so dry that fissures ran through the earth at its bottom. It looked as though someone had recently pulled aside the vegetation along the bank to reveal its thirsty depths. Rocks and boulders of all sizes populated the ravine as if they'd fallen from the cliff above. Then my attention turned to the other white objects littering the scorched hollow.

At first I thought they were the skulls of steers. Misshapen steers. But no. I looked more closely and saw they were human skulls. And arm bones. Leg bones. Pelvic bones. The ravine held the scattered remains of human skeletons. I remembered the skull that the coyote had whisked through the ceremony on Saturday night. Maybe I hadn't imagined it after all. My heart began to pound. And then Kaya turned to us with a remote look in her eyes.

"We were a small tribe," she said hypnotically. "And that was our home, as far as you can see below. The Americans thought they'd find gold on our land, so we had to be removed. We were rounded up and told we'd be taken care of, given food and medicine, if we surrendered to federal authority. The American soldiers at the fort told us that we'd be protected. So we showed up in Santa Fe, trusting, emaciated. We stayed for weeks and weren't given our rations. Still starving, we decided to take our chances and return to our village. Then one night the American soldiers came with guns. We tried to escape by running up the mountain, but they hunted us. They shot us in our backs, stole what little we had. Mutilated our bodies. I can see it happening. It's happening right now. They threw our corpses in this ravine."

I stood staring at her in shock. We all did. This fugue state was similar to the one at the airfield, but more emphatic.

More . . . focused. And a thousand times more powerful, considering that she was standing among the evidence of the destruction she described.

Kaya squatted in the ravine and trembled as if from some deep reservoir inside. She seemed to be experiencing the massacre herself, in real time.

"Here's where my mother was shot," she said, fingering the dirt. "She was trying to protect me. She wore my baby sister in a papoose on her back. The vigilante came up and ripped her from my mother's body. He threw her in the ravine, which flowed with water back then. 'Nits make lice,' he said. Then he stabbed me through the heart with his bayonet. He pulled my kachina doll from my hands, said he'd keep my teeth for himself as trophies and give my doll to his daughter as a souvenir. He cut off my mother's private parts."

One thing hadn't changed after Jay's ritual: Kaya still couldn't cry.

"Kaya," I pleaded, unable to raise my voice above a whisper. It wouldn't have mattered if I'd screamed. She was somewhere else.

We hadn't read about this massacre in school. We'd never heard of this mass graveyard on the mountain. No marker or monument commemorated the deaths. How had Kaya known? She seemed to have a photographic memory for events that happened long before she was born. Even before her great-grandparents were born. But that couldn't be. Could it? Maybe if we just . . . waited it out, these images would disappear, like the ones on her legs that my swimming pool had swallowed.

Ellen started to retch in the sagebrush. Thomas, Kit, and I huddled together, unable to do anything but listen.

"I'd already seen the soldiers kill my father," Kaya went on. "He was a great warrior. But he didn't try to fight. It didn't matter. They shot him in the back as he rode away. Then they stole his horse." Kaya was getting more agitated the more she abandoned herself—and us—to her story. She began to pace back and forth in the ravine, touching the bones one by one.

"Kaya," I said, "talk to me. Where are you right now?" She closed her eyes.

"Riding through a canyon pass. Shots ring out. I think my eardrums will burst from the sound. Artillery fire echoes off the canyon walls. My father. . . ."

I thought of the reassuring sound of my dad's cough in the night.

"What is this feeling?" Kaya shrieked. "There's a bullet in my chest. It's moving through my lungs. It's sharp, it's terrible, it makes me want to be dead. What are all these feelings that make me want to be dead?"

I thought of what it must be like for people who'd been deaf their whole lives to hear for the first time. Or for blind people who could suddenly see. But this was the opposite of one of those miracles. Kaya's bold entry into the world of pain was catastrophic. She wasn't prepared. In that moment, if I could have given back her analgesia, I would have, without hesitation. One person should not have to feel so much.

"History forgot us," she howled. "History stampeded over us, over my people. The settlements and cities of America are built on bloody ground." She hugged a small skull against her chest.

"Come on, Kaya," Thomas said gently. "It's getting cold. We need to make camp. We can't fix the past tonight. But we can talk about it, together."

"The bones," she said. "My family, lost. We were a great nation."

"You still are," I said. But then, shamefully, the first image that came to my mind was an old Indian man I'd recently seen curled up behind the gas station with a bottle in a brown paper bag. I thought of everything that had been stolen from him.

"Nothing," Kaya said, "will ever be the same."

I thought I heard a baby crying. It was as if the sound was coming from the bones. The smell of burning wood flooded my nostrils.

Looking to Thomas for help, I saw from his collapsed shoulders and distressed eyes that he felt as impotent as I did. What could we possibly do for Kaya? I felt like one of the scientists of the Manhattan Project as I watched my bomb explode on the horizon, my black hole of all that is good. I regretted my callous experiments.

Kaya took off running through the ravine and began scrambling up the cliff face that towered over it. Thomas tried to grab her, but she was too quick. Within moments she had climbed to the top as skillfully as a wild mountain sheep. She stood dangerously on the edge of the precipice, her proud body silhouetted against the darkening sky. She pulled something from her pocket. Her bear totem? No, a razor.

"Oh my god," I said. "Thomas." I reached for his hand.

"She's reliving something up there," he said. He was spellbound by the sight of Kaya's figure on the cliff. He gazed up at his burden-sister with what looked to me like profound understanding. He could see how bad it really was. I felt terrible for him. For Kaya.

You know those moments when time slows and you remember something so strange, so random, yet so vivid? Some memory you didn't even know you'd latched onto? As I gazed up at Kaya on the cliff, I remembered a presentation Kit had once given in history class, about a ruthless attack on the Navajo Indians in 1805. When five hundred Spanish soldiers invaded the Diné's sacred Canyon de Chelly in northeastern Arizona, they discovered more than a hundred Navajo women and children seeking refuge in a lofty cave. Before all the Indians were massacred, one old woman tackled a Spanish soldier who'd climbed up the towering rock. Rather than see him violate their time-honored Chelly defenses, she wrapped herself around him and then jumped off the cliff, sending them both plunging to their deaths. The Navajo call this site "The Place Where Two Fell Off."

I needed to get to Kaya before she did something drastic. I took off running, clambered up the steep, loose rocks that led to her aerie. I barely noticed the cacti and brambles that cut into my legs, drawing blood. They would slow down anyone who might follow, but of course I didn't feel the pain. As I reached the peak, I narrowly avoided stepping on a rattlesnake. It hissed and then lunged at my hiking boot, but I leapt out of the way. By the time I reached the top of the mesa, I had lost a visual on Kaya. Then I heard her.

"Look at me," she said, yanking up the legs of her pants.

24

THE SAME PICTOGRAPHS THAT KAYA had drawn on her legs in black pen on Monday afternoon were now carved into her flesh. Carved, as in with a knife. Freshly bleeding. I thought I was going to faint. I could imagine how much pain she was in. And she wasn't done. With a razor blade, she was still cutting symbols and patterns into her skin. Every time she dabbed away the blood with her shirtsleeve, her thighs glistened with pictographs we'd only seen previously in museums etched on leather and buckskin, the careful record keeping of an unknown Indian chief.

"Oh my god," I said. "Kaya." My wounds were nothing compared to hers. My pain was nothing.

Thomas and the others were trying to find a safe way up the incline that Kaya and I had mounted so easily. I heard the rocks tumbling under my friends as they shouted desperately for us to climb down.

"I never should have let her come," said Thomas, slipping down the face of the cliff as he fought for leverage.

"Oh my god," Ellen said. "I can't get up there. What do we do? Lo, do something!" The ritual had taken us way too far.

This was what Jay and Thomas had warned me about. Why hadn't I listened?

"Tonight I represent my people," Kaya said. "Even though my ancestors lie in the bone pits before us, their suffering is far from over." Something barked behind her, and a coyote appeared through the rocks. Kaya stooped over and began petting her between her ears. The striped black ear markings told me that the coyote was Dakota, but I saw no sign of Jay. I longed for any adult presence, but it was just me, Kaya, a wild animal, and all of our sordid American history facing off on the cliff. Kaya stepped closer to the ledge and slipped slightly, sending small stones skittering into the ravine.

"Kaya," I said. "Please." With every step I made toward her, she made one in the opposite direction, bringing herself precariously close to the rocky abyss below. I stayed still, too afraid to move. Dakota retreated to a nearby bush and began licking her haunches.

Kaya looked at me intently, and at that moment I felt that she could see straight into my neurons. I felt that she could hear the music, both good and bad, that my thoughts made. I felt that she could see all my colors, all my wishes. I felt that she could see into my soul itself. And I didn't know if the outcome of this scrutiny would be positive. My hair bristled like a coyote's under her gaze. I clutched the deer totem around my neck.

"You already know what I'm going to do, Lo," Kaya said. "And that's okay. But you can't stop me." I *had* to stop her. The week couldn't end this way. The ritual was supposed to heal us all, not destroy my oldest friend.

"Kaya," I said. "Please. I'm begging you. It doesn't have to be like this."

"No," she said. "It does. What has already happened is too grim, too devastating. I cannot stop seeing the lives that were lost. I feel them, Consuelo. In my gut, in my heart, I feel the wounds. They're everywhere. Their history is everywhere." She bent down and dug her fingers into the earth, then rubbed dirt into her leg where the cuts formed the body of an Indian warrior being dragged behind a horse.

"But Kaya, there's also hope. Can't you feel that too?" I should have taken her to Canyon Road, so she could see the rosaries hanging from the branches of the tree at sunset. I should have taken her to the natural hot springs, so she could feel the warmth penetrate her bones. I should have driven her past the peach orchards that grew along the Rio Grande. I should have taken her up in one of Thomas's hot-air balloons so she could view these mountains from the heaven above them. I'd kept these experiences to myself while she had been alone with her tragic history. I'd been stingy with my joy, just as I'd been stingy with my burden.

"No more hope," she said. "Only pain."

"We love you," I said, my voice breaking. "We need you. Can't you see that? We can't lose you. *I* can't. Please talk to me, Kaya. Let me help you. We are all here for you. We promised to take care of each other. Remember?"

"The tangible me—the me with a body—is lost," she said. "All that remains now is my soul. And it's been seized for a higher purpose. It's not your fault, Lo. I don't blame you. But my soul is already spoken for. It wants to return to its native community."

Then she wrapped her arms around me. Was her fervor due to the fact that she meant it as a last embrace? Or because she wanted to hurl me off the cliff with her, like the Diné woman from the story? Over Kaya's shoulder, I saw Dakota running toward us. She looked murderous, as if she planned to attack. I struggled to extricate myself from Kaya's arms and position myself between her and her savage fate.

I would fight Dakota. I would protect Kaya. I would fight history. Only my animal nature could save her.

Then I felt Dakota's jaws clamping down on my forearm. I felt the pressure of the bite, but not the teeth themselves. I snarled at Dakota. I yelped and spurred her on, even though I could see her bite penetrate almost to the bone. I wanted her to tear off my arm and then go for my jugular. I wanted her to shred my ruined nerves. I wanted to assume all the destruction, so Kaya would be safe. When Dakota lunged at me again, I flinched. A lifetime of pain had trained me well. Burdens couldn't be undone overnight. I still dreamed of pain. My body still had its memories.

"Kaya!" Thomas shouted from behind us. "Consuelo!" We turned to face him. Dakota released her grip. Thomas had mounted the cliff. He approached cautiously. His bare legs were bleeding from the brambles on the mountain.

"Kaya," he said, "you're not alone. We can get through this."

For a few seconds she seemed to entertain this hope. Then her face became resolute again. "No," she told Thomas. "I'm sorry, but it's too late."

25

AND THEN KAYA TOOK HER position at the edge of the rock, and, before Thomas and I could reach her, she leapt.

She simply disappeared over the precipice. Silently, like sand. Like a wisp of ash. Dakota unlatched her jaw from my arm, as if to let me know her work there was done. By the time I made it to the edge of the cliff, Kaya's body was already sprawled at unnatural angles in the ravine below.

Ellen and Kit had never made it up the steep embankment, so they were the closest to her. Ellen scrambled to Kaya's side while Kit stood frozen, stunned. From above I stared in shock as blood pooled under Kaya's beautiful head. I crumpled to the ground. Meanwhile Thomas sprang into action. He pulled off his shirt and wrapped it around my arm. It took me a second to recognize what he was doing. Then I saw his white V-neck turn red around my wound.

"No. Go to her. Please, Thomas. Save her."

"Stay here," he said, and then began half sliding and half falling down the less steep part of the cliff where he'd ascended. I stared into the ravine.

"No," I said, as I waited for Kaya to get up. "No," I said, as I watched Ellen and Kit try to move the boulders that encircled her broken body. "No," I said, as I heard Ellen screaming, "She's not breathing! Kit, she's not breathing!" Kit pulled Ellen to him, hiding her eyes from Kaya's traumatized figure. The blood on her bare legs formed an intricate network of streams, obscuring the carvings.

Then Thomas reached Kaya's side. He took her pulse. He tried to breathe life back into her lungs. And then he just sat next to her, lowered her eyelids, crossed her scarred arms like a shield across her chest as she had so often held them in life. Kit pulled a blanket from his backpack and gently laid it over her body.

I smelled rich, pungent wood smoke, though I still couldn't see any sign of fire above the trees. They weren't burning. We were burning. I pulled my cell phone out of my pocket and stared at the numbers I needed to press. It seemed like it took me an eternity to dial 911.

26

AS WE WAITED FOR THE rescue crew to arrive, Thomas mounted the cliff once more to clean and bandage my arm with the first aid kit he'd packed. The white bandage went around and around while my eyes stayed fixed on Kaya's shape under the blanket far below. I couldn't feel anything. Not the coyote's wound on my arm. Not my grief. Not the chill that had begun to set in with the sunset. Thomas had put on his hoodie over his bare torso and brought me my sweater. But I refused it. The fabric felt foreign and repulsive. Too soft and warm for me, for this life.

It was a long time before Thomas decided I was ready to descend. I went straight to Kaya's side. I touched her face. I told her to get up, that everything would be okay now. That we'd all switch back and life would return to normal.

But I couldn't stop crying. This wasn't right at all. I should be strong now, free of pain. I shouldn't be able to cry, and I'd cried more this week than I ever had before. Maybe Jay should have just let me stay sick. Sometimes being well was more confusing.

Circle home, Lo.

Where is home?

Kit made a campfire in the ravine, not far from Kaya, to keep us warm while we waited. The flames bounced shadows of boulders across her body as though trying to nudge her awake. A tendril of smoke snaked into the sky above the mountain as if it was signaling something. What was it trying to tell me? I needed answers. I needed Jay.

The EMTs worked for an hour to retrieve Kaya from the rubble of rock and bone that surrounded her. They insisted on treating my arm, though the bites weren't that deep after all, as if the coyote hadn't really meant to do lasting damage. I declined a rabies shot. I knew it was my disease, not hers, that had driven Dakota to attack.

Thomas told the rescue crew that Kaya had accidentally fallen off the cliff while we explored the ravine together. It was just a tragic hiking accident that happened while we were playing hooky. Had nothing to do with souls or spirits of the dead or American history or our dumb problems that we'd been so desperate to unload that we'd put our friend in mortal danger.

Now that the worst had happened, Thomas didn't seem so afraid anymore. Even hiking down the mountain by flashlight behind Kaya's body, he didn't falter once, and he made sure that we didn't either. Then I had a thought that temporarily woke me from my daze. I wondered if his burden was gone forever. If it had died with Kaya. And I wondered if I would eternally carry her analgesia now that she had breathed her last. I looked down at the bandage on my arm and regretted everything I'd done.

Messing with nature, messing with my particular lot of suffering.

But if I were to carry Kaya's burden, I would honor it. I would not complain. It would be her legacy.

We followed the rescue crew and Kaya's stretcher back to solid, level earth. Then we said goodbye to our beloved friend. Before she was put in the flashing but dreadfully silent ambulance for the long drive back to Santa Fe, Thomas tucked their shared bear totem into his pocket, and I placed our deer in her hand, closing her ragged fingertips around it before they went cold. Then the four of us who remained tore down the road back to Pecos Park. It was the only place that seemed right. The only place that held any hope.

Kit searched for quiet music on the radio, but all we heard were emergency broadcasts about the flames just north of us. We switched off the warnings and drove in silence. I took a detour to avoid the roadblock I heard was installed on the road to Los Alamos. We accelerated into the smoke.

Which brings us back to the beginning.

27

MY HAND FLASHED THROUGH THE flames in the center of the Pueblo kiva. I dropped Kaya's baby tooth in the middle of the hallowed fire. It just seemed right to burn the relic like coal. I could not keep that reminder of her body.

But was I myself a reminder of her body?

Thomas stood up on his blanket and limped to the time-worn wall encircling us. He seemed infinitely weary as he leaned his head against the stone pillar that kept the roof from collapsing. He was done fighting.

"We just need to return things to the way they were," he said. Maybe he hadn't given up on me after all. He walked toward the fire, kicking up a small cloud of glittering sand. I couldn't stop myself from morbid speculations. Were the burned remains of ancient bodies mixed in with the granules? Kaya had told us what had happened on this land centuries ago. What had happened to her people. And now she'd met a similar fate.

"We just need to be ourselves again," Thomas continued. "We can't bring back Kaya, but we can reclaim our old identities. No matter how heavy they are. No matter how much they hurt."

I shuddered, but I knew Thomas was right. Our past selves were the only options we had left. Those imperfect selves were the only ones who still had a chance of surviving.

The sunrise beamed down through the keyhole in the roof and mingled with the smoke and flames, as if the rays had been waiting throughout the dark night for a worthy dance partner. Dance. . . . It had just been Wednesday night when we all moved in the casita together, but now it seemed like lifetimes ago. One lifetime.

I made up my mind to do everything I could to save these three people. They had become my friends. And one of them had become much more than that. If Jay's magic was strong enough to turn a deer into a bear and a mountain into a volcano, then maybe it could turn death back into life.

28

"JAY," I SAID TO THE solemn man standing near the ladder. "Please, bring her back. You have to bring her back."

"Bring her back?" he said.

"Yes. You have to save Kaya."

"We can't resurrect her, Lo. But we can set her free."

"No! I don't accept that. There must be a way. You've got to know some magic for . . . accidents. There must be another ritual. Look in your bag. Look in your pockets. Spit on me. Smudge me. Do something, anything. Kaya wasn't supposed to die. You have to see how wrong this is—"

"Kaya is gone," Jay said, "and there's nothing we can do. While we can grieve the loss, we cannot undo it. We can let it shape us as Kaya was shaped by her own losses. Strong souls like your friend's can persist long after the body has departed, but unfortunately you cannot reverse her physical fate."

"So that's it?" I said. "She's just . . . dead?" Like Karine. Another person I loved, gone. What kind of a miserable *shape* could I make from this? All I could think of was a heart broken down the middle.

"Kaya's soul was too fluid, too porous," Jay said. "It couldn't establish boundaries."

"So she was punished for that?" Kit said.

"She was not punished," Jay said. "Nor was she rewarded. She simply was. She simply fell."

At that moment I wanted to fall too. In some ways I felt I already had. It had never been my body at stake this week. It had always been my soul.

"My darling children," Jay said. "You've gone astray. You need to return to the right path. I trust you to find it." Then, without another word, he made his way up the ladder.

"Where are you going?" I shouted as he disappeared through the smoke hole. "Come back and help us!"

But then I realized that we didn't need him anymore. Jay's magic still remained in the kiva, circulating among our bodies. And I alone knew how to use it.

29

"HE'S NOT COMING BACK," I said, getting to my feet. "I'm going to conduct the ritual without him."

"Wonderful," Kit said. "And what exactly qualifies you? Were you a spiritual guru in a past life? Or did you just play with a Ouija board once at a sleepover? Right before your Agua girlfriends put your bra into deep freeze?"

"Please, Kit," I said. "I got us into this, didn't I? Please give me a chance to make amends. I think I know how."

A calm descended on our chamber, and our previous bickering seemed to dissolve with the night. Thomas sat silently, back in hibernation. Next to him Ellen painstakingly scratched Kaya's name into the kiva wall with her lighter. Suddenly even the graffiti and other modern markings in the chamber seemed sacred in their own way. Though the story they told might not have been beautiful, it was true. And utterly human.

"Did everyone bring their totems?" I said.

Kit reached inside his pocket for Ellen's raccoon. Ellen untied my horse from her neck, and Thomas withdrew Kit's rabbit from his pocket, as well as his and Kaya's bear. I was the only one without a totem to give back. I clenched my numb and empty hand. I knew exactly what I wanted to say.

"Thomas, Ellen, and Kit. My friends. This week we have all proved to ourselves and to each other that we are more than our burdens. We know now that our burdens can never define us, that pain is a part of life that we cannot ignore or fight off or destroy. We can only accept it and live in its moments, just like everything else. We must take the lessons from this week and live with souls full of light and purpose, full of each other, and especially full of Kaya. Now we are ready to receive back our burdens. With gratitude for what they have taught us." I approached Ellen, who was more pensive than I'd ever seen her.

"Ellen," I said, "I hereby take back my symptoms. . . . I see now that the reason I was suffering so much is because I was trying to do it alone. Now I feel that I can accept my illness, whatever it is. With a community to support us, we can accept anything." Ellen handed me the horse. I seemed to feel its power in my palm.

"I'll be right there with you, Lo," she said. "Like you were there for me this week. I promise." I hugged her.

Then Ellen walked over to Kit, who faced her fearlessly. "Kit," she said, "I hereby take back my burden. Through watching you this week, I've seen that life doesn't need to be clouded over with fear . . . or masked with drugs. Now I just want to take the bad with the good. I want things to be *real*. By always looking for an escape hatch, I miss the beauty around me. Now I will try to see clearly." Kit placed the raccoon in her palm.

"You're part of the beauty," he said. "We want you here in the real world. With us." Ellen drew the raccoon to her chest and held it there for a moment, meeting Kit's undaunted gaze with her own.

Then Kit turned to Thomas. "Thomas," he said, "my brother. I take back my fear. I'm sorry that I made you scared. Before this week, I never would have thought that was possible. We can recognize that human beings are vulnerable without being paralyzed by that knowledge. And there are good, helpful spirits who work in the dark. Not just monsters." Thomas gave Kit his rabbit, then pulled him into an enduring bear hug.

Now Thomas stood quietly with his totem. "If I could speak to Kaya right now," he said, "I'd tell her. . . ." His eyes filled with tears. "I'd tell her that I'm sorry for what I inflicted on her. Seeing her on the mountain last night, it was like I recognized my own trauma for the first time. But there was no time to help her process and . . . metabolize what she was reliving. Without being able to make sense of her suffering, or dull its immediacy, she was . . . doomed. And I see now that . . . I can't go that same route. I have too much to live for. I think . . . I *know* that if I face my past now, with the help of others, I can heal." I wrapped my arms around him.

We didn't expect to feel the effects of the swap right away, if at all, and so we simply sat on our blankets, waiting for the day to be over, communing with our individual thoughts. Which all centered on Kaya, if my own focus was any indication.

Before we could leave, I knew there was one final thing I needed to do. "I'm going up," I said, "but you all take as long as you need."

Back out in the open, the clouds of smoke from the north were smaller, sputtering. My father had put out the fire, as I knew he would. At a higher elevation from where I stood, the bones of Kaya's ancestors awaited consecration. Many miles away, Kaya's bones also waited.

And then I was dancing. Something in the air—maybe smoke, maybe gold—compelled me to move. There, in the desert, in the daylight, all by myself, with no music, I danced. So Kaya's spirit would find peace, I danced. So we would all be kinder, more accepting of our differences, and of our own faults, I danced. So we would not just destroy each other, but instead open our eyes to the miracle of being alive, of being so similar, even in our suffering, I danced. The smoke and the fire and the blood and the light were all in my body, and I lifted my arms to the sky with grief and with joy. I felt that I was drawing rings around my body and then finally shaping them into a world.

30

ON SUNDAY MORNING I WOKE up early, roused by the familiar pounding in my head. I'd been dreaming that I was limping across the desert with a broken foot when a magnificent horse rode up behind me, her flanks tattooed with images of gentle faces both human and animal. I climbed on her back, and we galloped toward the ocean.

Lying in bed, my foot throbbed precisely where it had in the dream, but I knew that it wasn't broken, only sprained. And I knew that, somehow, I was still being carried. I smiled through the pain.

Seymour darted acrobatically across my window screen. I guess only one superhero remained in my bedroom, and that was okay with me. I dressed and took my pills for the first time in a week, then crossed the hallway to the door I hadn't opened since July. Karine's wheelchair still sat empty in the corner of the spare bedroom. I kissed the horse totem in my right hand and then wrapped its string around the wheelchair's handle.

"You have given me a great gift," I said, feeling my aunt's energy swimming through the room. "An awakening. I am ready to accept it now." The horse swung back and forth slightly on its string, catching the light from the window and casting it upon the shrine of family pictures on the mantel. Soon I would add the painting that Kaya had given me, just as soon as I sketched her body into the scene, so the three of us would be dancing together always.

———

"*Buenos mañanas*," I said when I walked into the kitchen. My parents weren't eating. They were too busy drinking coffee and monitoring my every movement. All of Saturday night's careful apologies about the illicit camping trip and my explanations for Kaya's accident and my subsequent disappearance had only served to make them more worried about me.

"How are you feeling this morning?" Mom asked.

"I miss Kaya." She nodded, knowing fully what I felt.

"And physically?" she said, looking me up and down.

"A little achy, but alive," I said, limping to her so I could kiss the top of her head. "And glad to see you." I began chopping up peppers for the McDonough Sunday Morning Chili Challenge. If it turned out that habañeros were an offbeat home remedy for MS, I'd be in remission in no time.

"We're glad to see you too," said Mom. She had already arranged a visit to Mrs. Johnson that afternoon. We were bringing food and flowers. And memories. Ellen, Kit, and Thomas were going as well. We wanted to tell Kaya's mom how special her daughter was, and not just because she couldn't feel pain.

"Remember, baby," Dad said, "no matter what the doctor says tomorrow morning, we'll get through it as a family." Oh, right. My neurologist appointment. How could I have forgotten? Little did Dad know that I'd already been healed by a medicine man with no fancy degrees on his wall. He lived in the wild and had no prescription pad beyond a pouch of animal totems. Even though he couldn't eliminate my MS, or whatever I turned out to have, he had made me better. He'd reminded me of who I was beneath my errant DNA. I had a life that transcended my illness. MS. My Salvation.

"I know, Dad," I said. "It won't be the end of the world, either way."

———

Thomas and I met at the Psalms airfield before the usual post-church rush. I saw him before he saw me. He didn't wear a hoodie, so I could see that his face was grave and lost in thought as he tinkered with a burner. But he brightened the moment our eyes met. *Circle home, Lo.*

"I missed you," I said, resting my head on his shoulder.

"I missed you too." When we finally withdrew from our embrace, we both had to wipe away tears. We were together, but Kaya was still gone.

"Are your symptoms . . . ?" he said.

I nodded. "And you . . . ?"

"My memories are back," he said. "But they feel a little different now. More like shadows of the real thing."

I squeezed him tight. "That's good," I said. "Shadows mean the sun is shining."

"Consuelo, I've seen…and done…many horrible things. I'm afraid you only know a fraction. Things as bad as what happened on Friday night. Though in some ways that was more brutal because I'd let myself care. Deeply. But now…. Now I think I can mourn without reliving the trauma. It hurts—it hurts bad—but it's not crippling, you know? Because of this week, I don't feel as separated from my inborn nature, and I feel this sense of self and strength rising to help me. Does that sound foolish? Do you know what I mean?"

"I do. And I feel the same thing." Thomas pulled away slightly and tilted my chin in his fingers, gazing into my green eyes that might one day go blind again. I would remember every detail of his face.

"And I think," he said, "that I can also…feel love again… especially now that I have you."

"What are you saying?" I knew exactly what he was saying, but I wanted to hear the words.

"I love you, Lo." The happiness that swelled inside my body at that moment dwarfed any pain I could ever feel.

"I love you too, Thomas." I think from the moment I'd seen him standing at the Agua wishing well, I'd loved him. And each little glimpse of his soul since then had only made me fall deeper. He was a poem that spoke to me. He was a song. We stood there kissing as the morning breeze tumbled over us and the blue sky became our own private vault of atmosphere, keeping us safe.

But not Kaya. She was outside our vault now. Her energy was elsewhere. And yet . . . I could still feel it.

"I was thinking," I said, moving my lips away from Thomas's but keeping his body close, "about how a lot of native tribes didn't keep a written history. So most people in the outside world don't have any idea how they danced, how they laughed, how they loved their babies and celebrated each other. . . . All of that happy, abstract stuff is sort of skipped over by the history books. But that doesn't mean it's lost. I think suffering is only part of the picture. The Indians were tricked, killed, even massacred. But that joyful energy, that music that they made, can still survive. When you think about it. Just like our dead can survive, as long as we keep them in our hearts."

"You're right," Thomas said. "Let's remember Kaya the way she lived." I closed my eyes and pictured her riding a bike like a mustang through the streets of Santa Fe. I pictured her racing around a Zozobra picnic blanket with heaven in her hands. I pictured her childlike expression as she comforted me in the car on the way to our first—and her only—ritual, responsive to my suffering even though she had no reference points for pain.

"Hey, guys," said a new voice. I opened my eyes to Ellen's gentle, sober face. Kit stood beside her with his arm around her shoulders. I hadn't realized how much Kit and Ellen had bonded during the ritual week, but in hindsight it was only natural that they should get together. They had both crafted thorny exteriors to hide their fundamentally tender souls. When they were finally able to ease up on their defenses, they discovered kindred spirits on either side.

"We thought we'd find you here," Ellen said. I hugged her. Our group wasn't complete, but it was still full of love.

"How are you guys feeling?" I asked, after we'd dried our fresh tears.

"New and old at the same time," Ellen said.

"I know what you mean," I said. "It's like being reborn, but in your same old body."

"Good, though," Kit said.

"Yes," Ellen said, clasping him to her. "Good."

Though everyone had shed their adopted burdens after last night's ritual, we didn't feel that we'd regressed. Something had happened to us over the course of the week to forever alter the angle of our energy. We had roused our dormant souls and bared them to the light, and to each other. Now we felt a truth and a . . . harmony to our lives, an inner wellspring that could weather any drought. At least that's what I sensed when I admired the faces, simultaneously brave and vulnerable, of my friends.

"Does anyone want to go on a trip with me after school tomorrow?" Kit said. "There's an Indian reservation around Four Corners that I've been wanting to check out. I'm doing research for a short story."

"Oh yeah?" I said. "What's the story?"

"It's about a beautiful Zuni girl who dies. Her parents take her body to a mountain and bury her in the space between boulders. They pray over her body for three days, until they're sure she's taken refuge in the next world. Then they leave her to the rocks. And then her story really begins." Ellen reached for his hand and squeezed.

"That's kind of cool," I said. "So in your story, life doesn't start properly until after death." We were all quiet for a moment.

"Is your arm okay, Lo?" Ellen said.

"Yeah," I said. "It's actually . . . a relief to feel it."

A coyote howled in the infinite distance behind the airfield.

"Did you guys know that in Native American legend," Kit said, "the coyote is responsible for death? The story goes that in the beginning, people lived forever. But the coyote alone knew that the world wasn't large enough to hold all the people, so he tricked the dead into staying away, even though it made the living sad. The coyote alone knew that sometimes we have to die."

I touched the bandage on my arm. "Maybe Dakota knew that too," I said.

Thomas looked up at the sky thoughtfully, as if searching for one of his balloons. "You can wish for a different life all you want," he said, coming back to earth and to us, "but in the end we're all guided—whether by an animal alter ego, or a shaman, or the spirit world . . . or whatever—to be where we need to be. Or just to *be*. And I don't know about you guys, but it makes me feel safe. This week has convinced me that each one of us has a powerful soul that can communicate with something that transcends . . . us. And that same soul can give us direction along the way. If we know how to listen.

As long as we pay attention to life—all of life—and keep our hearts wide open, we'll be protected. We just have to tune in."

I thought about how I used to read energy as music and think people were different strains of the same song. Somewhere along the way I'd stopped listening. I'd had to block it all out because it was too much. I hadn't wanted to be so sensitive to the sounds of the world. It was a liability to feel everything—like my aunt's pain, like my mother's grief that her little sister had died before fulfilling all her dreams. Like my conflicted body. But maybe it was a gift to be burdened, because then you could change. Then your soul could be enlightened. Now my ears felt open again to what everyone intoned.

"And we can't get rid of human suffering," I said, picking up Thomas's thread. "We can't block out what happened to Kaya. But there's something to be said for feeling pain, in all its various songs and colors. Because it can inform us."

Any number of energetic forces can make us see more clearly. Sometimes just seeing that other people are suffering is enough to forge a blessing of compassion. You can't make your burdens disappear by putting them into a burning man or into a prayer book or even into someone else. You can only make a healing miracle in your own mind.

Epilogue

ON THE DAY WE GRADUATED from high school, I decided to be late to the school-wide party Kit was throwing at Fort Marcy Park. I made a note on a slip of paper and took it to Shell Rock, where Kaya had once planned to hold her seventeenth birthday party. This was my final burden, and I'd borrowed it from the Indians. "Nothing lives long," the note read, "only the earth and the mountains."

I released it into the May sky and watched it float away. It was part of the transient air now, drifting east and west in the same currents that carry tribes, children, and balloons. I watched the note until it disappeared into the airstream along with the fragrance of juniper, along with a hint of water just beneath the surface of the desert. Circling home.

Just because it's paper doesn't mean it has to burn.

Acknowledgments

Sometimes I think that acknowledgments should occur in the middle of a book instead of in its final pages, because the halfway point has always been the clutch moment for me as a writer. That's where I worry that I'll never finish or that I'll never do justice to the story I want to tell. In those intense times of doubt, a relentless cheering section makes all the difference. *The Way We Bared Our Souls* met with its own midlife crisis, but I was able to make it to the end with the help of the following people:

My mom, who first drove me across the Mississippi.

Matt, who let me bounce ideas off him about rodeos, California, and young love on our long walks around Brooklyn.

My siblings, especially Stephen, who managed to support my writing despite my rejection of all his YA book ideas.

My "co-*madre*" Susannah, whose lifelong spiritual guidance informed this novel.

My cousin Margo, who was always ready to celebrate with me every accomplishment, however minor, throughout the writing process.

Charles, who remains with me long after death, and whose face I often saw when I moved Thomas through the world.

Lance Weisand of Albemarle High, who first awakened me to the darkness of American history, while also giving me hope that our nation's ideals could prevail.

Gloria Loomis and Julia Masnik, whose enthusiasm for the project at times dwarfed my own.

My late father, whose paperback westerns and Native American histories I still read when I miss him. And who was also on that long-ago trip across a great river.

Finally, this book would not have made it five pages, let alone to the middle, without the devotion of Liz Tingue at Razorbill. Though as my editor she was always savvy, insightful, and exacting, she was (and remains) first and foremost my friend.